TRANSCENDENTAL

Transcendental

PERSEPHONE AUTUMN

Transcendental

PERSEPHONE AUTUMN

BETWEEN WORDS PUBLISHING LLC

Transcendental

Copyright © 2021 by Persephone Autumn

www.persephoneautumn.com

All rights reserved.

ISBN: 978-1-951477-22-6 (Ebook)

ISBN: 978-1-951477-23-3 (Paperback)

ISBN: 978-1-951477-44-8 (Hardcover)

Editor: Ellie McLove | My Brother's Editor

Proofreader: Rosa Sharon | My Brother's Editor

Cover Design: Kat Savage | Savage Hart Book Services

BOOKS BY PERSEPHONE AUTUMN

<u>Lake Lavender Series</u>

Depths Awakened

One Night Forsaken

Every Thought Taken

<u>Devotion Series</u>

Distorted Devotion

Undying Devotion

Beloved Devotion

Darkest Devotion

Sweetest Devotion

<u>Bay Area Duet Series</u>

<u>Click Duet</u>

Through the Lens

Time Exposure

<u>Inked Duet</u>

Fine Line

Love Buzz

<u>Insomniac Duet</u>

Restless Night

A Love So Bright

<u>Artist Duet</u>

Blank Canvas

Abstract Passion

<u>Novellas</u>

Reese

Penny

<u>Stone Bay Series</u>

Broken Sky — Prequel

<u>Standalone Romance Novels</u>

Sweet Tooth

Transcendental

<u>Poetry Collections</u>

Ink Veins

Broken Metronome

Slipping From Existence

Poisonous Heart

Beneath Wildflowers

PUBLISHED UNDER P. AUTUMN

<u>Standalone Non-Romance Novels</u>

By Dawn

*For anyone who has suffered a lost love.
For finding the strength and courage to
fall in love again.*

Once my forever after,
You faded from my grasp.
All I have are memories,
Mental images of us last.
My mind won't let go,
But my heart says it's time.
Will you forgive my weakness,
If I make another mine.

—*Persephone Autumn*

ONE

Fletcher

I CRUMPLE the paper and throw it across the room with the pencil.

Dropping my head in my hands, I grind the heels of my palms to my eyes. Pain lances the backs of my eyes and I gladly endure it. Physical pain at least lets me know I feel *something*. Something other than failure.

"Fletch, take five."

I peer up and catch Jonathan's worried gaze. "Yeah, sure."

Placing the Fender Redondo on the stand, I take a deep breath and rise from my lucky chair. Which hasn't provided much luck as of recent. I walk out the studio door, down the hall, and step into the early summer sunshine.

The sun beats down on my skin and I close my eyes. Absorb the ultraviolet and bask in the heat. After a beat, I amble across the lawn toward the hackberry tree and sit on the wood bench near the trunk. Tipping my head back, I gaze up at the lush greenery and the kaleidoscope of butterflies fluttering between the branches. They flap their delicate wings without a care in the world. I envy them that.

"You feeling alright?"

I startle as Jonathan sits beside me. His eyes on my profile as I keep my focus on the mass of butterflies. The single question loaded with several behind it.

Am I alright? It's a legitimate question. Because I don't feel like myself. Haven't for some time. And I have no idea how to fix what is wrong. Wouldn't know where to begin.

"Not so much." I drop my gaze from the tree and meet his eyes. "I feel… lost."

He props an ankle on his knee. Laces his fingers in his lap. Bites and releases his lower lip, again and again. Pondering how to broach the subject of my obvious blockage. Then he meets my gaze. The corners of his eyes crinkle as they turn down. The corners of his lips following the same action.

"What's changed?"

If I knew, would I be in this predicament? That is what I want to say. But I keep the thought to myself. Instead, I think back over the last few months. Over the time just before. Think of all the possible reasons why my creativity seems to have flown out the window and drifted with the wind.

What of significance has happened in the last three to four months?

I broke up with Renee. But honestly, that was more a relief than burden. She had been driving me up the wall with her constant need to know where I was and what I was doing and who I was with. We had only been dating two months and she acted as if we'd been married a decade. Not that I think marriage equals partner paranoia, but she definitely took the concept and ran with it.

If anything, breaking things off with her *inspired* me. The sudden urge to write songs about crazy exes sat at the end of my pencil. But, in the end, I thought it better not to take that avenue.

What else?

I stare at the house Jonathan and I use as a recording studio, zoning out with my eyes glued to the pale blue siding. My mind surfs through countless memories in search of something, anything, that may stand out. That may give me an indication as to why I am failing at the one thing I love and do well.

And just before I throw in the towel, a memory slaps me in the face. But I don't feel this one moment is the sole reason for my recent lack of inspiration, but it definitely left its mark.

"Not quite sure. Only thing I come up with is a conversation I had with my father in early April. But it was the same shit as usual."

Jonathan nods subtly. "Only my business if you want to share. But if you want to talk about it, I'm here."

I stare down at my lap, feeling less myself than ever. Curling in on myself isn't generally my style. If anything, I usually grab shit by the horns and tug with every ounce of force. But why does my father make me feel this way?

Small. Meager. Pointless.

Unlike the man beside me. Jonathan North. Not just my music producer, but also my stepfather. More of a father figure than my own has ever been. Never once has Jonathan made me feel worthless. Or like my music had no soul or purpose or voice. On good days and bad, Jonathan has always lifted me higher.

I huff and focus on speaking rather than feeling. Because if I actually *feel* the words my father spoke to me, I may believe them.

"As usual, he asked when I was going to grow up. When I was going to get a *real* job. Earn a *real* living."

"And what did you say to him in return?"

"That I *am* a grown man. That my music is more real than his lackluster managerial job."

Heat spreads across my chest and up my neck the more I think about it. About the man who has never believed in a damn thing I have done; not as an adult or child. Never supported my dreams. Never praised me for the unbelievable recognition I have received in the music industry.

It pisses me off. Makes me volatile and pushes me to the breaking point.

"Sorry you're having to still deal with this, son. But don't let him get under your skin. You're so much better than that. Don't stoop to his level."

Jonathan is right. I know this. And yet, for some reason, this single event resonates deeper than any previous. I just suppressed it along with every other time my father has deemed my career worthless. Not as if he has been a role model in any capacity.

But is it too much to ask for him to care? For my father to actually say something positive about me or my life. He may not have been the man I spent most of my time with growing up, but he is still my father. And for some reason, at twenty-nine, I still want him proud of me. Of my talent and skill and accomplishments. To hug and congratulate me for all the blood, sweat, and tears I have poured into my music. To smile and say, "I'm proud of you, Fletcher." Why is extending positive accolades so difficult?

"Trying not to, but damn is it challenging."

I lean forward and rest my elbows on my knees. Stare at the grass and fallen leaves beneath my sneakers. Jonathan rubs his palm on my shoulder briefly in an effort to soothe my internal wounds.

At least I have him. At least I have someone who smiles and cheers me on when I turn out a new song. Someone who gives me positive feedback when I play a new tune I've been toying with.

"You need a break, son."

I peer over my shoulder at him. His face more serious than ever. More sympathetic than harsh.

A break. I roll the idea around in my head. Ponder over the possibilities. At this point, not like I would lose valuable time in the studio. I haven't written or produced a new song in so long, no one would notice me taking time off.

But I can't just take time off. Time away should be enlightening. Invigorating. Rejuvenating.

"Say I take a break." Jonathan nods. "What the hell do I do with myself? Lounging around by the pool isn't the answer. If anything, it may create worse problems."

"Agreed. Let me talk with some buddies in the business. I remember Chad or Bonita mentioning a retreat one of their musicians went to last year."

"Retreat? Like sit in a circle and talk about your feelings?"

Jonathan laughs. "No. More like a place away from the city. Hiking and scenery and doing artsy shit to inspire yourself. There may be organized events, but from what I remember, they aren't required attendance."

A retreat. Going to the middle of nowhere to find myself. To find my muse—because she definitely abandoned ship and left me high and dry.

No harm, no foul. Right?

Honestly, I am open to anything at this point. And if going out of town to who knows where is what I need, then I am game. There is nothing to lose by me going off and getting away from everything that bogs me down.

"Talk with whomever and get more information on this retreat."

Jonathan pats my back before rising from the bench. "Once we finish up here, I'll touch base with them. As soon as I know more, you'll know more."

Standing, I come eye to eye with Jonathan. Time has been good to him over the years. Probably has more to do with how happy he is with Mom. Their constant smiles and need to be near one another. You would think it easy for me to be inspired by them alone. Wish it was that simple.

"Thanks, Dad."

Although Jonathan isn't my biological father, although my biological father still resides aboveground, I have always deemed Jonathan as Dad. For me, the title gets awarded due to his tenderness and desire to see me fulfill my dreams. As a boy, he told me I didn't need to call him dad out of obligation. I simply stated he felt like my dad.

"Sure thing. Let's clean up and call it a day." I nod and follow him inside. "And if you're interested, your mother is making her famous garlic chicken. Ann will be over for dinner too."

Family dinner actually sounds great after another frustrating day. And passing on Mom's garlic chicken is out of the question.

"Count me in. Should I see if Mom needs anything?"

He opens the door to the studio, shaking his head. "Nah. You know how well stocked our pantry is. I'll call and let her know to add another plate. She'll be excited."

We go about our own routines of straightening the studio. Nothing extensive, just picking up trash and setting things as they were when we arrived. Although this is mainly my studio with Jonathan, he works with other clients here. So, we do our best to behave as if it isn't ours.

On our way out, I toss the trash in the bin outside. I wander over to my car and holler to Jonathan that I will meet him at the house after a brief stop at my own.

As I start the engine and buckle my seat belt, I stare at the quaint house in front of me. The pale blue siding and white trim. The landscaped yard, neatly trimmed hedges, and blooming flowers.

This studio has always been my happy place. My solace. A place where I felt most myself.

And for whatever reason, that peacefulness has evaporated. Hopefully this retreat Jonathan mentioned can help lead me back. Back to myself. Back to inspiration. Back to life.

Because without my music, who am I?

TWO

Fletcher

THE PLANE HITS the tarmac at the small county airport in Northern California and the first thought I have is I landed in the wrong place. Although the sight of old warplanes intrigues me, I cannot help wondering why they just sit here. Unused. For incoming passengers to view.

Odd.

As the plane slows to a stop, I peer out the window at the structure smaller than most homes in Los Angeles and wonder how this place exists. How such a minuscule building houses all the necessities to shuttle people into the sky and bring them back safely to the ground.

Once the plane reaches a stop, two workers on the tarmac wheel over a large metal ramp, butting it against the plane door. Minutes later, the door flings open and the steward announces we may disembark. Gathering my carry-on from the bin, I weave my way off the aircraft and step out into the early Northern California sun.

The bright sun pelts my exposed skin as my hair ruffles in the gentle breeze. I slip my sunglasses down from the top of my head. Stare across the cloudless skyline and take my first deep breath during my time away. The cooler air coats my lungs and wakes me up. Starts the process of revitalization.

This is exactly what I need. A different view. Less city noise. Quiet that only comes with solitude.

July in Southern California isn't quite as pleasant as here in the north and I welcome the change. Until recently, there has not been a time where life warranted change. A time when my originality ceased to exist without change. The whole shift has me befuddled.

But that is why I am here.

Many people shrivel under change. Others stand on the sidelines, silent. But I am neither of those people. Me? I am the type to stretch my arms wide and demand change. As a musician, change is essential. Yes, keeping to the root of who you are is vital. But not evolving into a better version of yourself is a setup for destruction.

"This way, sir," an older woman calls from the small building. "Your luggage will be at baggage claim momentarily."

For a split second, I open my mouth to ask where baggage claim is, but stop myself knowing I will see it as soon as I enter the small structure. And I prove myself correct.

While I wait for my suitcase to appear on the small belt, I open Uber on my phone and request a driver.

Suitcase acquired, I roll my luggage out the door and into the parking lot, waiting near the curb. Minutes after I have my luggage, my ride drives up and I am on my way.

The petite woman driver, maybe in her early forties, makes idle chitchat as she heads for my destination. Nothing monumental, just questions as to my visit.

Less than twenty minutes pass before the car turns onto a narrow two-lane drive. I gaze out the window at the forest of tall redwoods flanking the path. The greenery dense and serene. Other trees fill the landscape as well. Moss dangles from high limbs. Ferns grow on the bark of others. Wind rustles the foliage and the dancing leaves have me mesmerized. A sea of brown and green. Off in the distance, I spot a deer, eyes focused on the car as it passes.

After a few minutes, the trees thin. The Maya-blue sky becomes more visible. And the drive weaves more to the right and splits off from the opposing traffic. I lean forward, staring ahead as if this will help my vantage from the passenger seat.

My first thought… the images online do this property no justice.

An enormous mansion comes into view. The exterior cloudy gray with charcoal-gray tiles on the rooftop. Walls jutting out and retreating to form the oddest construction. One end of the building mimics an updated castle turret.

While the opposite end resembles modern, angular architecture. Not a single wall is without windows. Some small single panes. Others ten feet tall.

The landscape between the drive and the mansion is packed with sculpted shrubs and bushy trees. A small walkway from the drive to the building winds around flowering plants and beneath small pergolas covered in blossoming vines.

My driver rolls to a stop at the entrance of the pathway under a tall, stained timber-frame carport. Without a word, she exits the car, retrieves my luggage from the trunk, and sets it off to the side of the car. I exit the car and meet her beside my suitcases.

"I could've gotten them from the trunk, but thank you."

"No problem." She smiles. "Part of my daily workout."

And before I manage another word, she strolls back to the driver's door, gets in the car and drives off. Unlocking my phone, I add a healthy tip to the ride before I forget.

Then, I stand alone. Under the covered patch of drive, I inhale deeper than ever and allow the cool air to pierce my lungs. Shiver as it fills each lobe and fissure in the mirroring organs. Close my eyes as the breath passes out through my lips.

When I open my eyes, I take another look around. Absorb the earthy tones—rich browns and mossy greens. Inhale the robust scent of the soil, piney evergreens, the perfume of blossoming flowers, and salt in the air. Everything about this place is vastly different than where I live. Not just the potent smells and stimulating scenery, but also the heady energy buzzing in the air.

I haven't been here ten minutes yet and already feel invigorated.

Steering my luggage up the winding path and through the gardens, I approach the main entrance to the retreat. Tall doors made of glass and oak welcome me. *Soul Sanctuary Retreat* etched in the panes.

The door swings open as I reach it. A woman with gray hair and laugh lines near her eyes leans against the panes with a larger-than-life smile. Clad in a loose white linen top and matching pants, Birkenstock sandals, and a chunky purple crystal hanging from her neck, she radiates light and positivity as she welcomes me with open arms.

"Mr. Lockwood, I presume."

I stop and extend my hand. "Please, call me Fletcher."

She reaches for my hand with both of hers and cradles it. "Jessimine Hill. Welcome to Soul Sanctuary."

I glance down at our joined hands and question how her touch is so warm. So gentle. A combination of the best hug and the slow radiating warmth you feel when drinking hot coffee or tea. Although the embrace extends no farther than my wrist, it feels as if she holds me close.

"Thank you. Happy to be here." I wheel my luggage inside and she shuts the door behind us.

She guides me toward a tall counter, steps around it, and taps on the keyboard hidden from view. A few clicks of the mouse and she peers back up. Laying an open folder on the counter, she explains more about the retreat and my stay.

"Mr. Lock— Fletcher, looks as if we'll have you here for two weeks. We have you set up in the Buttercup cottage." She removes a brochure from the folder, unfolding it to display the map. Pointing, she continues, "If you follow this path when you walk out back, it will lead to your cottage. Yours is at the tail end of the path, past the Elderberry and Snapdragon cottages." Jessimine hands me a key. "The cottage has a full kitchen if you decide to use it versus dining here. If anything is missing —linens or amenities listed—please let me know."

I take the key as she folds the brochure and tucks it back in the folder. Glancing around the open main residence, I note several of the branched-off spaces used for the workshops mentioned online. The website spoke of several workshops—painting, yoga, music, meditation, and more. No doubt the folder in my hand provides a long-winded breakdown of them all.

Tucking the folder under my arm, I wheel my suitcases away from the check-in desk. "Thank you, Jessimine." She smiles as if we have been friends for years. "Think I will get settled and read over all the retreat has to offer."

Jessimine steps out from behind the counter and escorts me toward the back area of the main residence.

"Let me get the door for you." She opens the door and points off to the left. "That will take you to your cottage."

I exit and head for the path constructed of large slate pavers, soft fine grass growing around the edges. As I stroll along the trail, I gaze at the abundance of colorful flowers. They grow in bushes. Lush and radiant. Perfuming the air and waking my eyes.

As I near the end of the trail, my home for the next two weeks comes into view.

A rustic wooden cottage painted the same cloudy gray as the main residence. Two large windows sit on either side of the white door, a wreath of greenery and yellow flowers at the heart. A pair of Adirondack chairs on the porch with a table nestled between them. And a sea of small yellow flowers on the tips of grassy bushes surround the cottage.

Buttercups. Fitting.

I unlock the door and step inside. The sun filters through the windows and brightens the largest one-bedroom home I have set foot in.

To my left is a small dining area with a rustic wooden table for four—the wood various shades of brown, red, and sand—a cushioned bench against the wall and two chairs opposite. A black geometric light fixture hangs above the center. At the heart of the table is a black runner and a small vase of buttercup flowers.

Beside the dining, the kitchen looks much the same. Open wooden shelves line the wall over the sink, housing canisters and dishware. Mugs hang on black iron hooks, resting against a white subway backsplash. Granite countertops rest over black cabinetry with silver hardware. Edison bulbs hang from the ceiling, nestled in silver cages. And off to the right, pots and pans dangle from more black iron hooks.

Off to my right, the living quarters and small hall to the bed and bathroom.

The living room is quaint. On the windowless wall is a small white sofa resting on a rope-corded rug. A low wooden coffee table inches in front of it with potted greenery and candles at the center. Opposite the couch sits two matching chairs with a small table between them and beneath the window. A stone fireplace at the end of the room with an alcove to hold logs. Black light sconces on the walls above the couch and chair. Ivory curtains dust the floor and frame each window.

"Wow," I breathe out. I haven't been here long, yet feel as if I landed in some alternate reality. One filled with nothing but opportunity and peace. Exactly what I have searched for.

Rolling my suitcases toward the small hall between the kitchen and living area, I step into the bedroom and breathe deep. It may not be the decor I would choose for my own home immediately, but there is something so serene about the space I can't ignore.

The far wall is mostly windows. A small, padded bench at the base lined with pillows. The perfect view of the Pacific just past a small cluster of trees. An iron-framed king bed swallows the center of the room, adorned with a plush white comforter and mountain of fluffy pillows. A walk-in closet with a stacked washer-dryer on the wall butting against the bathroom. Framed botany photos artfully placed on the walls. And a tall, handcrafted wooden dresser opposite the bed.

I park my suitcases near the foot of the bed and wander across the hall toward the bathroom.

"Will I want to leave this place in two weeks? Jesus."

The large clawfoot tub screams for my attention as I enter the bathroom. Silver antique fixtures with a hand-held sprayer at the center. On one side, a matching pedestal sink. On the other, the toilet with wooden shelves above matching those of the kitchen. Fluffy towels, wicker baskets, and small plants and candles resting on the wood.

"Seriously, how the hell did Jonathan's friends hear of this place."

One thing I note, there is no television in the entire space. Nor a radio—although I did spy a record player and wireless speaker in the living room. Other than that, entertainment is solely up to me—whether I join people in the main residence or discover something to do in my cottage.

Either way, I have a feeling the next two weeks will be the best I have had in months. Maybe years.

THREE

Madeline

UNPACKING the last items from the suitcase, I tuck them away in the dresser made for two. But not before one last inhalation of my favorite nightshirt. The basic white cotton men's undershirt, nothing special to an outsider. For me, though, I never travel without it.

After I stow the suitcase inside the closet, I wander over to the padded window seat. An abundance of decorative throw pillows and a blanket lying along the ledge beneath the expansive window. The perfect place to read a book or daydream.

My toes bump the base of the seat as I stare out the window. Blues and greens and browns consume most of the view, added sprinkles of pink and yellow and white here and there. The ocean travels farther than my eyes see. Tall trees, lush and scrawny and everything in between, occupy the space between the cottage and the Pacific. The occasional flowering plant or bush adds life to the otherwise earthy view.

"Breathtaking," I mumble. "Don't you think?"

Per usual, there is no answer. Silence. Always silence. Such unwelcome silence. A silence I am incapable of fixing. Silence that never ends.

I close my eyes and press a palm to my sternum. The throb beneath the thick bone is the reason behind coming to the retreat. To lessen the ache. To discover some form of happiness again. To exist in the world without pain. At least that is what everyone else says it will do.

Taking a deep breath, I wander out of the bedroom and go to the dining table. As I open the folder and stare over the activities and events listed, my pulse kicks up a notch. The idea of joining strangers to paint while drinking wine or sitting with others at a bonfire while they chat or any of the other long-listed items kicks my breathing into high gear. Has my newfound anxiety front and center.

"Take a breath." Chris's voice is strong. The balm I need.

Why is his voice only noticeable when I panic? When I travel toward melancholia? But still off in the distance, the same as his touch.

How I miss his warmth. The way he used to trail his fingertips over my palm, up the inside of my forearm, along my upper arm until he clutched my shoulder and held me close. I miss the tingle beneath my skin. The burn it created—not only where he touched me, but throughout my body.

I would do anything to feel that warmth again. Anything.

After another scan of all the possible itinerary items, I decide to join whoever is in the main residence kitchen to help cook dinner. Although lunch passed not long ago, I imagine the kitchen is constantly busy. Cooking isn't my forte, but it is a menial task I easily get swept away in. As long as there is a recipe or guide, I shouldn't burn or undercook anything.

I wander back to the bedroom and change into more comfortable attire. After I check my appearance in the full-length mirror, I pluck my key from the dresser. A hand-carved wooden oval reading *Snapdragon* dangles from the ring.

As I exit the room, I don't look back. Don't voice my departure. My inclination to leave a note serves no purpose. Not anymore. Not for months.

The door closes with a soft click as I step onto the front porch. I insert the key, lock the door, and take a deep breath.

Two weeks. Will two weeks make a difference? Can two weeks lessen the constant pain in my heart? Change how deeply rooted the hurt resonates? My family seems to think these two weeks will make a world of difference. And maybe they are right. Maybe two weeks away from home and reminders and day-to-day life is a step in the right direction.

After another deep breath, I tuck the key in my pocket, step off the porch and follow the trail back to the main residence.

Within seconds, my chest feels lighter. The sun beams down and heats my skin, the fiery ball closer to the Pacific than the midpoint of the sky. I breathe in the saltiness of the sea and fragrance of blooming flowers and robust foliage. Detect the chirps of distant birds and chatter of other patrons as I near the main residence.

Although the retreat is roughly an hour drive from home, this part of Northern California holds a wholly different energy. First off, being yards from the ocean versus miles births new life. The constant breeze from the water comparable to a new breath of existence. The salty air a fresh and welcome change.

Can't remember the last time I felt the ocean air on my skin. Not that driving to the bay or ocean from home is a feat. I just haven't had the desire to go.

Not alone.

But here, in this magnificent place... I feel more alive than I have in almost a year. Which adds a new layer of guilt to my subconscious. The weightlessness I experienced minutes ago is now gone. Consumed by the shame of experiencing joy when happiness should be the last emotion I feel.

I have come to accept the weight will always be there.

Pressing on my shoulders. Compressing my heart. Draining the air from my lungs.

Regardless, I will move forward. Continue down my path on wobbly legs. The path that still exists, narrow enough for one. Even if it is the path I least expected.

As an older man exits the residence, he holds the door for me and I thank him. The small entryway off the back of the residence reminds me of a small greenhouse, except modernized. Gray, porous concrete walls on either side span ten feet from the door into the residence. Vines crawl up the walls with bold green leaves and small white flowers. On either side of the doorway are tiered wide shelves with several different potted plants—aloe, herbs, succulents, flowers, tomatoes, garlic, root vegetables, lettuce and more. Overhead, potted plants hang from wall to wall rods. Some with flowers, others just green.

I have yet to enter the kitchen, but it already feels as if I am in the pantry. The perfume from the fresh herbs alone invigorates my weary mind.

Wandering farther inside, I glimpse the rooms as I pass them. Later, I will take a more detailed tour of everything. For now, I just want to reach the kitchen and busy my hands.

A few more turns and I land in a kitchen big enough to fit three of mine inside it. The room houses the largest refrigerator I have ever seen, two industrial gas ranges with more knobs than I am used to seeing, and enough counter space to have a dozen people in here at the same time and not feel crowded.

As I step farther into the kitchen, I take notice of three other people. The woman who welcomed me at check in—Jessimine—and two men, one older and the other closer to my age. Each has their hands busy with different tasks. Their eyes downcast and absorbed by the task at hand.

But not a minute passes before Jessimine looks up from the pile of fresh herbs she cuts with quick precision. She sets the knife down on the cutting board, casts a smile so bright it practically blinds me, and wanders in my direction.

"Ms. Reynolds, so nice to see you again. How can I help?"

I peer over at the two men engrossed in whatever they are cooking. The perfume medley of rosemary and citrus and garlic float in the air, and my mouth waters instantly.

"The information in the folder stated I could help in the kitchen."

Her smile brightens further as she steps closer and wraps an arm around my shoulders. "There's always plenty to be done here in the kitchen. Come with me."

She guides me to where she stood when I entered the room. Small piles of thinly sliced herbs sit all around the cutting board she uses. Another pile of larger leaves sits off to the side, waiting for the chopping block. I stare at it all, wide eyed, and swallow.

Before I squawk out my hesitance to use such a large knife on the small leaves, she guides me farther down the counter. When she stops, I stare at the jars and bowls of ingredients in an attempt to decipher what it is I am doing.

"Would you mind helping with the bread for dinner?"

I peek left then right, in search of the bread she references, guessing she needs me to slice and plate it. But there is no bread on the counter. And with striking clarity, I stare at the jars on the counter again and realize I am *making* the bread. From scratch. With my hands.

Not that I am opposed to such things, but I didn't grow up in a household where we made bread from scratch. Heck, before Chris and I started dating, I'd never had anything except inexpensive white loaf bread in lackluster packaging. Not that we ate *fancy* bread. He simply introduced me to foods I had never eaten.

"Everything is here," Jessimine states as she waves her hand over the line of ingredients on the counter. "I planned to start the bread after finishing with the herbs." She reaches for a cookbook behind the large flour canister and starts thumbing through the pages. When she lands on the page with the bread recipe, she sets the book on a wooden stand that holds the book open to the appropriate page. "Here's the recipe. Take your time and don't worry about the end product."

Although I am appreciative of her reassurances, I cringe and flatten my lips as the skin between my brows tightens. Most of the food I cook at home is basic. Meals I made with Mom as a kid. Casseroles or simple meals made with pasta or rice. For the most part, Chris cooked all the creative and healthier meals.

But that hasn't happened for months. In its place, takeout or delivery or microwavable meals.

"Thank you, Jessimine." At least this will keep me distracted and my hands busy for some time.

"You're welcome, sweetheart. If you need an ingredient I forgot, another bowl or utensil, let me know."

She resumes her spot at the cutting board of herbs while I read over the bread recipe. I slip an apron on over my clothes and give the recipe one last once-over. It all seems straightforward, so I dive in and get myself elbow deep in flour minutes later.

By the time Jessimine finishes her task, I strain to finish kneading the dough ball in front of me. But I don't give up. The activity provides a catharsis. A release everyone says I need, but I have waved off for some time. Having this small chore has provided me an outlet. A way to channel the emotions I stow in the corners of my mind.

Jessimine grabs a bowl and starts another loaf beside me and, for a time, we work in silence. Peaceful silence. Before she begins kneading her loaf, she adds some of the herbs she cut and spreads them evenly throughout the dough. Then, she plops the ball of dough in front of me and throws me a smile.

I knead the new loaf while she starts a third. This process goes on for a while longer and I am grateful she took over the blending stage. When the loaves are ready, she pops them in an oven the size of three standard ovens. And it isn't the only one in the kitchen.

Untying the apron at my waist, I tug it off then wash my hands at the sink. Jessimine steps up to my side, ready to do the same.

"Thank you," I say with much sincerity.

She glimpses my profile. "For what?"

Not as if I am a special case and she granted individualized permission for me to join her in the kitchen. But being at the retreat—although I fought the initial reason for coming—has already brightened the shadow cast over my heart. The darkness may never vanish completely, but I can accept a lesser version.

"For letting me help."

Before long, the rest of dinner comes together and we add the food to platters and baskets and deep dishes. We carry the meal out to the community dining area, where a wooden table large enough to comfortably seat twenty consumes most of the room. I follow Jessimine and we set the food down on the two buffet cabinets along the wall. The cabinet wood matching the dining table.

Within minutes, guests pile their plates high with food and sit at the table, and I follow suit. As I sit in my chair, ready to dive into the delicious meal, my mood shifts back to its former gloominess. My mind automatically drifts to Chris. To missing his presence in the chair beside me; his warmth and his smile.

Jessimine pats my shoulder on the way to her seat. "Thanks for all your help. Hope I'll see you in there again during your stay."

"Sure you will," I mutter more to myself than her.

After a few bites of dinner, I can't help but feel someone's eyes on my profile. It isn't uncomfortable, but I feel it nonetheless. Without making it overtly obvious, I pick up my water glass and take a drink while scanning the table. It takes me a moment to scan the length of the opposite side, but I stop when I reach the opposite end.

A man with thick, shoulder-length brown hair studies me without care. His gaze more focused on my fingers than my eyes to notice I have caught him. But the second his eyes lift to mine, they widen a beat before he drops his chin and his skin pinks.

Behind his curtain of hair, I swear the corner of his lips quirks up. For a split second, my heart stutters and my palms sweat.

Admiration and the delight it brings are natural. Normal. Healthy.

So why is my chest constricting? Why does this fraction of time feel so wrong when everyone has told me it is common? Typical. To feel attraction to someone else. For someone else to find me attractive. To experience human nature.

Because I can't just move past what happened. I can't move past the rift. They say time heals all wounds. But should all wounds be healed? Should they scab over and fade away? Be forgotten as if they never existed in the first place?

What happened can never be forgotten. But how do I *live* and not forget?

FOUR

Fletcher

GOD, that was embarrassing.

Nothing like being caught staring. Although, the dark-haired beauty didn't seem as fazed by the notion. And the idea of her accepting my admiration creates an unfamiliar warmth beneath my ribcage.

At first, I had been scoping out the other guests. One by one, glancing at each face and wondering why each sat at this table. Came to this retreat. I wondered, *Are they here because they feel a piece of them is missing too?*

When I had reached the opposite end of the table, my eyes landed on her.

Quiet. Demure. Lost in her own thoughts. And a brittle sadness in her facial expression and body language. Not something the average person picks up on, but I see it. See how she wants the world to perceive her versus how she feels inside. The two in complete contradiction.

For a moment, I had studied her. My gaze had dropped from her face and landed on her hands. Hands tell a story and say things people try to disguise from their eyes and lips and voice. As a musician, I find myself gawking at people's hands more often than not. The shape and length of the fingers and nails. Whether the skin is smooth and supple, rough and calloused, or thin and weathered. Hands speak a language all their own.

And that is where my eyes were focused when she caught me.

Embarrassing. As. Hell.

But something instinctual tells me she doesn't take offense.

As I stab another bite of chicken and lift the fork to my mouth, I peek through my now fanned-out hair and toward where she sits. Her focus zeros in on her own meal, but I don't miss the gentle smile on her lips. And I don't know why, but the subtle gesture adds a zing to the warmth billowing in my chest.

A hand lands on my shoulder and I startle.

"Sorry." I peer up and Jessimine winces at my side. "Just wanted to check how your meal was and if you got settled in your cottage."

I give her a smile and nod. "No need to apologize. I was lost in thought." Her shoulders relax. "And every-thing is perfect. Thank you."

She pats my shoulder. "Well, let me know if you need

anything." As she starts back to her own seat, she pauses and faces me briefly. "After dinner, there'll be a fire down at the pit near the beach. Join us."

For a split second, my gaze drifts to the sad woman at the end of the table. I wonder if she will be at the fire. If she will sit bundled in a blanket, chilled by the ocean breeze, and stare at the flickering flames as they dance in the darkness.

I hope so. Even if we don't speak, I would like to see more of her before the night ends.

"See you there," I tell her.

She throws me a warm smile before resuming her seat at the table.

The remainder of dinner is a mix of light chatter and a delicious dessert. I talk with a couple—Mark and Caleb— and learn their trip to the retreat is just to get away from the city and all the busyness that comes with being constantly connected via electronics. Mark works in technology and almost never gets a day away from his laptop, tablet or phone. Caleb tends to terminal patients in a San Francisco hospital as a nurse. His getaway reasons are different than his husband's, but just as taxing.

When dinner finishes, I ask them if they plan to attend the fire. Once we deposit our dishes in the tub, the three of us wander from the main residence and navigate our way down toward the beach.

The pebble path winds its way through gardens of greenery and flowers; the blossoms fragrance the air and have me breathing more fully. Two curves and fifty feet later, the path opens up to a large outdoor sitting area with an enormous fire bowl at the heart. Orange and yellow flames already ablaze. Twilight on the horizon. The breeze off the ocean not enough to disrupt the flames, but noticeable enough to create a shiver.

Large boulders rest behind the seating and encircle the area, leaving an opening for the path we came from and a path toward the surf. Grassy plants and wildflowers grow sporadically in the space between the boulders and the chairs and couches. Soft pads and throw pillows sit on wide wood pieces of furniture. Small tables available between every other seat. Trees and thick shrubs behind the boulders, hiding the area from the residence and cottages. A small stretch of the beach visible from any seat around the fire.

Peaceful. Welcoming. And the perfect way to end the evening before bed.

Me and the guys plop down on one of the couches and resume talking about our lives away from here. And the fact none of us take time away often enough. Honestly, the notion of vacation to many nowadays is an anomaly. Too many of us feel our worth is determined by how many hours we work, how much we accomplish or how many awards we receive. In truth, neither time nor accolades influence worth. Respect in all forms, on the other hand, is invaluable.

Just as I start to tell Mark and Caleb about my recent shortcomings in the studio, I *feel* my chest warm as it did earlier. The familiarity makes me stutter to a stop and scan those who have since joined us. A slow perusal of faces; many of them lost in their own conversations while they enjoy the beautiful evening.

Until I land on her. The dark-haired beauty from dinner.

She sits directly across from us, eyes fixed on the fire but not seeing the flames or feeling the heat.

Can't quite put it in words, but her melancholy calls to me. Whispers unintelligible words in my ears and beckons me closer. Urges me to engage with her.

As before, she sits alone. Unspeaking. Not interacting with any of the other guests. Her knees are drawn to her chest, arms wrapped around her bent legs and hugging them close.

I bring my attention back to the guys, let them finish sharing their thoughts, then excuse myself. As I rise from the couch, a nervousness I haven't experienced in years swallows me. For a beat, I reconsider my decision to sit on the opposite side of the fire. To go sit with Mark and Caleb or flee for my cottage. The last time I felt anything remotely close to this was when Tricia and I first dated. And what I felt for Tricia didn't compare to the sensation coursing through my bloodstream now.

But that relationship ended years ago. And inevitably ruined most I have had since. Not that my one-to-two-month flings could truly be anywhere near a legitimate relationship.

Oddly enough, I just haven't found anyone since who makes me want to settle.

Leisurely, I stroll around the fire bowl and head toward her. I capture her appearance as the firelight dances over her skin. The soft edges of her jawline and prominence of her cheekbones. The thickness of her brows at the center before they thin closer to the lateral edges. Her perfectly even plump lips, free of gloss or color. Her soft, narrow nose.

But none of those tugs at me. Not the way her eyes do.

The fire reflects in her round orbs, but there is no sparkle. No twinkle. No passion. Instead, her eyes hold despondency. Desolation. And some blend of pain and grief.

Feet away, I slow my short stride before I come to a stop in front of her. When I don't move past her, she breaks her concentration from the fire and lifts her chin to peer up.

Her eyes widen and a subtle hint of blush skirts across her cheeks. The response boosts the growing warmth under my sternum.

"Are you…" I pause to lick my lips. Then I take a deep breath and start again. "Are you okay?"

Almost imperceptibly, she tightens the grip on her legs. Her breath hitches for a beat. And she blinks away the glassiness in her eyes.

"Yes, thank you." Voice so soft. Timid. Apprehensive.

I point to the vacant seat beside her. "Would you mind if I sit?"

Her eyes widen again as she clutches her necklace and toys with whatever pendant lies nestling beneath her shirt.

I follow her fingers as they move left and right, over and over. In the dim firelight, I can't make out the object on her necklace. So I ignore it and lift my line of sight back to hers.

"It's okay," I say, giving her the option to decline. "I'll go back to where I was." As I pivot to step away, her voice halts my next step.

"No. Sorry, I'm being rude. Of course you can join me." Her voice still holds all the same features as a moment ago but with a touch more volume.

I settle into the seat next to her and try my darnedest to not stare at her partially shadowed profile. But every few seconds, I have to remind myself to look elsewhere. To glimpse the skyline as it shifts from pastels to a medium gray blue. Take in the gradual silhouette of the evergreens as nightfall approaches. Scan the cluster of people surrounding the fire, chatting as if they have known each other years and not hours.

From the corner of my eye, the woman tucks her necklace back into her top then hugs her legs with both arms again. She shivers but tries to mask it as she adjusts her position in the chair. Automatically, I wish I had a coat to offer her. Or an overshirt. Something to give her an ounce more warmth.

Summer is still young, so the temperatures haven't hit their peak yet. Northern California also doesn't experience the same summers as it does in the southern half of the state. Plus, with the sun now below the horizon and the added breeze from the ocean, the chill isn't unexpected.

"Would you like to scoot closer to the fire?" I offer, still not facing her head-on. A voice in the back of my head tells me not to shift my gaze and I don't stop to question why.

My eyes on the flames, I pick her up in my peripheral. Spot her slight adjustment to face me more, but not fully. As tempted as I am to make visual contact with her, to connect with her close up, I keep my line of sight on the fire. And I wait.

Wait for her to speak up. To make the next move, whatever that entails. Because the voice in my head also tells me something critical happened to her. Something irreversible. Something that has left a permanent scar no one will ever see or feel except her.

"If you don't mind."

Worries over others' feelings above her own—noted.

"Not at all." I rise from my chair and scoot it closer. "Do you need help? They're actually quite heavy."

She starts moving the chair without issue. "I got it. Thank you."

Once we sit back in our seats, I extend a hand in her direction. "I'm Fletcher. Or Fletch. Whichever you prefer."

Her eyes dart from my hand to my face and back down again, unsure. Just as I start to pull my hand back, she takes it in hers. In comparison, her hand is small when enveloped in mine. Soft where I have calluses. Dainty versus brawny. And it feels and fits perfectly.

But that isn't what stands out. Those are simply side notes.

What stands out strongest is her fire. A heat similar to when you wrap your hands around a mug of fresh hot coffee. Searing, yet you don't want to let go. You just want to bring the mug closer.

To not come off as a creep, I let go.

"Nice to meet you, Fletcher. Madeline. Or Maddie, if you like."

"It's a pleasure, Madeline." The temptation to call her Maddie sends tingles up my spine. In a good way. But nicknames are generally reserved for close friends or family. They are personal and come with time. And I rather like her full name. "What brings you to the retreat?"

The minute progress we made in the last few minutes evaporates with my question.

Her face pales. The shiver from a moment ago was nothing in comparison to her shudder now. Although our chairs don't touch, I feel her tremble in my bones. And I can't explain why.

I wish my desire to reach out and hug her wouldn't be perceived as awkward or creepy. But truth be told, we are strangers. And an unfamiliar man embracing a woman inevitably makes the situation uncomfortable.

So, I tuck my hands under my legs and pin them to resist temptation.

"Sorry. If it's personal, you don't have to answer," I say.

Beside me, her body sags as she exhales. "Thank you. Just been going through a difficult time."

"Me too. Although, something tells me my difficulties are minuscule in comparison." She remains tight-lipped, so I carry on. "I'm a musician. And as of recent, I haven't been able to create. So, I came here for a change and to reenergize what I have apparently lost."

Madeline twists in her chair to face me; half her face aglow from the fire, while the other half remains hidden by shadows. Similar to how we only see one side of the moon; the dark side always mysterious and captivating.

"What type of music do you create? Not sure if that's the proper terminology."

I shrug. "Your wording is fine. I write whatever comes to me. Most people say my music is dismal and too real. But they continue to listen. And I continue to channel what I feel here." I lift a hand and rest the palm just to the left of my sternum. "That's all that matters."

She focuses on the hand I have yet to drop. Studies it intently for seconds or minutes or hours until she breaks contact. Her eyes fall to her lap, a fresh glaze glints in the firelight.

Whatever has her ready to unhinge emotionally, I let her process it at her own pace. Give her the opportunity to speak when she feels ready.

"How do you do it?" she whispers, eyes still downcast.

"Do what?"

"Create such painful pieces of art."

Good question. Most who produce emotional art like

me usually have tragedy in their past. Loss or heartache or abuse. The possibilities are endless. The only one I have experienced was heartache, I suppose. But I'm not sure my one long-term relationship is the sole reason I write the music I do. We simply grew apart. Both of us.

My only guess is the pain correlates with the history my father and I share. My birth father. But that is something to explore on another day.

"Not sure. It just comes to me. It's what I feel most when I sit down with my guitar."

She parts her lips, poised with a follow-up, then presses her lips back together. Her eyes narrow a hint; her brows scrunching to form a *V* between them.

"What is it?" I ask.

Her eyes meet mine and a hint of the blush I saw earlier paints her fire lit cheek. "Would you play for me sometime?" Voice so soft, I barely discern her question.

The intensity in my chest magnifies. "Would love to. Another night, though."

A gentle smile lifts the corners of her mouth. We don't speak another word as we sit comfortably by the fire.

One by one, the other guests leave. I have no clue what time it is, nor do I care. What I do know is, this is the first time in months I don't feel lost. The fog that has lingered for months seems thinner. A bit easier to navigate through.

Is it this woman? Am I a magnet for the dispirited? Are the melancholy people of the world my inspiration?

All valid questions, none of which I have answers to.

But I have time. Two weeks, to be exact. And who knows; maybe in that time frame, I will learn the answers.

I rise from my chair and set it back in its place. "Was nice to meet you, Madeline." I give her a gentle smile. "Have a good night. See you around."

"Good night."

And with much reluctance, I abandon her and head for my cottage. Alone and a tad lighter than I was when I arrived.

This retreat may be exactly what I need.

FIVE

Madeline

I HOME in on Fletcher's backside as he disappears into the night. Close my eyes the moment he disappears from view. Clasp at my necklace and draw the weight out from beneath my shirt, twisting the piece at the heart.

What the hell am I thinking?

Eyes popping back open, I lock onto the flames just feet away and get lost in the flicker. Zone out and remember a time when I would never consider looking at another man. When the man I loved—love—made me smile and laugh. When we went on spontaneous adventures and lay under the stars without care.

But that no longer happens.

Now, there is just… nothing.

I tuck the necklace in my shirt and rise from the chair.

After I set the chair back to its original position, I wander the path that takes me back to my cottage. Back to silence. Back to the all-consuming loneliness I have experienced for more than half a year. A solitude I never asked for. A solitude I never wanted.

As I approach my cottage, a dim light ahead stops me in my tracks. The soft glow barely catches my eye farther down the path, but I see it. Curiosity gets the better of me and, instead of turning toward my cottage, I amble toward the light.

The more steps I take, the more I hear the soft strum of a guitar. No lyrics follow the gentle notes. The melody subdued and woeful. Similar to the beat of my heart.

The path ends as another cottage comes into view. Light spills from a window covered with gauzy, white treatments. And a man sits in the dark on the porch, bent over a black acoustic guitar.

Eyes trained on the man in the shadows, I step off the path and hide behind a nearby tree. The tree doesn't disguise me well, but the absence of city lights helps keep me hidden from view.

And for a time, I simply watch him play his guitar. Watch the silhouette of his fingers as they sweep the strings. Listen to the subtle tune and close my eyes. Allow the chords to vibrate through me and settle somewhere deep inside. An empty place.

When the strumming stops and the chirp of cicadas takes over, I try to make myself small behind the tree trunk, worried I have been caught.

But then his front door opens, then quietly clicks shut. Holding my breath, I ease out from behind the tree and peer over at the cottage.

Inside, he moves into the kitchen. Between the distance and the gauzy curtains, my view of him is limited. So, I step closer. Probably close enough to be considered intrusive. But intrigue has me doing things tonight I never would have in the past.

I tiptoe up to the porch and over to the window. Little by little, I lean my head to the side and peer through the sheer curtains. And see nothing.

Without warning, a silhouette shifts much closer than expected and I step back, slapping a hand over my mouth.

He stands within reaching distance—if a wall and window weren't between us. I don't move. Don't breathe. Don't make a sound as I wait for him to step away. My heart pounds a vicious rhythm as I lie in wait. My lungs burn from oxygen deprivation. But I remain rooted in place, palm to lips, until he closes the second row of non-transparent curtains.

The moment he does, I bound off the porch and bolt down the path toward my own cottage. Adrenaline pumps through my veins as the cool ocean air licks my exposed skin. When I reach my own porch, I stop, bend at the waist, and slap my hands to my knees.

"I almost got caught," I whisper into the dark, working to regulate my breathing.

Fletcher.

His cottage is less than a hundred feet from mine on

the opposite side of the path. This little fact does nothing to help settle my rapid heart rate. And for that, guilt washes over me anew.

I stand tall, close my eyes and shake my head. A bubble of emotion erupts in my chest and has my heart beating a turbulent rhythm. Shame. Remorse. Disgust. My line of thinking, my strayed thoughts, are unacceptable. Aren't they? *Yes, they are unacceptable.* I should not be thinking of or gawking at other men. Not even obscured and from a distance.

I retrieve the cottage key from my pocket and unlock the door. Everything is exactly as I left it hours earlier. Not a paper out of place. All the lights out except a dim lamp on the bedside table I flipped on before leaving. The bedding tidy and the bathroom pristine.

What I wouldn't give to have a piece of dirty laundry to pick up after. Or to adjust the comforter because there is too much on one side.

Going about my nighttime routine, I change into pajamas, brush my teeth and brush the knots from my hair. I toss my laundry in the closet near the stacked units and promise to deal with them tomorrow. Then I slip under the bedding and close my eyes at the chill of the linens. A chill that greets me every night. A chill I can't shake, no matter what I do.

After flipping off the lamp, I roll onto my side and stare out the window facing the ocean. Stare at the moon as it glows in the inky night sky. Tonight, the moon brings me a sense of calm. Fills me with hope and peace.

Two emotions that have been absent from my life for months.

As I close my eyes and bunch the bedding for comfort, the sight of Fletcher in the dark strumming his guitar flits in my head. Followed by the sound of Chris's voice… telling me he loves me.

I pinch my eyes tighter. Wish for some higher power to alleviate the hollowness beneath my breastbone. Pray for an explanation as to why all of this has happened. *Is* happening. Why I am swarmed with grief and despair as well as a hint of delight and hope. Can pain and promise coexist?

But no answers come. Not in this cottage and not tonight. How could they?

And I hate myself for my line of thinking. For my indecision. For the ease with which I dismiss a love that once monopolized my every waking moment. A love that I miss with every breath I take.

The saddest part of all… I don't remember the last time I felt that love. By means of his words or touch or even the scent of him on my skin. Too much time has passed.

And that love is just… gone.

SIX

WHEN I ARRIVED at the retreat yesterday, I had my doubts about finding inspiration here. How could I not? I never needed a setting change for my creativity to flow. I simply channeled different times in my life. Different people. Different experiences with those people.

But none of that had been working. None of my usual tactics sparked my muse. So, this place was the alternative. A retreat in the middle of nowhere, Northern California.

The entire property, or at least what I have seen thus far, is breathtaking. A definite change of pace and scenery from the usual concrete jungle I see day in and out. This place is so… green.

Not just green. Earthy. Colorful, but not like the city.

The air invigorating and crisp. The sky bright and wide. And the quiet… the quiet is like nothing I have known.

Yes, I have traveled. Visited various places within the country. But, for the most part, I stayed in the city. It isn't often musicians record or perform in the woods. Not that I am opposed to such an intimate idea.

But this place is different. The energy in the air, from the earth, makes me feel like a different person. Someone new. Refreshed. As did the dark-haired beauty from last night.

Madeline.

Our conversation had been minimal. A brief introduction and light exchange. More of a one-sided conversation, which I didn't mind. I had no qualms being more vocal while we sat fireside. Before I came to sit by her, something told me she wouldn't reveal much. The sadness in her eyes, perhaps. And I was—am—okay with this.

How easily I got swept up in just her presence. At dinner, the subtle and embarrassed glance. By the fire, the way her skin glowed and was obscured by the orange flicker. She holds an air of mystery and disparity. Elegance and simplicity.

And more than anything, I want to know her.

After I left her at the fire last night, inspiration hit. Nothing outlandish, but inspiration nonetheless.

As soon as I walked into the cottage, I scooped up my guitar and sat on the porch, shrouded in darkness. And with an unfamiliar ease, the tune and lyrics spilled from me. A heartbreaking theme slowly carving itself to life in stone. When I reached the end, I went inside and prepped for bed. But not without jotting it all down.

This morning, my conversation with her last night feels dreamlike. A hallucination I conjured to appease my lackluster mind. But as I stroll into the main residence for breakfast, I spy her across the room. Any notion I had of last night being a figment of my imagination vanishes.

I rush through the line and fill my plate with an array of breakfast foods. After I grab utensils, I dash toward the empty chair beside her. As I take a seat, I note she still has a healthy amount of food on her plate.

Perfect.

"'Morning," I say as I place a napkin in my lap and spear the fruit on my plate.

From the corner of my eye, I catch Madeline shifting her focus from her plate to me briefly. A gentle smile tugs at her lips. "'Morning."

For a moment, we sit in silence and eat our breakfast. I make a point not to stare, but I find my focus on her hands often. Right holding her fork; left in her lap, occasionally lifting her napkin. Her fingers are slender, long, delicate. Nails free of polish with only a hint of white past the pink. No rings or bracelets. Although, I swear I spot a pale line on the skin of her left ring finger.

Hmm, interesting.

As the food on our plates slowly disappears, I itch to spark a conversation with her. To know her, little by little. A voice inside me warns this woman isn't like others. Not someone to take for granted or treat frivolously. That tragedy mars her life, that her past hovers close and has her hesitant to move forward.

What exactly that tragedy is remains a mystery. A secret that is not my place to investigate.

I swallow and spear the strawberry on my plate. "What's on your agenda today?"

She sets her fork down before turning to face me. With a shrug, she says, "Not sure. I may just wander the grounds. There are several hiking trails. What about you?"

Would it be too forward of me to ask to join her? We don't know one another. If I ask, will I make her uncomfortable? No one else appears to be at the retreat with her. Of course, I base this on the fact she has eaten alone twice in less than twenty-four hours and no one joined her at the bonfire.

I look up from my plate to meet her eyes. "Not sure. Mind if I join you?"

In my periphery, she wrings the napkin in her lap. The gesture is minute and somewhat hidden by the table, but I notice. Not that I will mention it to her.

"Um…"

"Madeline, you can say no. Promise it won't hurt my feelings."

She clutches at her shirt near her sternum, presumably taking whatever pendant she spun on her necklace last night. Confusion flits across her features—her eyes narrow briefly as her brows twitch. Just as I open my mouth to speak again, her expression straightens and she drops her hand back to her lap.

"No. I mean yes. Of course you may join."

"Are you certain? Don't want to make you uncomfortable."

Slow and steady, she nods. "Yes, I'm sure."

We finish our breakfast with minimal conversation. When our plates are empty, we carry our dishes to the bin and deposit them. Without a word, we weave our way through the residence and out the back door into the bright sunlight.

And for some reason, as I walk beside Madeline, I suddenly feel thirteen again. Awkward and shy and fumbling. Unsure of where to keep my hands. Should I fold them across my chest? Pin them at my sides or stuff them in my pockets? This is far from a first date, but the jitters and apprehension of being alone with this woman resemble exactly that.

Get it together. This is just two adults going for a walk. Nothing more.

I gesture to the path in front of us. "Lead the way."

Her cheeks pink and I can't help but smile. Her bashful response intrigues me. I am far from the best judge of age, but if I guessed, I would say Madeline is older than me. Not by much, but older. I see it more in the way she carries herself than any facial feature. A wisdom that only comes with time and life.

"Um, I'm not quite sure where to go. There's a trailhead not far that splits to some of the different trails."

I remain a step behind to her right. "Surely, there's a sign at the trailhead. We can figure it out from there. But you'll have to lead for now."

For a few minutes, we follow a sidewalk toward the tree line. Neither of us says a word, but I absorb the moment. Take in the casual mid-thigh khaki shorts and loose cream top she wears with a pair of everyday sneakers. Today, she has her hair in a ponytail; the ends of her hair dusting the neckline of her shirt.

Most would see her as casual and comfortable. Ready to conquer the day.

But those who have spoken with her or sat within ten feet of her may know otherwise. Those familiar with her, even in the slightest, may pick up on the constant fidget of her fingers. Or the occasional stutter in her step. And maybe even the sporadic pitch in her breath.

I may not know this woman well, but she lives and breathes her story. Maybe, before we go our separate ways, she will speak it too.

We come to a stop when we reach a large display; a map shielded behind plexiglass. And from what I can tell, most of the trails are lengthy. But I spy one much shorter and point to it.

"Maybe we should take the shorter one. Not sure about you, but it's been a while since I've hiked."

"Been a while for me too." Her tone somber before she shakes it off and continues. "Come on." Then she bolts for the trail and I stumble to catch up.

Gravel crunches beneath our shoes as birds chirp from

the trees. For the most part, shade covers the trail. The temperature still mild and a touch cooler under the tree canopy. Madeline's hair sweeps to one side as a gentle breeze rustles through the trees.

And for a moment, I simply gaze at her profile. Study the contours of her jaw and nose and brow in the light of day. Guilt rears its ugly head for ogling a woman who appears heavyhearted, and I mentally slap myself. But then I look at her and see it is also her sorrow that continues to lure me in.

As ashamed as that makes me, I cannot help myself.

I take a few longer strides and walk side by side with her, keeping with her pace. "So, Madeline." She peers over at me, but doesn't slow her gait. "What is it you do for a living?"

I hate small talk. Hate it with a passion. It feels empty and meaningless. But Madeline isn't someone you ask the deep questions without adding a level of comfort—trust—in first. For all intents and purposes, we are strangers. It surprises me already she was okay with me tagging along. Yes, this retreat isn't cheap. But just because people have money, doesn't mean they are safe.

She slows her pace to a more casual stroll and I adjust my stride. "I help manage a doctor's office. Nothing glamorous. At times, I feel more like a secretary."

"Don't downplay your role. I'm sure you work hard and the doctor appreciates you."

A soft smile curves the corners of her mouth. "Thank you." And for two steps, she glances over at me. "Even though you've never been to the office or seen me working, that was nice of you to say."

We step up onto a wide bridge; a fresh water stream rushing beneath it. Madeline steers over to the rail, rests her forearms on the edge, and gazes down at the stream. I step up beside her and mimic the action.

"It's beautiful here," I whisper. "Don't know about you, but this isn't the typical landscape I see every day." She nods, but doesn't speak up. "And it's so quiet here."

"Too quiet," she mumbles. Her words almost inaudible, but I hear them. And the strain behind them.

I lift my gaze from the water and meet her profile. Surely, she feels my eyes on her, but I don't look away. Can't look away. And like a creep, I lean a fraction closer.

"Does the quiet bother you?"

She swallows and lifts her left hand to clutch her shirt. As she does, I notice, just where her thumb meets her hand, a small freckle. The small brown spot no bigger than a felt-tip pen mark on her skin. But, to me, it stands out. Has me observing the rest of her hand for other marks I potentially missed.

Then she drops her hand and I shake off the trance.

"Yes and no."

For a brief moment, I forget what I asked and retrace my mental steps. Oh yes, I asked if the quiet bothered her.

"Why both?"

Hopefully she didn't notice my lag in response.

"Years ago, I loved the peace that came with certain

types of silence. Nowadays, it feels as if all I have is silence. Undesirable silence."

"What changed?"

She whips her head my direction, facing me head-on, eyes wide and a slight shake to her head.

"I… I don't think I can talk about it."

Guilt consumes me for the second time in less than an hour. Something or someone recently hurt her. And I just dredged it up. *Way to go.*

I rest a hand on her bicep—neutral territory, right?— and rub slightly. "Hey, you don't need to tell me anything. Alright?" She nods and deters her eyes back to the water. "Just trying to make conversation. How about you tell me something random."

She meets my gaze again and, for the first time, I get an up close and personal view. Her irises an earthy brown, rimmed in a bold brown black. Eyes as mysterious as the forest around us, and equally as enchanting.

"Like what?"

I break eye contact and get lost in the endless greenery. "How about your favorite color?"

She hums and shifts her weight from left to right. "Blue, like the sky." Then she nudges me with her elbow, which surprises me, and I bring my focus back to her. "What about you?"

"Mine isn't as unique. Kind of predictable, actually."

A small *v* forms between her brows as she tilts her head to the side.

"Black." I point to my shirt, a generic plain tee. "Majority of my wardrobe is black."

"How is that predictable?"

I shrug. "Maybe because of the music I create. I figure most people would assume I'm always sad. And most people associate sad with the color black."

"I don't," she whispers.

"Don't what?"

"Associate sad and black. If I paired a color with it, I'd choose maybe gray. Like a looming storm. The dark clouds edging closer, but just out of reach. The opposite of a bright, sunny day."

Her analogy more spot on than most. Yes, most wore black to funerals. Or you saw it on the loner kids. But to associate the color with sadness is stereotypical. For me, I considered it vast opportunity. Not necessarily emptiness, but an openness to anything. Endless possibility. Infinity.

"Your reference seems more fitting." She smiles then returns to studying the stream; a soft rose hue tints her cheek as she shuffles her feet side to side. *Compliments make her uncomfortable.* "Do you want to continue the trail?"

This seems to alleviate her worry somewhat. "Yes, please."

We wander from the bridge and follow the gravel path once more. Just the two of us, out in the thick of nature, listening and observing and existing in the same space.

Silence with Madeline isn't insufferable. If anything, I rather enjoy the stillness and serenity. So very different than sitting alone at home, although neither of us speaks or touches. Just her vibration next to me sparks new life in my veins. And I don't quite know what to think of that yet.

"Do you have any hobbies?" I ask, my focus on the curve in the trail up ahead.

"I paint." She sighs. "Well, I used to paint. Years ago."

I want to ask why she no longer does, but stop myself. When I asked her to elaborate why she did and didn't like the quiet, she froze. So, I will try another tactic.

"Can't say I've done more than paint by number." She laughs, but it almost sounds forced. I smile anyway. "But I did see a painting room in the main residence and considered giving it a try. Maybe you can give me a few pointers when I do."

"Maybe," she answers, voice laced with hesitance.

We amble through another curve in the trail and head in the general direction we started from. But we don't take the bend at the same speed and angle, and her forearm brushes my knuckles for a split second.

The microblip of time feels infinite. Her body barely grazes mine, yet heat coats my skin like a fresh sunburn. My throat dries as a light sheen of sweat layers me from head to toe. And a small whirlpool swims beneath my diaphragm.

Just as quickly as our skin meets, though, she yanks her arm away. She wraps her arms around her center and hugs herself fiercely. And without warning, she picks up speed and storms off.

"Madeline, wait!"

No matter how quickly I move to catch up, she darts away faster. The forest starts to thin and I spot the rooftop of the main residence through the trees. One last time, I pick up the pace. But it is no use. Madeline has a solid seventy feet on me.

The exit to the trail becomes visible and, just before she disappears from view, I swear I hear her sobs echo in the trees.

I skitter to a halt, staring where she stood moments ago. "Sorry," I whisper into the trees, hoping maybe they will carry the message to her.

SEVEN

Madeline

I JOG the path that leads back to the cottage; a river of tears streaming down my cheeks. Tears loaded with sadness and anger and frustration. But most of all, self-hatred.

Fletcher's touch had been accidental and innocent. No more than a light brush of skin. But my mind blew the soft graze completely out of proportion. Made it seem much more intentional. Potent. Desirable.

The worst part… I longed to feel desired in that way again.

How many months have passed since I last felt wanted? Truly wanted. When was the last time a man looked at me and saw me as desirable? When was the last time *anyone* saw me as something other than a listless woman? Months. Too many months.

As much as I yearn to be found appealing in such regard, guilt holds me captive from those luxuries. The guilt-ridden pressure more powerful than Neptune's gravity. More consuming than any first kiss. More acute than an open wound.

My feet crunch against the gravel as I push myself harder. Last thing I need is someone stopping me to ask why tears stain my cheeks. To try and heal the scar forming down the midline of my heart.

No one can cleanly seal that fault line. No one.

I reach the cottage porch and dig the key from my pocket. With a shaky hand, I shove the key in the lock and turn before rushing inside. As the door slams shut, I press my back to the wood and slide down to the floor. I tug my knees to my chest and drop my forehead as the monsoon of tears rips free.

The hollowness that has taken up residence between my breasts for far too long swells in size. Like a black hole, it sucks any and all joy from deep inside. Steals remembered smiles and once-upon-a-time laughter. Robs me of long-lost touches and dreams of forever. Swindles away every last happily ever after I once thought existed.

I fist my shirt and clutch the necklace beneath the cotton. Cling to the life I always wanted. A life I will never have. A life ripped away from me far too early.

"S-so sorry," I sputter out, sobs racking my body. "I should have t-tried harder. Should have done m-more."

For a moment, nothing but silence surrounds me. A silence that has slowly driven me mad with each passing day. Unhinged me to the point my family and closest friends pooled enough money for this trip. Regardless to my protests, they all said coming here was for the best. That it would help. That it would heal.

How can anything help? How will two weeks at a retreat fix this?

"Don't cry." Chris's voice echoes in the silence; and for the thousandth time, I wish for his touch. An impossible touch. *"I hate seeing your tears."*

I lift my head from my knees, eyes closed. If I open my eyes, nothing but disappointment will follow. Disappointment at what I will see. Disappointment at what I *won't* see.

Instead, I press my palm to the floor and lean to the side until my cheek cools against the wood. I curl in on myself and sob. Shed tears as the pain splits me in two. Clutch my chest as my vision blurs.

Just before I drift off, Chris whispers, just out of reach. *"I love you."*

EIGHT

Fletcher

THREE DAYS. I haven't seen Madeline for three days. Not at breakfast or dinner. Not at the nightly bonfire or in the painting room during the day. If it were any other person here, I wouldn't worry.

But Madeline isn't just anyone.

From the moment she appeared in my orbit, I gravitated toward her. The weighted pull impossible to ignore. Comparable to how the moon revolves around the earth—constant and wobbly and necessary.

It isn't just her outward appearance that draws me in—although her beauty is undeniable. More than anything, her deep-seated dejection calls out to me. The sadness she carries so heavily on her shoulders.

Does that make me unbalanced or out of my mind? Probably. But I don't care.

As I walk through the dining area, I spot Jessimine and am half tempted to ask if she has seen Madeline the last few days. I portion a little bit of everything onto my plate before collecting a napkin-wrapped set of silverware. Just as I wander toward the vacant chair beside Jessimine, I glance to the line of guests still waiting to fill their dinner plates and see Madeline.

I halt in my tracks, refusing to look away until she notices me too. An older woman steers around me and takes the seat I originally intended to take. But I no longer care.

Madeline peers over to the table and locks eyes with me. A deafening whoosh pulses behind my ear as we hold each other visually. The guests in front of her have moved forward, but she hasn't taken a single step. Her feet rooted in place as we exchange silent questions and explanations.

After a beat, I give her a slight nod. My way of telling her everything is okay. That *we* are okay. Not that there is much of a *we* to begin with.

The corners of her mouth tip up just enough for me to notice. The motion subtle and soft. An affirmation.

She breaks our contact to step forward and fill her plate. While she collects her dinner, I locate two empty chairs, hoping she will sit beside me. When I survey the line, I don't see her. Before taking another breath, I scour the room as my heart hammers with unparalleled intensity.

Until she sits in the vacant chair to my side.

Her presence alone regulates my vicious heartbeat. Attunes my breathing. Sings the melody inside me, just out of reach.

"Hi," she breathes out.

"Hey."

We exchange smiles. A silent forgiveness given and taken. She doesn't bring up her absence and I don't question it. Something tells me she won't give an answer even if I did ask.

Although we barely know each other, it feels as if I have known her for years. An old friend. A best friend. Maybe even a long-lost love.

I shake off the last thought. The last thing Madeline needs is someone causing her discomfort or assuming a false role in her life.

"Sorry I missed—"

I hold up a hand to stop her. "No need to apologize. For the other day or any of the days since."

She audibly exhales and drops her shoulders. "Thank you."

"No need to thank me. Just glad to see you now."

She grants me a bigger smile before picking up her napkin-wrapped silverware and unraveling it.

We eat our dinner in companionable silence. Every now and again, I feel her eyes on my profile. Studying me. A pulsing energy vibrates off her and ripples over my skin. Waking every molecule beneath the surface. Entering my bloodstream and coursing through my veins with an exquisite cadence. A sweet refrain I cannot wait to translate with my guitar.

Light chatter fills the room around us, but we finish our meal without a word. Followed by dessert in the same fashion.

I have only had one long-term relationship, but I can't recall a single time when I felt so utterly comfortable just being in the same space as her. Not like this. Not like when I am with Madeline.

Even the women I casually dated had a constant need to speak. At times, it felt as if they were narrating themselves to the world. The constant need to translate their every thought for all to hear. I found it odd. It also made me wonder if maybe they never got enough attention as a child. If people ignored them with frequency. Or maybe the opposite.

But Madeline isn't like other women I have known. She has gentleness and reservation. Soft edges that have been hardened by her past. And although she speaks in hushed tones, instinct tells me she isn't naturally so reticent.

Once she sets her fork on her empty plate, I take both our dishes to the bin.

"Thank you," she says upon my return, a pale pink coloring her cheeks. Pink has never been a hue I preferred, but I am discovering a new love for it. "You didn't need to do that."

"I know, but I wanted to." I extend a hand to her,

mentally prepared for rejection. "Would you like to go sit by the fire with everyone?"

Unexpectedly, and without hesitation, she takes my hand and rises from her seat. The soft warmth of her skin a juxtaposition to my calloused cool fingers, and I can't help but savor our differences. Where she is smooth, I am rugged. Her skin scorches mine as if we have been at the bonfire hours already.

How can such a stark contrast feel so perfect? Why have I never noticed such differences with any other woman I have spent time with?

But what I find most fascinating, she doesn't drop my hand the second she stands. In fact, it seems as if she tightens her hold.

"I'd love to."

We exit the main residence, hands clasped, and I can't help but wonder what has happened with her over the last three days. What did she do? Had she been alone? When she jogged off the other day, I heard her sobs. She had been upset. More than imaginable. But why?

I replay the day in my head. Our walk along the trail. For the most part, it had been quiet. Peaceful. We talked here and there; a slow introduction to each other. Everything had been great. Until I accidentally grazed her forearm.

The flare of heat across my skin when we touched has been permanently imprinted in my memory. No woman has left such a lasting effect. Marked me so thoroughly. Did I do the same to her? Is that why she ran off?

Did the heat between us frighten her?

I hope not.

As we walk into the seating area near the fire, I let her guide us. Not just to a place to sit, but also to what happens next. Surprisingly, she continues to hold my hand. After our brush on the trail and her reaction, I assumed Madeline would avoid me the rest of my stay or hers. She has proven me wrong, thank goodness.

She steers us toward a couch on the far side. Our hands break apart as we sit and a chill sweeps over me at the loss. Does she feel an inkling of the magnetism between us? The building intensity?

God, I feel as if I am drowning in it. Not that I mind. If anything, I beg for more.

She shivers, her leg brushing mine in the process.

"Cold?"

Extending her palms toward the fire, she shakes her head. "Not really."

I stare at her profile in the firelight and memorize the play of shadows on her jaw, her cheekbone, where her brow meets her temple. She watches the fire and I watch her. The bat of her lashes with each blink. The occasional tuck of her lips before she sweeps them with her tongue. And the gentle rise and fall of her shoulders with each breath.

Madeline bewitches me. Without trying, she captivates me; wordlessly beckons me closer. And like a fiend, I lean in, breathe her air, and commit every delicate curve and subtle sound to memory. I compartmentalize each fragment alongside the way her touch triggers life inside me.

"Do you want to move the couch closer?"

Measured, she rotates her head to face me. Eyes a sparkling blend of mystery and darkness and amber, dancing in the firelight. I hold her gaze. Match her ferocity. Hold my breath until she answers.

She leans back, eyes still on me. "No. This is good," she breathes out with a shake of her head.

Reluctantly, I break eye contact to sit back and stare at the fire with her. For a moment, neither of us says a word. Don't move.

Lost in thought, my mind strays to missing her presence over the last three days. Not that either of us is obliged to spend time with the other, but I hadn't seen her anywhere. I had at least expected to see her during breakfast or dinner. But I hadn't. And I wondered if she had checked out.

The idea of her leaving the retreat without a word did strange things to me.

On the first day, I thought maybe I missed her in passing or she had decided to spend time in her room or cottage. God, I didn't even know where she was staying on the property—not as if I could ask anyone either.

Midway through the second day, an imperceptible eddy swirled beneath my diaphragm. An incomparable nervousness. I don't think I had been that fidgety since freshman year of high school. And I had no idea what had come over me. No other woman has provoked such restlessness in me, awake or during sleep.

By the start of this morning, I wanted to crawl out of my skin. At breakfast, I stared at the chair she previously occupied in the dining room. Hoping against all hope she hadn't left. Desperation crept in. Had me hiking all the trails and searching all the rooms of the main residence. And with each step I took, each second without knowing her whereabouts, the anxiety weaving a web beneath my ribcage grew thicker, more constricting.

But the moment I laid eyes on her tonight; every missed breath came rushing back. Every skipped heartbeat escalated my pulse. That thick web of fear dissipated.

And now that she exists in my bubble again, I don't want to miss an opportunity.

"Is everything okay?"

Her eyes trail the flicker of the fire. "Yes and no."

I audibly swallow, hesitant to ask the next question. "Did I do something wrong?"

She drops her gaze to her lap then picks at her fingernails. I want to reach out and rest my hand on hers. Tell her if she doesn't want to answer, she doesn't have to. But I resist the urge. Instead, I sit patiently and wait for her response. Give her time to choose whether or not to answer.

"No," she whispers, head downcast.

"Do you want to talk about it?"

This draws her attention back to me. With our connection, I let her know she isn't obligated to tell me anything.

That her company is enough. But if she does want to tell me, I will listen.

She closes her eyes, and I instantly hate the barrier between us. Hour-long seconds tick by before she meets my gaze again. And what I see there is heartbreaking.

I doubt she will own it aloud, but Madeline suffers. In this moment, I see her pain in every line and crinkle marring her beautiful face. I see it in her glassy, veiny eyes. In the wobble of her chin as she fights the impulse to cry. In the way she wrings the hem of her shirt in my periphery.

What happened to this beautiful woman?

"I should." A quiet sob rips from her chest and she clamps a hand to her mouth.

God, I want to wrap my arms around her and hug her pain away. But I don't want to be intrusive. Insert myself when inappropriate.

Rather than overstep the boundary she has laid, I ball my hands at my sides and slip them under my thighs. "You don't have to."

Her glassy eyes hold mine as she clamps down on her lips. "I know. But for the first time, I want to." She swallows. "Maybe not tonight, though."

"Not tonight," I echo with a nod. As we sit in easy silence, an idea sparks to life. "Do you have plans tomorrow?"

"No. I considered checking out the art rooms, but nothing is set in stone."

Now or never, Fletcher. What's the worst that could

happen? I don't want her to reject the idea, but I prepare myself for the possibility.

"Would you like to do something with me tomorrow?"

I don't miss how she wrings the hem of her shirt again. Or how her eyes dart as she ponders the idea. But I won't rush her into making a decision.

Sooner than expected, she responds, "I'd really like that."

As much as I don't want the evening to end, I am eager for tomorrow. A real chance to get to know Madeline. To learn more about her life. What makes her smile. And what shadows her heart.

If luck is on my side, maybe she will let me in. Even if just a blip on her radar.

NINE

Madeline

FROM THE MOMENT I woke this morning, an untamable cloud of energy has swirled beneath my breasts. A mix of fire and excitement and anxiety. As of now, I don't quite know how I feel about it.

Last night, I took a leap. Stepped well outside my comfort zone. Did something I never imagined. Embraced the possibility that something else may be able to bring me joy. Solace. Or maybe even… love.

Three days of self-induced confinement. Three days of tears and pleas and questions. Pleas for forgiveness. Questions about whether or not I was doing the right thing and if I could actually do what so many had suggested. Tears over moving forward to find happiness again.

Does it make me a bad person to want more? To crave something other than pain and heartache?

If either of those questions had been asked a week ago, two weeks ago, a month ago, the answer would have undoubtedly been yes.

In the beginning, family and close friends understood my need to be a recluse. To bury myself under the comforter for days on end and not surface for air or food or human interaction. But as time ticked on, as month after month passed by, everyone worried for my well-being. Worried whether or not I needed professional help to move on.

How do I move on, though? And why is it acceptable to move on?

So many other women have stood where I stand. Wore the same shoes. Yet, they stood their ground. Held firm. Didn't let others sway their choice.

Why couldn't I?

Over the last three days, I allowed myself time to answer this question. I stepped outside myself and tried to see everything from different perspectives. Replayed the advice and voiced concerns of those I love most. More importantly, I questioned what Chris would want. If anyone's opinion mattered more, it was his.

Yesterday morning, when I woke with puffy red eyes and a minimally sutured heart, a realization struck.

All Chris ever wanted was for me to be happy.

Once, he told me he hated when I cried. Sad or happy, he never wanted tears to stain my cheeks. *The world needs your smile,"* he'd told me. *"Give it. And don't let anything steal it."*

The longer his words echoed in my memories, the more I cried.

I don't want a limited, half-lived life. But how do you smile after you lose the one person who made it shine the brightest? Gifting someone my smile nowadays feels like betrayal. Foul and inappropriate. Loathsome.

Until I met Fletcher.

The way he regards me is different. Everyone familiar walks on eggshells around me since… but Fletcher doesn't know me. Not the way family does.

To Fletcher, I am mysterious and fascinating. An enigma. A cryptograph to decipher with special glasses and a secret decoder ring. And part of me wonders if he unknowingly has the tools.

When he looks at me, he *sees* me. Although he hasn't stated as much, he sees the hurt. The only difference when he sees it versus my family and friends, he doesn't dig. He doesn't insist I speak up and voice the madness cycling in my head. Doesn't suggest therapy or "getting out there." He simply asks if I want to talk about it.

He makes me *want* to talk about it. Yet, I still bite my tongue.

I swipe up my cottage key from the table and head for the door. "Maybe today I'll find my voice," I mutter to myself as I lock up.

Just as I step onto the gravel path and walk toward the main residence, I hear my name called out. I stop and spin to see Fletcher twenty feet back. Although fully aware his cottage is an easy one-minute walk from my own, I startle at seeing him.

I skitter to a stop, lift a hand and wave. "Morning." My eyes rake over him in a shameful manner and I quickly shift my gaze to the trees.

When he reaches me, the smile he flashes heats me more than the summer sun. I inwardly cringe at how easily this man makes me feel emotional connections I never experienced prior. Not even with Chris.

Do these feelings make me a horrible person? Do they make me subpar? In my eyes, yes.

Once upon a time, I made an unbreakable commitment. A pledge. Although I am not to blame for the severance of that commitment, it still knocks me breathless when I ponder a future without it.

"'Morning. Headed to breakfast?"

I nod subtly. "Yes. Figured I'd see you there."

"Shall we?" He gestures for me to walk.

The gravel crunches beneath my Converse as I take one, two, three steps before Fletcher falls in step beside me. We walk in silence from our cottages to the main residence, soaking up the beautiful morning. The sun beams behind the tall tree line, slowly ascending. Birds call out to one another, swapping morning songs. Woodland creatures wake to scavenge the earth for breakfast. It is all so picturesque and peaceful.

Today, I dressed in minimal layers. Denim shorts, a cotton tee with a flannel over top, and Converse. Although the morning air has me rubbing my upper arms, the summer sun will warm my skin for most of the day. So, being able to peel off the flannel and kick off my shoes is a nice option.

"What are we doing today?" I ask as we step inside the main residence.

Fletcher side-eyes me. "Would you be upset if I kept it secret? Just for a bit."

Would it upset me? No. It has been a while since anyone surprised me. With outings or gifts or gestures. Several of my friends admit to not liking surprises—the idea makes them anxious or skeptical or wary. Me, on the other hand, I love surprises. Love the ripple of nervous energy flowing through my limbs. Love the excitement encompassed in the not knowing; in the mystery. And I love the fact that someone wants to make me breathless and jittery with thrill. To me, surprises are a sign of affection.

Does this mean Fletcher holds affection for me?

And why does the idea of such a concept send me soaring through the clouds with a constricted heart?

"No, that's fine," I tell him as we enter the main residence.

For some reason, breakfast is busier than ever this morning. Days of the week mean nothing at the retreat— every day is the weekend while here. Perhaps it is the time. Usually, I don't arrive until an hour after either meal starts. Maybe I subconsciously did so to prevent long lines and loud chatter.

With full plates, Fletcher and I find seats near a window to eat. Bite by bite, we clear our plates in peaceful silence. When we finish, Fletcher takes both our plates to the bin, stopping to speak with Jessimine on his return.

And for a moment, I guiltlessly stare after him. Survey him foot to crown. Take in his relaxed posture and ease at speaking with others. How he toys with something in his pocket—not out of nerves—but doesn't remove it. The way his fingers bow and curl when he lifts a hand to tuck loose strands behind his ear.

Fletcher moves with such finesse. Similar to the way a dancer glides when they walk, but different. As if he hears music in everything; ebbing and flowing around it, with it. Synergistically. Instinctually. Every step a drum beat. Every hand gesticulation a strum of the guitar. And every smile the lyrics to a memorable melody.

As the last idea passes through my mind, Fletcher peers over at me. Catching my eyes on him. Heat crawls up from my chest to my throat, resting on my cheeks. The corner of his mouth tips up in a half smile.

I have the sudden urge to ditch my flannel and fan myself.

When he refocuses his attention to Jessimine, I gulp down the last of my orange juice before loosening my flannel to allow for more circulation. Just as I unbutton the last button, Fletcher steps up to the table. The ivory buttons of his white linen shirt crowd my vision. After several ragged breaths, it dawns on me that I am staring at his abdominals. Granted, they aren't visible through the material, but it doesn't stop me from conjuring the image.

I swallow and peek up. His eyes study me with familiarity. An ease I don't quite understand since we barely know one another. And for a moment, I relish in the comfort I see; feel. I settle on the unique coloration of his irises—like golden sunlight trickling through the lush foliage of vibrant green trees—and note I will never stare into the forest canopy without thinking of Fletcher.

He extends a hand for me to take. My gaze instinctively travels down—to his lips, down his throat and over his Adam's apple, along the vertical line of buttons, until I veer off to his arm. As my eyes trail along the inside of his forearm, I spot a small tattoo between his watchband and the start of his palm, close to his thumb. Unable to make out the symbol, I make note to ask him later.

I place my hand in his and rise. Jitters erupt beneath my diaphragm. Delight flows in my veins. Soon, Fletcher will disclose his surprise plan for our day together. And no matter what it is, I already know it will be enjoyable.

"Do you need to get anything from your cottage before we go? Sunglasses? Sunscreen?"

"If we'll be outside, those things may be a good idea."

We stand near the exit of the main residence, our hands clamped. In this moment, I feel twenty years younger. Sixteen and on edge about my first real date. Wondering if my date will ask me out again. Tense about kissing; not knowing if I kiss well or poorly.

Fletcher gives my hand a light squeeze then drops it.

"Yes, we'll be outdoors. Why don't you go get what you need and meet me back here in fifteen minutes."

Fifteen minutes. That will give me time to ditch the flannel I no longer need and grab a few essentials.

"Meet you back here."

I wander out of the main residence, but Fletcher doesn't follow in my wake. As I round the bend that leads to the path for our cottages, I peek over my shoulder and spot Fletcher. He watches after me; contentment smoothing the hard lines of his face and jaw. Admiration and reverence tipping his lips up into a smile. And just that look alone has me walking faster.

But what does any of it mean?

TEN

ONCE MADELINE DISAPPEARS down the path toward the cottages, I waltz back into the main residence and beeline to Jessimine.

After Madeline agreed to spend the day with me, I fumbled through the brochures and guides to find something to do. Most of the activities listed in the generic, colorful trifold were group related. I wanted to have Madeline all to myself.

So, I enlisted the help of Jessimine. And she didn't let me down.

As I round the corner back into the dining area, Jessimine spots me and nudges her head toward the kitchen. I cross the room and pass the dwindling crowd of retreat guests, a smile shared here and there, and enter the colossal kitchen.

Impatient, I lean against the counter and tap my fingers on the outside of my thigh as I wait. I drum the beat of "Dream On" by Aerosmith, barely making it past the intro when Jessimine steps in the kitchen. Her face glows with pure delight. Teeth bright against her sun-kissed skin. An extra bounce in her step.

Is this because of me? Or did she have an exceptional conversation with the gentleman she spoke with before following me into the kitchen? I can't be certain.

"Thank you for doing this, Jessimine."

She strolls past me and pats my shoulder. "No trouble at all. Glad to help."

I stare after her as she opens a closet or pantry door then disappears inside. A moment later, she exits with a lidded wicker basket hugged to her chest. For the next few minutes, I follow her with my eyes as she coasts from cabinet to cabinet, plucking an array of items.

With each new selection, she adds it to the basket and goes for another. Mixed nuts and dried fruits. A loaf of crusty bread. A variety of cheese, meats, and olives. One by one, the basket fills, but not before she sets plates, cups, and cutlery inside.

"You're a godsend," I say as she hands over the heavy basket.

She smiles up at me with a glint in her eye. "Nah, I just want everyone to enjoy their time here. And if that involves filling a basket with food, so be it."

I step forward and wrap an arm around her shoulders. "Either way, thank you."

When we break apart, she waves me off. "Now, go. Get out of here. Enjoy this beautiful day."

I exit the kitchen and wander through the residence until I step out into the morning sun. Before leaving my cottage earlier, I double-checked the weather. A reassurance the day still held blue skies with occasional fluffy clouds.

Unhooking my sunglasses from the front of my shirt, I slide them on and tip my head back. The sun glows just above the eastern tree line. Cumulus clouds float in the cerulean sky like loose cotton balls. Wayward strands of hair tickle my face in the gentle breeze.

I close my eyes and inhale deeply. The salty ocean air fills my lungs as the sun warms my skin. A quiet rustle stirs from the trees nearby, most likely from the natural inhabitants. When the sound is replaced with the steady crunch of gravel, I open my eyes and level my gaze.

Madeline steals my every breath. Robs my ability to speak. Ripples my thought patterns like a skittering pebble across the water. I don't question it. I simply bask in the sensations.

She stops an arm's reach from me. Dark sunglasses shield her eyes from view, but my face heats from her gaze. A subtle smile softens her lips and I swallow down my desire to feel them.

"Ready," I croak.

Almost imperceptibly, she nods. Is she worried her voice will crack too?

I proffer my empty hand and smile. When her fingertips graze my wrist and slowly trek down my palm to take my hand, I breathe again. New life fills my lungs and wakes every dormant atom in my body.

Without a word, I lead us toward the trailhead. Jessimine informed me one of the paths ends at a river where the retreat has canoes, kayaks and paddleboats available for guests. They placed signs along the river to guide everyone on the water. She also let me know of some places to stop and wander.

"We're hiking?" Madeline asks as we start down the trail.

"Yes and no."

Her gaze on my profile is a heatwave, but I keep my eyes forward. Even under the tree canopy, she will see the flush spread up my neck to my cheeks. The crimson doesn't embarrass me. If I am honest with myself, I want her to know how she affects me. How my pulse stutters and breath hitches. How my skin heats and an invisible energy stirs to life at my epicenter. That she has influence over me.

But, for now, I keep these details to myself.

After another bend in the trail, the trees open up and the river comes into view. The river seems more a stream, but is wide enough to let boats pass without concern.

"Thought we'd go canoeing. Is that okay?"

I hadn't considered that she may not like the water. Or

that she may not be able to swim. *Shit.* But before I second-guess every idea I had for the day, she stops my tailspin.

"Yeah. It's a nice day to be on the water."

We hoist a canoe off the rack, put on life jackets and load up. She situates on the bow seat and grips the sides as I push off and hop in. I pick up the paddle, steer us to the middle of the stream and follow the current.

Hour-long minutes pass as we float on clear water. Madeline stares into the trees and occasional canopy as we glide past. She balances her weight and leans over the edge to peer into the water. Or maybe check her reflection. Regardless, I cannot take my eyes off her.

When the canopy opens up, she drops her hand to the water and skims the surface with her fingertips. Chin resting on her other hand on the canoe edge, I memorize this moment. The tranquil way she watches the water part under her touch. The softness on her face as she relaxes out in the open. This side of her… I want to see more of it.

I have seen her relaxed before now, but not to this degree. Madeline seems to be in her element. Her body less rigid, less on alert.

I hate to disturb her peace. Frankly, I am more than willing to sit here and ogle her all day. But I also want to enjoy conversation with her. To learn more about who Madeline is and what she likes. Little tidbits to tell me more about her. Pieces to tuck away for memories and, if I am lucky, the future.

"Have you been on the water before?"

She rotates to face me better; her fingertips still toying with the water's surface. The sun glints her face in such a way, I see through her dark lenses. And the way she studies me. I hold her gaze, although I doubt she sees the intensity in my eyes.

"Yes, but not since I was a child. My parents took us out a few times each summer."

"In the Pacific?"

"No. The campground we went to in the summer butted up to a lake."

I paddle and steer us toward the right bank. "Just you and your parents?"

She nods. "And my little brother. He made camping adventurous, even as we aged."

"Ah, yes. Us boys can do that." I chuckle and she joins in. But I don't disregard the fact she just revealed another piece of herself to me. I revel in it.

As the front of the canoe meets soil, she lifts her head and scans the area. Jessimine told me which markers had trails, lookouts, and tables for lunch. This stop is for the lookout tower.

Once we have the canoe out of the water and in the shade, I grab the basket and guide us down the path. Although we won't be eating here, it isn't smart to leave the food unattended with animals in the area.

The river just out of view, I startle when Madeline slips her hand in mine. The gesture is unexpected, but welcome. I glance down at her next to me and smile as hundreds of scenarios whip through my head. Scenarios I shake away.

"So, what's out here?"

"Jessimine says this trail leads to a lookout tower."

"This trail?"

"Yeah. Guess there're several trails off the river. Thought we'd check out two or three."

From the corner of my eye, I glimpse her smile. "Sounds nice."

We take our time on the path, looking up into the trees and into the woods on our way. After roughly fifteen minutes, the base of the lookout tower comes into view. When we step up to it, my eyes drift up the wall to the top. The tower is easily four stories, if not more.

"Wow," we say in unison, then laugh.

"Ready for this?" I jerk my chin toward the stairs.

She nods. "No, but let's go."

I gesture for her to take the lead and follow at her pace. The last time I climbed this many stairs was years ago. By no means am I old, but this lookout tower reminds me of the last time I worked out. And the tower isn't four stories; it is six.

When we reach the top landing, every step up was worth getting here. I jerk to a stop as my eyes widen at the three-hundred-and-sixty-degree view.

From here, we see the tops of the trees for miles and the ocean even farther. I imagine this place would be a photographer's wet dream. As a musician, inspiration has hit me more in this place than anywhere else in the last several months.

I set the basket down on a bench and take my phone out. Opening the camera, I switch it to panoramic and capture the scenery.

"If you don't want to be in the picture, now's your chance to move," I say as I spin around. As suspected, Madeline shuffles out of the way.

Before I leave this place, before we go our separate ways, I hope to get at least one picture of her. Madeline is ingrained in my memory, but physical images are perfect for those times when you question reality.

When I finish the picture, I open it and show Madeline.

"Wow."

"My thoughts exactly."

We stay at the top of the tower until the sun nears mid-sky. We stare at the treetops, the ocean, the river below. A few times, when she looks the opposite direction, I peek her way. Take in the sight of her with the ocean at her back, with the wind kicking up her flyaway strands. No matter the lighting, backdrop, or elements, Madeline enchants me.

Before she catches me in the act, I look away. Back out at the trees. I close my eyes and get lost with the clouds.

I know the exact moment Madeline sidles up to me. She doesn't touch me or make a sound. Although my eyes are closed, I sense her inches away. Arm so close, if I shift my weight, mine would brush hers.

"Are you okay?" she whispers as if a crowd eavesdrops nearby.

Eyes still closed, I take a deep breath. "Yeah. Just soaking it all in." I open my eyes and face her. "All of this… it's so new to me."

Up in the lookout tower, life has new perspective. Up here, so many aspects of my life feel inconsequential. Other aspects hold more significance. Most of all, I identify the emptiness inside. The hidden or lost pieces that have thrown me off balance.

Would I have recognized this without Madeline here? Is it this place or her that gives me clarity? Maybe it is a little of both. But without her, I wouldn't have come here today. To the tower, to this view.

She lays her hand over mine on the rail. "It's new to me too."

With her hand on mine, we both stare out to the horizon. When she takes a deep breath, I flip my hand over under hers.

"Should we head down? There're more sights to see."

She clutches my hand. "Only if you agree to come back here with me before we leave the retreat."

My throat dries and I swallow. "Of course."

Hands clasped, I grab the basket as we take our time down the stairs and back to the canoe. We drift away in the water and it feels as if a piece of me stayed on shore. Something about this place is magical; unexplainable.

At the second stop, both of us remain reserved until we reach the wooden picnic tables.

Funny enough, I have never been so reticent around a woman. Same can be said about the women I have dated.

Not that Madeline and I are dating. We are simply enjoying each other's company while here.

But I like her muted strength and solemnity. The more I get to know her, the more my gut instinct repeats it probably isn't in her nature to be so restrained.

"Hungry?"

She peers up at me, the edge of her lip pinned between her teeth. The sight wakes me up from the haze I had been in from the tower. Rather than open my mouth, I wait for her response.

She releases her lip and swallows. "Mmhm. What's for lunch?" I don't miss the off-key tone in her voice.

We dig out the feast Jessimine packed and fill our plates. Over the next hour, we eat and drink and get to know each other better. Madeline tells me a little about her parents and younger brother. All of them live within miles of each other in Northern California. Much as I want to ask what part of Northern California, I bite my tongue. If she wants me to know, she will share. I tell her about my parents—leaving out the unsavory parts—and sister. When I mention my dad, I refer to Jonathan. If Madeline and I evolve into something more, I will consider mentioning my father. Until then, he isn't worth the wasted time.

With full bellies, we pack up the leftovers and walk the small trail hand in hand.

Madeline next to me feels right; natural. Would she say the same about me? Or is she appeasing me? God, I hope her touch isn't pity on me for her reaction the other day.

"So, what is it you do in the real world at the doctor's office?" I ask as we hit the end of the trail and turn back.

"The real world?"

"Yes, the real world." I jut out my chin. "This place is a distant planet we never knew existed."

She chuckles and tips her head back to look into the canopy. "Suppose you're right." She levels her head and a sadness blankets her features. "I manage the office and sit at the front desk on occasion. Nothing that requires several degrees."

Is she ashamed of her job? Is that why her face fell? Or is it something else?

"Some of the best jobs don't require degrees. As long as you enjoy what you do, that's what matters."

I studied music throughout public school, but I never attended formal training or education after high school. Unless I plan to do the technical side of music, there is no reason for me to shell out thousands of dollars.

"True," she whispers.

Why do I get the feeling it isn't her specific job that has caused the mood shift? Maybe someone in the office makes her uncomfortable. The remote thought burns white hot in my solar plexus.

I squeeze her hand. "You okay?"

Sticks crunch and snap under our feet and she doesn't say a word. But I have learned Madeline will speak when she is ready. So, I wait her out. She doesn't make me wait long.

"Yes. It's just…" She stares out into the trees. When I glance at her profile, I see her lips tucked between her teeth as her chin wobbles. She wipes at her eyes and takes a deep breath. "I haven't been at work for months."

Whatever the reason, I doubt it has anything to do with her coworkers.

"Want to talk about it?"

She shakes her head. "One day, but not now." I latch on to *one day* and embrace the possibility of seeing and talking to her in the future. Beyond this place.

"Whenever you're ready."

We make it back to the canoe and hop in. The remainder of our time on the water is spent in silence. She toys with the water as she did earlier. I paddle the canoe and split my focus between the river sights and Madeline.

One day.

What did she mean when she said that? One day before we leave the retreat? Or after we leave? Seeing Madeline once we leave this place seems like an impossibility. Maybe she meant we will keep in touch. Talk on the phone. Send texts or emails. But that feels so high school. Like those times when you wished everyone a great summer in their yearbook, jotted KIT above your phone number, but most didn't keep it touch.

Madeline is more than a generic line everyone dishes out, but doesn't mean. She is the type of woman you have meaningful conversations with. The woman you treasure and treat with reverence. The woman that makes you whole when you feel anything but.

So, when she says *one day*, I have to believe she means a day in the future. Off this property. Away from this retreat. If she does, I will find a way to make it happen.

For Madeline, I will do anything.

ELEVEN

Madeline

TODAY HAS BEEN a whirlpool of emotion. Spending time with Fletcher has been wonderful. But time with him also feels more intimate than I care to admit.

I don't remember the last time I smiled or laughed like I did today. Not since…

Fletcher brings out a side of me I thought vanished with Chris. His patience and respect have me reminiscent. And I don't quite know how I feel about it. The similarities both men possess confuses me at times.

What does this mean? I gravitate toward the same "type" of man? Is this normal?

When it comes to physical features, Chris and Fletcher are polar opposites. Chris's military-cut blond hair versus Fletcher's unruly, shoulder-length brown locks. Chris stood closer to my height; where Fletcher could easily rest his chin on my head. And Chris had a body similar to a runner—slender and fit; where Fletcher stretches shirts taut with muscles I daydream of touching.

But when it comes to personality and traits, the similarities are difficult to miss. Aside from the patience of a saint and endless respect, both men possess an unmatched tenderness. Equally devoted and attentive. If I took the time to know Fletcher more, I don't doubt he'd have even more in common with Chris.

And that scares me to the bone. In both good and bad ways.

The canoe slows to a stop on the dirt where we started our adventure. An adventure I thoroughly enjoyed. It reminded me of spontaneous trips from years past. Escapades with no map or agenda. Impromptu fun.

"Thank you for today," I say as we tuck away the canoe.

Fletcher picks up the basket and sidles up to me. "You're most welcome."

I take a deep breath. *It's okay to feel the way you do. It's normal. Human nature.* I reach for Fletcher's hand and my heart quivers at how perfect it feels around mine. Warm. Rough with occasional softness. Strong. His hand hugs mine as if it were made to fit.

We amble up the path toward the main residence without hurry. The sun dips closer to the west horizon. Birds chirp in the canopy, but quieter than when we walked this path earlier.

Warmth fizzles and expands in my chest like a star being born. The more time I spend with Fletcher, the more I open up to him, the more noticeable the sensation.

I don't want to question it. Yet I do.

I question how something so strong, so powerful, can be felt after only knowing him such a short time. Does this make me a bad person? For disregarding Chris so easily. Am I smothering memories of Chris with thoughts of and emotions for Fletcher?

Without hesitation, I reach up and clutch my necklace through my shirt. I squeeze the band at the heart and close my eyes briefly as a shuddered breath leaves my lungs.

Fletcher tightens his hand on mine. Comforting me. "You okay?"

Our feet crunch the gravel another ten feet before I nod. "Yeah," I answer with sandpaper on my tongue.

His gaze heats my skin, but I don't look up at him. Can't. If I do, the dam will burst. The tears I refuse to cry will barrel out. My resistance to open up fully with Fletcher will shatter. And now isn't the time.

I get enough sympathetic stares, shoulder pats, awkward hugs and painful smiles. The last person I want pity from is Fletcher. It would wreck me.

He edges closer to my side. Brushes his arm with mine as his gait slows to a stop. His breath warm and irregular on my hair as he leans into me. I close my eyes, wait for his lips to press my crown. But he inches away before any contact. He lingers in my orbit, a moon balancing an ecosystem. Not always visible, but a constant presence.

"One day," he whispers. He straightens, but doesn't step forward.

"One day," I repeat.

Fletcher takes my plate and his to the bin in the dining room. Throughout dinner, Jessimine side-eyed and smiled in our direction. The wrinkles near her eyes and lips softened as they scrunched together. An odd but gentle sight. Just like the one I see now.

The man beside her gets up and goes toward Fletcher. Then Jessimine heads my direction. I feel fourteen again. Like the time my mother pulled me aside and we had "the talk" after she caught me kissing a boy from school.

"How was your day?" She sits in Fletcher's chair.

I reach for my water, take a sip and give myself a moment to organize my thoughts. The cool liquid soothes my dry throat, but not my nerves. Why does her question make my palms sweat?

I set the glass down. "Good. Yours?"

Jessimine scoots closer. Her eyes narrow infinitesimally as she regards my brief, vague response. She tilts her head marginally as her lips curve up with affection.

"Good, honey." She pats my hand. "Was beautiful outside. Don't you agree?"

I nod. "Yes." Over at the bin, Fletcher engages in a similar conversation with the man. He glances my way with a half smile and shrugs. I turn my attention back to Jessimine. "Was nice to be on the water, too. It's been a while."

Jessimine prattles on about the different canoe trails set up. I hear but don't absorb her words. Instead, I zero in on Fletcher. The way he animates his hands as he talks. The flex of his forearms and length of his fingers. How his eyes widen and brows inch up with his exuberance. And how every few words, he peeks over at me with the hint of a smile.

"Shall we?" Jessimine asks.

I press my lips in a straight line. *Shall we what?* "Sorry, what?" I ask as heat crawls up my neck.

Jessimine gives me a knowing smile. "Head out to the bonfire. Shall we?"

"Oh." I shuffle to stand and smooth out the nonexistent wrinkles on my shirt. "Yes, I'd love to."

We amble through the residence toward the back. Jessimine holds the door open for me and I step through. But she doesn't. In her stead, Fletcher sidles up to me and takes my hand. We both glance over our shoulders and spot Jessimine and the man side by side in the residence.

"Well, that was awkward." Fletcher chuckles.

"Uh, yeah. Felt like the time my mom asked a hundred questions after my first date." My cheeks heat. Thank goodness the sun has set and the sky is dark enough to shadow my skin.

Fletcher squeezes my hand and guides us toward the fire. "Same. Paul gave me the third degree. Asked questions not even my parents would."

"Paul?"

We close in on the fire and Fletcher gestures for me to pick our seats. I choose a loveseat on the east side of the fire, allowing a view of the ocean. We sit and I bring my knees to my chest while turning my palms to the fire. From the corner of my eye, Fletcher takes in my profile.

"Yeah, Paul," he croaks then clears his throat. "Jessimine's partner."

"As in personal or business?"

He shrugs. "Maybe both, but definitely the first."

Well that explains the tag team tactic in the dining room. I laugh and shake my head.

"What?"

"They swarmed us like sharks the second you stepped away. Think it bugged her I didn't say much."

Fletcher inches closer and bumps my shoulder with his. "Don't worry about it." I tilt my face to catch his better in the firelight. "Probably just being cordial. See how we enjoyed the food and the day."

He explains it with such ease. As if these conversations happen often. Under normal circumstances, they might. But nothing about us is normal. Both of us came to this retreat for very different reasons. His more simplistic than mine. And I may not reveal mine before we leave this place.

Part of me wants to, though. Part of me wants to open up to Fletcher. Cut the sutures holding my heart together and let my truth spill out. But I won't. Not yet. Not enough time has passed.

"It's okay, ya know," he whispers a breath from my hair. "You don't need to say anything. Not unless you're comfortable."

I twist to face him, his face inches from mine. The fire glows like sunshine on his forest irises and I get lost a moment. Lost in the idea of moving forward. Of opening up and being myself again. Someone I haven't been for so long. Someone I hope still resides inside me. I like her. Enthusiastic Madeline. Fun, driven Madeline. Open book Madeline.

"I want to, though," I whisper almost inaudibly. The backs of my eyes burn as my vision blurs. My throat swells and I swallow past the thickness. I stare into his eyes, seek comfort from his steady gaze and bite my inner lower lip. "I don't want to be this way anymore."

He takes my hand, his eyes not straying from mine. His thumb strokes small circles over the center of my palm. "What if I like the way you are?"

I close my eyes, welcome the temporary darkness and shake my head. When I open my eyes, Fletcher invades all my senses. His forest-fire eyes locked with mine. His breath stutters and coats my lips. I gasp and inhale his clean cedar scent. And something inside me shifts. Settles. Finds peace.

"What if this isn't the real me?" I choke out.

He gives a small, lopsided smile. "Might not be you all the time, but it's still you. The sad part."

Oh, god. Does he know? What happened and why I am here? My eyes dart between his and dig deep for answers to questions I haven't asked.

"Wh-what do you mean?"

"Madeline..." His thumb continues to circle my palm. He reaches up with his free hand and tugs gently on the end of my hair. "I don't know what happened to you, but you wear your heart on your sleeve. From what I see, anyway." He pauses, frees my hair then brushes his knuckles along my jawline. Suddenly, there isn't enough oxygen in the atmosphere. His eyes follow the motion a beat before lifting to meet mine. "Not everyone is as observant."

I swallow and sigh, relieved my emotional meltdown isn't blasted in neon lights. In the same breath, I freeze. The relief all but temporary. Shoved aside as Fletcher strokes my jawline again. As his touch sparks a fire beneath my skin. As his eyes scream emotions I haven't experienced in far too long. Emotions that riddle me with guilt to feel again.

"Fletcher..."

He searches my gaze. "Yeah?"

I lick my lips and his eyes drop to follow the motion. "What's happening?"

His eyes shoot to mine, a slight twitch to his brow. "Don't really know." He toys with my hair again then drops his hand. "Does it bother you?" I tilt my head. "Me touching you. Does it bother you?"

It should bother me. Should make me shy away and crawl into a corner. The band over my sternum burns my skin. A reminder why this whole scenario *should* bother me.

But it doesn't.

For the first time in months, I feel *alive*. Not just physically, but also mentally and emotionally. And it scares the hell out of me. After Chris and what happened, being close with someone terrifies me to no end. Not because I believe myself incapable of loving again. Quite the opposite.

What if I open up again and the same thing happens? What if I *lose* him? Lose myself again?

Fletcher lights every star in the night sky. Brightens the darkness with his gentle touch and wondrous soul. If his light fades, though, I fear I won't survive the dark again. Fear I won't return.

And I won't risk him for selfish reasons.

"It should, but no," I answer and tremble with my level of honesty.

"Why?"

I close my eyes and pinch my brows. "Why what?"

His fingertip paints the edge of my chin. "Why should it? Why doesn't it?"

I barely hear the words with his breath so close to my

lips. But I refuse to open my eyes and check. Refuse to read the emotion on his face and let them register with my heart. Not yet.

I clutch the band beneath my shirt. Fist the cotton around the thick metal. The backs of my eyes sting. Saliva pools in my mouth. And it hurts to swallow.

"I should feel guilty," I choke out. A tear slips free. "Ashamed." I open my eyes and take in a blurry Fletcher. "But I don't." Another tear spills down my cheek. "And that seems much worse."

Fletcher cups my cheek and rests his forehead to mine. The simple touch the most intimacy I have felt in far too long. Guilt tells me to pull back, to not let this man I barely know touch me like a lover. That this is wrong.

Chris pops in my head. His kind eyes and sweet smile. How he wrapped me in his arms and held me close. His shy touches and gentle kisses. Chris will be forever tattooed on my heart. Every touch and kiss and breath we shared.

"It's okay to be happy without me." The last words Chris said come back to haunt me. *"Maddie, it's okay to move on. To find love again."*

I screw my eyes tight and rock my forehead against Fletcher as the searing pain of my past rears its ugly head.

People move on every day. Move past pain and heartache. Learn to smile and laugh and love again. But how? How do you move on when you vowed to love someone all your life? Can I move on? Can I love someone new and still love Chris? Friends and family and therapists all say moving on is possible. That there is nothing wrong with wanting to live life, even with someone new.

Fletcher swipes a thumb over my tear-stained cheek. "Hey," he whispers and I open my eyes. "You don't have to tell me." I nod imperceptibly. "But please don't torture yourself. Don't burden yourself with some ideal. You're allowed to *feel*, Madeline. Regardless of what anyone says."

I laugh without humor. "That's the thing, though."

"What?"

"Everyone close to me has said the same. That it's okay to move on." Chris's family said as much the last time I saw them. The first time I showered and dressed to look nice rather than out of necessity.

"You don't have to tell me what happened. But can I ask one question?" I search Fletcher's eyes, see nothing but his affection for me and nod. "How long?"

Of all the questions he could have asked—questions I have been asked countless times—he chooses to ask how much time has passed. Not "who was the man?" or "what happened to him?" or "were you there when it happened?" like every other person who coddles my *situation*.

Fletcher knows whatever happened was bad. Devastating. *Flip your life upside down* painful. He knows this because he sees past my carefully stacked brick wall. Sees the frail woman with fragments of her heart in her hands.

And he wants to know how long. How long since a

man has touched me, kissed me, loved me. Because Fletcher cares about me.

"Seven months," I choke out and fist my necklace tighter.

Fletcher toys with my hair then grazes my cheek with his knuckles. "Not long at all."

TWELVE

Fletcher

TOMORROW. All of this ends tomorrow. Tomorrow, we head back to reality. A reality where I don't see Madeline every day. A reality where I probably won't see her much at all.

What a sad reality.

The past several days have been nothing short of life changing. Madeline and I have connected on an emotional and spiritual level. Not in the sense of talking about faith or religion. More like that, deep down, "my soul recognizes your soul" connection. And yet, we have done nothing more than enjoy each other's company, share great conversation and hold hands.

But it ends tomorrow. And I have no idea where that leaves us.

Madeline plans to return to work. Since her tragedy seven months ago—which I still remain oblivious to—she has sheltered at home. Stopped working and grocery shopping and practicing most daily activities. She came to the retreat—her family's doing—to get perspective. To step back and look at life through a different lens. To discover how to move forward with her life.

From our first day here, Madeline has grown. Not necessarily moved on, but made forward strides. In the last few days, she has smiled more than all the previous days combined.

Her smiles knock the air from my lungs. Makes my heart beat a new rhythm.

Does that happen with her too? Will tomorrow rob her of this newfound joy? Does she smile more because of me?

I throw the blanket off my legs and roll to the edge of the bed. "Ugh…" No sense lying here with my head in the clouds.

Today, I need to take advantage of every last minute with Madeline. Make our last full day together special. A few ideas come to mind, but I need to gauge how she feels.

After a quick shower, I dress and dash out the door. As I approach the Snapdragon cottage, Madeline comes into view. A brilliant smile adds a hint of rosiness to her cheeks. Hair—secured back—sways as she bounds my direction. Eyes shaded by dark lenses, but crinkled on the outer edges.

"'Morning," I say as she stops in front of me.

The last week, it has been like this. Not certain if it's coincidence or on purpose, but Madeline meets me outside her cottage each morning. We walk to the main residence hand in hand, enjoy breakfast together then hike a trail or walk the surf or sit in the sun and identify shapes in the clouds.

My bones lose shape at the idea of her peeking out the blinds, waiting for me each morning.

"Morning." Her smile masks the low enthusiasm of her voice. "Breakfast?"

I nod and take her hand. Gravel crunches beneath our feet as we amble toward the main residence. Every other step, I side-eye Madeline. Take in the shape of her lips and prominent cheekbones when she thinks my attention is elsewhere.

Until Madeline, I don't recall studying a woman so closely. And I don't mean "curvy" assets.

Madeline has a softness. Not quite demure, but she balances on the edge of reservation. Her sad side appeals to me, but her less subdued side beguiles me. When she cocks a brow and tips up the corner of her mouth. When she says something flirty but hides the words behind troubled eyes. Or when she bumps my arm with hers before resting her head on my shoulder.

Those small moments speak volumes. They speak of a once outgoing woman. Someone honest and caring and playful.

A woman I want more time with.

We round a dense thicket of bushes and the main residence comes into view. Each step forward is one less second of time spent together. Food is an obvious necessity, but I want to keep it short and sweet today.

Beside me, Madeline lengthens her stride and I wonder if the same thought crossed her mind.

Inside the dining area, we plate up minimal food and sit in the same chairs we have occupied for days. We wave and say good morning to others as they join. But for the most part, we eat in silence. Before long, I carry our empty plates to the bin and we wander out.

"Anything you'd like to do today?"

She tucks her lips between her teeth as we weave our way toward the exit. As we pass the art room, Madeline stops and tugs me back a step.

"We haven't painted the entire time here."

I drop my gaze to hers. "Would you like to?"

She nibbles at her thumb then nods. "Yeah. Think I would."

We spend the next three hours behind canvas on easels. Madeline studies the acoustic guitar and music sheets propped in the center of the room. Then she dips a brush in paint and flicks it across the canvas. While she paints the arranged piece—strange coincidence it was musical—I paint her.

Our easels angled enough she doesn't see my work. Which is good because one, I don't paint well. And two, I don't know how she would feel about me portraying her this way.

Will seeing this bother her? Does my painting her make me a creep? I pray the answer is no to both.

She sets down her brush, rolls her shoulders and stretches her neck. Her biggest smile yet brightens the room.

"It's been so long since I've done anything creative." She glances my way. "Thank you."

My brows bunch in the middle. "Why are you thanking me?"

"For letting me do this. For doing it with me."

I set my brush down and step closer to her. I drop my gaze and trace my fingertips along her forearm, following the action with my eyes. Madeline gasps but doesn't retreat from my touch.

For days, it has been like this. Subtle touches with deeper meaning. Most of the time, I instigate the contact. But every now and again, my heart stutters when she provokes connection.

With Madeline, I don't want to get carried away. Swept up in emotions that will set sail in less than twenty-four hours. Okay, they won't necessarily disappear. But the physicality we have shared will become a memory.

Am I a balm for her? A healing salve applied in time of need.

I want the answer to be a resounding no. But how can I think otherwise?

We haven't discussed what happens when we leave here. Neither of us has mentioned keeping in contact — over the phone or in person. Hell, I don't even know where she lives. A piercing beneath my diaphragm tells me it isn't far from the retreat, but I have no certainty.

When will I see her after we go our separate ways tomorrow?

I shake off the distress and step closer to inspect her painting. As the wet canvas comes into view, my breath falters. The backs of my eyes burn and I shake my head.

"How?"

Her lips upturn as she shrugs. "I love to paint."

As if that explains what I see. *"I love to paint."* Her words repeat in my head as I stare down at the canvas. As I stare down at painted tufts of hair and masculine hands with long fingers plucking guitar strings.

How did she paint this? Paint me? She hasn't seen me play. Or has she?

The first night here, I sat outside my cottage and strummed the inner working of a melody. The tune not quite strong in my head yet. Wasn't until four nights ago that I picked up my guitar again. After I said good night to her outside her cottage. After I desperately wanted to kiss her, but knew it was too soon for her.

That night, a song spilled from my soul, enchanted my fingers and bled from my lips. A song just for me. One I don't know I will share with the world. Lyrics and notes about love and loss and gravity.

Did she hear me? Quite possible.

Madeline may have followed me and watched me from a distance. Watched and listened as I spilled my heart to the dark of night. Spilled my truths when I thought no one heard.

But I don't regret the notion. If she heard me, she hasn't said as much. Hasn't asked who my muse is. And I don't think she plans to.

"I love to paint, too. But mine doesn't hold a candle to yours."

"Let's see," she says with a wave of her fingers.

Um… shit. Did I just walk myself into a corner? Set myself up for the worst last day with her?

She stares into my panicked eyes, brows at her hairline, hand still outstretched. The longer I make her wait, the more exaggerated her extended hand becomes. Like if she tries a different movement, I will cave and hand it over.

After too much time, her stool scrapes against the tile and she straightens. She sidesteps me and heads for the canvas.

"It can't be that—" She freezes. Her jaw drops and eyes glass over. She lifts a trembling hand to cover her mouth. "Fletcher…"

This is bad, isn't it? Shit. I need to fix this. But how? How do I explain why I painted her? Tell her she isn't just some woman I met at a random retreat. Or another random muse to boost my career.

No, Madeline is more. But what?

"Madeline, I…" Speechless, I fumble with what to say. "This isn't what it looks like."

I wipe clammy hands down my thighs. Look from her

to the painting and back to her. She studies the painting with reverence. Her eyes trace the lines and swirls and edges of paint. Her chest rises and deflates faster and faster. Chin wobbles as her eyes glass over. A tear slips free and rolls down her cheek.

I made her cry. And I have no idea if her tears are good or bad.

"Beautiful," she whispers almost inaudible then swipes under her eyes.

I contemplate my next words. Unsure how she may take them. But the clock is counting down. And time isn't on my side. So, I speak my mind.

"Yes." I lift my hand and brush my knuckles along her cheek. "You are."

Her eyes dart to mine. "Fletcher, I…" Her eyes rake over the painting again. "I don't know what to say. I… I…" She swallows and closes her eyes. "Thank you."

God, I want to kiss this woman. Not in some depraved way. But just touch my lips to hers. Feel her smooth, warm lips beneath mine. Hear her gasp at the contact. Catch her as she melts against me.

But she isn't ready. Not yet. Hopefully in the future. *One day.*

"You're welcome," I croak out. I remove the canvas from the easel and hand it to her. "For you. A gift to remember our time here."

She takes the canvas and gawks over it with tears on her cheeks. "I'll never forget our time here." Her eyes meet mine. "Never. But thank you." She removes her own painting from the easel and hands it to me. "And you should have mine."

This singular moment weighs heavier than any other we have spent together. Loaded with unspoken emotion and the desire for something neither of us is ready to explore. I may want her, crave her, make myself vulnerable near her. But if she isn't ready then neither am I.

Our time will come. I believe that wholeheartedly.

"I will treasure it always." And I have the perfect place to put it. "How about we put these with our things then grab lunch?" I suggest with the aim of lightening the dense air around us.

After lunch, we opt to walk the beach.

Thick grains crunch beneath our feet as we trudge along the coast. Salty air whips wayward strands of Madeline's hair across her face. But she doesn't brush them aside.

Her hand in mine, we stroll miles down the beach. Eyes on the water, on the sand, on everything but each other. On occasion, we stop to sit and watch the waves crash. Madeline plucks random rocks from the sand, surveys them, then discards them.

We sit on driftwood until the sun beams more west.

The silence stretches out between us, comfortable yet charged.

"Should we head back?" I ask, voice thick.

Madeline stares at the surf, eyes shielded by her dark sunglasses. "In a minute," she says, a somber edge to her words. She takes a deep breath, bends to pluck a rock from the sand and pockets it. "I'm ready."

Our walk back goes by quicker as the sun dances closer to the horizon. Too quick. With each step forward, I feel Madeline drifting farther away. Even with her hand in mine. She is here physically, but the rest of her seems to have gone out with the tide.

I squeeze her hand as the main residence comes into view. "Hey." She peers up at me. "Everything okay? You've been quieter than normal."

She bumps my arm with hers. "Yeah." She clears her throat. "Just thinking about tomorrow."

This explains her melancholia. Question is, what specifically has her sad? Much as I would love to be the reason she doesn't want to leave tomorrow, a pang in my gut tells me otherwise.

"We still have the rest of today."

She nods, but doesn't respond as we step off the beach.

Dinner drags on with more silence from Madeline. Until today, our shared silence radiated a green aura. Full of unspoken heart. But now, the green has muddied. Has grown dark and slowly fades.

Madeline slips back inside herself. Crawls back into her shell and shuts out the world. Shuts me out.

And I don't know how to handle this side of her. Don't know how to bring her back to the light.

After we both finish, I take our plates and cups to the dish bin. As I walk back to her, I pause and study her with open eyes. The same beautiful woman sits at the table, but isn't quite Madeline.

Her shoulders droop and head lolls. Eyes stare forward with vacancy. Lips dry and slightly downturned at the corners. She reaches up and clutches her necklace through her shirt.

I take a deep breath and vow to make her smile at least once more before we leave tomorrow. Back at her side, I extend my hand in her direction.

"Let's go sit by the fire."

She blinks a moment then takes my hand. We wander outside and sit on the same love seat we have sat on for the past week.

Tonight, everyone gathers at the bonfire. Most of us leave tomorrow. Leave this magical place and resume reality. This realization has us all quieter than usual. Introspective.

Madeline leans into me and rests her head on my shoulder. "I'll miss this."

I rest my cheek on her head and breathe in her subtle apple scent. "Me too." God, me too.

The next two hours go by in flickers and shadows with Madeline curled into my side. We whisper-talk about what we will miss most about this place. Neither of us mention each other, but the connotation hovers like a storm cloud.

At some point, everyone abandons us. We should go back to our cottages and sleep. But I don't want to miss a single second of Madeline molded against me. Call me selfish, I don't care. I want what I want.

"We should go," she whispers my unspoken thoughts. She lifts her head, but twists to rest her chin on my shoulder. "But I don't want to. Why can't we just stay here? In this moment."

I swallow past the expanding lump in my throat. Without care, I toy with the loose strands of her hair. Rest my forehead on hers. Close my eyes and breathe her in.

"Believe me, I want to. Badly."

When I open my eyes, I stop breathing. Her glassy eyes tug at my soul. "I'll miss you," she chokes out and nods. "More than I thought possible."

I brush my nose along the ridge of hers. Her lips a breath away. "Same." She licks her lips and I close my eyes, fight the urge to kiss her. "We should go," I say against my own wishes.

We both take a deep breath and break apart to stand. I lace her fingers with mine and guide us one last time toward our cottages. She tightens her grip on my hand while wrapping the other around my bicep.

Without hurry, we dawdle down the familiar gravel path. Madeline clings to me as if I might fade away. Breathes heavier. Her hand fidgets, loosening and tightening in mine.

Too soon, we reach her cottage. The Snapdragon.

Does she like snapdragons? I walk her to the door, release her hand and rock on my heels. Before I bid her good night, she snakes her arms around my waist and steps into me. I forget how to breathe. My heart rattles my ribcage. Then I remember how to breathe again, wrap my arms around her shoulders, hold her close and rest my chin on her head.

Madeline, in my arms, in an all-encompassing embrace, balances everything in the world. Settles every anxiety and soothes every fear. Her slender frame bends and curves in all the right places to match my own. Fits me with unorthodox perfection.

I never want to let her go. Never want this moment to end.

All too soon, her arms loosen and unwind from my body. But she doesn't step back. Instead, she hooks a finger in each of my front pockets and keeps her body glued to mine. Her breasts rise and fall and press my stomach, her breath hot just below the hollow of my throat.

"In another life…" she whispers near my skin.

I brush fingers down her spine then softly grip her hips. Kiss the top of her head, her forehead, each of her cheeks. Then rest my forehead on hers. Our noses touch. Lips close enough to taste.

"In another life."

Before our lips meet in the middle, she inches back and breathes deep. Then retreats one painstaking step at a time until she opens the door.

"Good night, Fletcher."

"See you in the morning. Sleep well."

She closes the door behind her and an overwhelming emptiness floods me. An excessive hollowness I can't shake.

I wake before the sun rises. Gather my belongings and pack my bags.

Today may be the temporary end of my time with Madeline, but at least we have the next few hours. And we have time to figure out what happens next.

I zip the last bag and do one last sweep of the cottage. Satisfied, I exit and head for the main residence, and one last breakfast with Madeline. As I pass her cottage, I slow down with the expectation to see her come out.

But she doesn't. I am half tempted to knock on her door, but remain rooted in place.

After staring at her cottage far too long, I all but sprint to the main residence. People swarm like bees outside. A buzz in the air as everyone comes and goes. Hugs and light chatter and promises to keep in touch. And I feel barricaded from getting inside. Getting to Madeline.

The urge to shove people aside builds with each passing second, but I weave past everyone with a cordial smile and wave. When I enter the dining room, I stop and scan the room and the taken seats at the table. More bodies whizz through than typical at this hour. Faces that have become familiar these last two weeks.

But none are Madeline.

Maybe she hasn't finished packing yet. Maybe my timing was off when I reached her cottage.

Just as I turn to dart out the door, a hand grips my bicep. I spin with a painful smile on my face, but it falls away when I see Jessimine and not Madeline.

"Good morning to you too, grumpy face."

I sigh and shake my head. "Sorry. Just thought you were someone else."

"Obviously." Her sad smile doesn't go unnoticed. I start to walk off again, but she stops me. "She left."

"What?" No way I heard her right. No way.

"About an hour ago, she left." I wince as a knife pushes slow and deep between my left ribs. "Not sure if it helps, but she'd been crying." Deeper, deeper. Twist.

I deflate faster than a balloon and pinch my eyes tight. Jessimine lays a hand on my shoulder and squeezes. Her touch doesn't console me. If anything, it drives the knife deeper. Expands the wound further.

"Did she say anything?" The words shaky and garbled as they leave my lips.

Jessimine rubs slow circles on my shoulder. "Sorry, Fletcher." She releases me and steps away.

So that is it. Madeline is gone. Like a specter in the

night. Vanished without a trace. No note, no goodbye. Nothing.

The hollowness from last night expands beneath my sternum. Swallows me limb by limb until Novocain replaces my blood.

She is gone. And she took a huge piece of me with her.

ONE YEAR LATER

THIRTEEN

Madeline

"MADELINE, YOU LOOK BEAUTIFUL." Sylvia takes both my hands in hers. "It's just dinner. Phillip and I will be there too."

Bless Sylvia and her overeagerness to soothe my shaky nerves. And get me "back out there"—her words, not mine. She is lucky my brother loves her so much. Otherwise, I would have shooed her away months ago.

"Why did I agree to this?" I mumble. Why the hell did I agree to a blind date, set up by my brother's girlfriend, when it is the last thing I want.

Because I want to appease her. Shut her up for just one night. Stop her constant interference with my nonexistent love life. Which I am quite content with.

Not that I wish it upon anyone, but if Sylvia lost

Phillip, she would understand my nonchalance toward dating. She would understand the barrier around my heart. A barrier only one person scaled.

But Fletcher is gone.

"You agreed to this because you love me." She flashes me her smiley profile. "And because it's time," she says a little softer.

I take a deep breath and give a slight nod. "Let's get this over with." I exit the bedroom before she rebuts my comment.

In the living room, my brother, Phillip, sits on the couch with the remote in his hand. He mindlessly scrolls through Netflix and watches previews. When I enter, he perks up and rises from the couch.

A gentle smile lifts the corners of his lips as he steps closer. He rests his hands on my shoulders before hugging me close. "You look pretty," he whispers in my ear. "Thanks for pacifying Sylvia." I hug him tighter. He drops his arms and extends an elbow my direction. "Shall we?"

I hook my arm in his, Sylvia takes the other and we leave. We drive into the city and I stare at the office buildings out the back window. Quiet contemporary music floats through the speakers as Phillip and Sylvia talk in the front seat.

The miles pass as the sky darkens. Phillip veers the car into the parking lot of a swanky restaurant. We get out and meander toward the entrance. A man in black slacks and a white button-down loiters near the front, his eyes scan the lot and light up when he sees Phillip.

My blind date. *Great*.

Phillip said he was older, but didn't tell me the age difference. Now, I see why. Hopefully, he just ages poorly. Because he appears more than a decade my senior. I don't mind age gaps, but the man looks old enough to be our father.

"Arthur," Phillip says. Ugh. He even has an old man's name. "How are you, man?" Phillip extends his hand.

"Phillip. Sylvia." He and Phillip shake hands. "Wonderful. And you?" Arthur glances my way. "You must be Maddie."

I extend my hand. "Madeline, actually." Anger floods me as I side-eye my brother. Only close friends and family call me Maddie. And in the company of just family, the occasional Maddie Mae slips out.

Arthur winces imperceptibly, glances at my brother then me as he takes my hand. He kisses my knuckles and a chill rolls through my body. "My apologies, Madeline."

I yank my hand away and cross my arms. Phillip senses my discomfort and suggests we head inside. The men walk together as Sylvia sidles up to me. She loops her arm with mine and rubs my bicep.

"Thank you for trying." She hugs my side and I nod.

The host seats us in the center of the restaurant. We sit three tables away from a small stage, my back to the stage and Sylvia opposite me. A server arrives at the table, relays the chef specials and says the music will begin soon.

I scan the menu with Arthur's eyes on me. My stomach

roils and I refuse to meet his unwelcome stare. Study my menu until the server returns. Shift my legs closer to my brother beneath the tablecloth, but don't bump him.

When I no longer have the menu to hide my face, I focus more on Sylvia and Phillip than Arthur. I don't mean to come off as rude, but this blind date wasn't my idea. And my discomfort has shot from three to nine.

Arthur creeps me out. Plain and simple.

Not long after the server walks off, I excuse myself and bolt for the bathroom. In the comfort of the posh stall, I plant my palms on the walls and breathe deep. Eyes closed, I pep talk myself. Tell myself to get through the evening and decline future dates.

The door opens and I hold my breath. *Clack, clack, clack.*

"Maddie? You okay?"

Sylvia.

I clear my throat. "Yeah. Be out in a minute." I flush the toilet to keep up appearances and exit the stall.

Sylvia greets me with a solemn smile. "Just wanted to check on you. Take your time."

She pivots to leave and I reach for her arm. "Thank you," I say when she looks back. She pats my hand and nods.

As the door closes, I step up to the sink and meet my reflection in the mirror. Stare at my lithe frame and gaunt cheeks. Narrow my eyes at the skin beneath them, the purple crescents hidden with layers of makeup. Drop my gaze to the rouge on my lips; something I haven't worn since my last night with Chris.

Something I regret wearing tonight.

Although unnecessary, I wash my hands then exit the restroom. Back at the table, our salads have arrived. And I am grateful to have something to distract me from conversation, even if I have no appetite.

A uniformed woman sets a stool on the stage as I resume my seat. Part of me hopes the music will drown out the possibility of conversation too. And continue throughout our meal.

I poke at my salad while the rest of the table engages in conversation. Someone taps on the stage microphone and introduces the entertainment, but I am too busy spearing the wilted lettuce to hear what he says.

The room goes quiet and I assume the musician steps on stage. Everyone except me faces the stage.

Guitar chords float through the room, permeate my skin and vibrate my bones.

I know this. How do I know this?

Realization hits. With a too loud clang, I drop my fork, but don't turn in my seat. Sylvia studies me and what I am sure is a jarred expression. She mouths, *"Are you okay?"* I subtly shake my head.

Then I hear his voice. Slow and melodic. The low timbre that now haunts my dreams alongside Chris. I pinch my eyes tight and swallow as I listen to him sing.

"It's all so dreamlike. A figment. A trick of the mind. I still feel… your warm skin near mine. Apple blossoms and rich brown eyes. Swirls of paint and perfect blue skies. Oh, how I wish… I should have stolen your kiss."

I spin to face the stage. My chair stutters and bangs the table. Phillip grumbles, but I ignore him. Ignore everything and everyone in the room.

Except the man on stage. Except the man pouring his soul out.

Fletcher.

Fletcher sits hunched over a black acoustic guitar. Clad in charcoal slacks and a black button-down, the top two buttons undone. His polished black dress shoes ebb and tap with the rhythm. A few strands of his secured hair fall forward, but he doesn't stop to tuck them away. He keeps his eyes downcast and closed and sings to himself.

With each new line and verse, I study the lines near his eyes. Scrutinize the way he pinches them tighter during certain lines. Surveil the furrow of his brow, angle of his head and occasional tuck of his lips.

The song ends with a layer of dejection. A sentiment that resonates in my limbs and roots me in place.

When he stops, I abruptly stand. The chair legs scrape the hardwood further. His eyes pop up at the disruption and meet mine. Neither of us moves for a moment. The audience claps, but our eye contact doesn't falter.

"Madeline?" he whispers into the mic.

And I bolt for the bathroom. I weave between the tables on weak legs and shove the bathroom door open. Again, I hide in the stall.

"No, no, no."

The door opens and closes. "Maddie?"

"In here," I tell Sylvia.

"You okay? What happened? Who is that?"

I heave and press my forehead to the cool metal door. Close my eyes and take slow, methodical breaths. Why am I freaking out? Why can't I stop freaking out?

"I… I'm fine." I swallow and take another deep breath. "That guy on stage, I know him. From the… retreat last year."

Sylvia quiets a moment. "Oh. Oooh."

Yeah, oh. A few months after the retreat, I told Sylvia about Fletcher. Not his name, physical description or in-depth details of exactly how close we became. But I did tell her he was the first man since Chris I had any feelings for. She also knows I left without saying goodbye.

Which is one of the reasons I have myself hidden in a toilet stall. Again.

"Please come out so we can talk. Feels weird talking to a door."

I sigh and unlatch the lock. The door swings open and she hauls me into her arms. She hugs me harder than anytime previous.

"I haven't seen or heard from him in a year. Which is my doing." I close my eyes and groan. "What do I say to him, Syl? After what I did, how do I approach him? He probably hates me."

Sylvia shakes her head and squeezes me tighter. "No, he doesn't hate you. You didn't see his eyes as you ran off. There's no hate whatsoever."

Why does that make it worse? Wouldn't it be easier if Fletcher hated me? Wouldn't it be easier to walk away and move on? That is what I told myself last year as I packed my bags and bolted from the retreat. Obviously, it didn't work.

My cheeks heat. "What do I say? There's no way I'll leave here without us talking."

Sylvia inches back and holds me at arm's length. "Speak your heart, Maddie. You don't have to spill it all in one shot. Just be open and honest. Tell him why you left early without saying goodbye. If he cares, he'll listen."

I go to the sink, wet a paper towel and pat my forehead and cheeks with the cool cloth. "Thank you."

She rubs a hand up and down my arm. "Anytime." Sylvia winces and I narrow my eyes at her. "What about Arthur?"

I roll my eyes and sigh. "Arthur was a no from the get-go. Syl, he looks older than Dad. Not really my type."

She laughs then loops her arm in mine. We exit the bathroom and she leans in close, whispering, "That's what I told Phillip. But men never listen."

Thank goodness Sylvia isn't Team Arthur. Otherwise, we would need some serious girl-talk time.

Each step through the dining area, Fletcher's voice grows louder. I want to look at the stage. Want to read his expression. More than anything, I want to apologize. But that will have to wait until later. When he finishes working and this horrible blind date ends.

Dinner goes slower than granny behind the wheel. I

spend half the time attempting eye contact with Fletcher and ignoring Arthur. Thankfully, Sylvia helps in the Arthur department, engaging him with idle chitchat.

When dinner finally ends, we all stand. I glance over my shoulder at Fletcher and he watches me with curiosity. I hold up a finger and let him know to wait. He nods subtly and continues playing.

We head toward the exit but stop short. Arthur spins and takes my hand, but I yank it away.

"Listen, Arthur. I had a really nice time." Arthur smiles but doesn't pick up the hint I am throwing down. *Great.* "But… I think it'd be better if we agree this" —I gesture between us— "isn't going anywhere."

How long has it been since I rejected someone? Have I ever? Too many years have passed for me to recall such an occasion. Regardless, it sucks.

His face falls. "I understand," he says with dejection in his voice. "For what it's worth, I had a nice time."

Really? This fascinates me more than anything. Especially since I spent the majority of dinner avoiding him or away from the table. But I won't harp on the matter.

"It was nice meeting you, Arthur." I extend my hand and he shakes, but thankfully doesn't kiss my hand.

Arthur and Phillip wander outside while Sylvia and I hang back. Soon as they are out of earshot, Sylvia throws questions at me one after another.

"What are you going to tell him? Do you want us to wait? Are you nervous?" She prattles on and on, and before long, I drown in the sea of anxiety.

I hold up a hand. "Syl, stop." She quiets. "First, I don't know what I'll say. No, please don't wait. I'll find a way home." I tuck a nonexistent hair behind my ear. "And yes, I'm nervous."

Sylvia takes my hands in hers and looks me in the eyes. "You'll be fine. Call if you need us." She drops my hands and pivots to walk off. But stops to look over her shoulder. "And I expect details later." I roll my eyes. "Good night."

"Night, Syl."

After Sylvia walks off, I go to the bar, park on a stool and order a drink.

Soon, Fletcher will leave the stage. And soon, I will have to speak with a man I never thought I would see again. A man I *wanted* to see again. A man I have thought about for the last year and regretted my decision to leave without a goodbye.

Fletcher.

FOURTEEN

Fletcher

I FOUND HER. Madeline is here and I've finally found her.

And I am stuck on this stage for another twenty minutes. Twenty minutes I would much rather spend with her.

When she signaled me to wait, a weight lifted off my shoulders. The moment my eyes landed on her in this ritzy restaurant, I feared her leaving without saying goodbye. Again. But that fear fizzled out with one simple gesture. One smile. A smile I haven't forgotten but missed fiercely.

I strum chords and croon lyrics to a thinning crowd. Two of the songs on tonight's set list were written with Madeline as my muse. The rest from previous albums.

I want to play all her songs. To her. For her. Would

that weird her out? Scare her off? For me to sit across from her, play my guitar and sing lyrics only for her.

My eyes don't leave her as she talks with a man near the exit. I grind my molars and force out lyrics until she shrugs and shakes his hand. The two men from her table walk out while she hangs back with a woman. They talk a moment. The other woman regards Madeline with concerned eyes. Holds her hands with tenderness. Then, the other woman leaves and Madeline wanders to the bar.

Where she waits. For me.

One last song. Three minutes of doing what I love. And it takes far too long.

When I finish, the crowd applauds. I thank them, set my guitar on the stand and all but run to the bar. I weave through the tables and several people stop me to extend kind sentiments. *"You're a talented young man."* and *"That was a beautiful set."* The list goes on.

I appreciate each and every kind word and don't brush them off—they pay my bills, after all. But I am desperate to reach Madeline.

Finally, I clear the tables and reach the end of the bar. Eyes glued to Madeline, I walk slower. Absorb her in a different light, different atmosphere. Cherish the soft, subtle features of her profile I missed the last year.

She still robs me of breath. Maybe more now than before. Time tends to do that to people. Alter the way you see the world or people. And Madeline stuns me.

As I approach her, she toys with a short glass on a

napkin. Twirls it and tears at the corner of the napkin. Her eyes downcast, focused on the swirl of clear liquid.

I ease onto the stool next to her. Her eyes close and she sighs. My heart rattles my ribcage like a trapped beast as we sit in momentary silence. One year ago, I loved the silence Madeline and I shared. But over the last year, silence has been torture. A brute ravaging my mind and heart. Tattering my soul.

She opens her eyes and twists to face me. "Hi," she says a breath above a whisper. Her eyes close again briefly as she tilts her head. "Sorry." Pain on her tongue and in her eyes.

I itch to touch her. To reach out and take her hand like I did on countless occasions before. To feel her warm, soft skin against mine.

But time changes people. And she may not welcome my touch as she once did.

"Hi." I swallow down the urge to tell her the apology is unnecessary. An apology she deems important. But I understand why she did what she did. "Thank you."

Her leg brushes mine as she swivels more my direction. I stop breathing and let the fire spread. Bask in the burn she creates in my limbs, my torso. A scorch I have missed since I last touched her. Since I almost kissed her.

I don't miss the way her breath hitches. The way her chest rises and falls quicker. But she recovers easier.

"How are you? Do you live nearby?" An edge of confidence laces her voice, but I hear the small stammer.

"Doing alright. I'm touring Northern California this

month. Then head back to LA." She nods and bites her lip. "How've you been?" I glance toward the exit. "Your friends seemed nice."

Madeline peers over her shoulder then meets my eyes. "My brother and sister-in-law thought it'd be a good idea to set me up on a blind date." I flinch, but she doesn't notice as she rolls her eyes. "I only accepted to shut them up, but told them they had to join. Arthur took the rejection easy enough when they left."

Arthur must have been the man whose hand she shook. A man who appeared decades her senior. Does Madeline prefer older men? If so, that tosses me aside.

"Blind date, huh?" I try for nonchalance. "Big brother not think you're capable of finding someone on your own?" I tease.

What the hell am I saying? And why the hell am I a bumbling fool with her now? This is Madeline. The woman I spent two incredible, life-altering weeks with. The woman I can't get out of my head, no matter what I do. For two weeks, we talked with such ease and familiarity. We sat in comfortable silence and melted into each other.

Has time changed us so dramatically? Can we not sit side by side and talk like we once did? Maybe it is the setting. The change of scenery and introduction of reality. Are we not the same people in this place? Can we be?

"Younger brother." Madeline tucks hair behind her ear. "Phillip means well. He just wants to see me happy again." Her eyes dart between mine. "But he doesn't know what will make me happy," she whispers the last words.

A bartender steps up. "Refill?" he asks Madeline and she nods. He looks my way. "Your usual, Fletch?"

"Please, Benny."

He steps off to make our drinks and Madeline furrows her brow. "How long have you been playing here? Thought you said you were touring the area this month."

When Jonathan set up my tour, mostly small events and venues such as this, I requested several to be in Northern California. I had no idea where Madeline lived, but I hoped to bump into her. So, I chose to play in cities closer to the retreat. The likelihood of seeing her—at an event or while I wandered the area—was slim, but I had to try.

Seems my instincts were spot on.

I won't mention that I arrived in the area a couple weeks early.

"I've played here several times during past tours. Tonight is one of a handful of times I play here this month."

Benny sets a clear bubbly drink with a lime wedge in front of Madeline. Then sets a Jack and Coke in front of me on a napkin. We both sip our drinks a moment, and I take the opportunity to look over Madeline with new eyes.

She wears a simple yet classy black dress that stops at her knees. Her arms bare, but shoulders covered with wide straps. The dress forms a V on her chest, hiding yet accentuating her natural curves. Just above her heart rests a silver necklace. With a thick silver band. A wedding band. A man's wedding band.

Flashes of all the times she clutched and fisted her chest come back in a rush. The faint untanned skin on her left fourth finger. Her sadness and hesitation. The day she ran from me when we touched the first time. She just told me her brother wants to see her happy again.

Oh, god.

People don't generally carry wedding bands close to their heart after a divorce. No, most only do such things after loss. Tragic loss. Could be another loved one, but my gut begs to differ. Wedding jewelry from family members gets stored in safe places in your home, not slipped onto a necklace and worn close to your heart.

I don't want to make this awkward. Or make her uncomfortable. But this possible realization has me stumbling in my head.

Shake it off, Fletch. This is Madeline. The same woman you met a year ago.

I swallow my assumptions and trudge forward. Now is not the time to broach such heavy topics. Now is the opportunity to pick up where we left off. Or start somewhere new.

"Would you have dinner with me?" I ask before I chicken out.

She sets her glass on the napkin then faces me with a pout. "I already ate."

Not a no. "Another night is what I meant."

Her lips curve into a breathtaking smile and I remind

myself to breathe. "I'd love to. You're here until the end of the month?"

"Yes." One last week. "I play tomorrow and next weekend. Then I leave for the rest of the tour."

Madeline looks over my shoulder and smiles. I turn to see who caught her attention, but no one is there. I pass it off as her thinking.

Her eyes meet mine again. "I'm free whenever you are."

I follow through on my urge to touch her and reach for her hand. She doesn't shy away. And when our skin meets, every emotion I felt a year ago slams into me at full throttle. Saturates and drowns me. My heart remembers the familiar rhythm it beat only when Madeline was near. My lungs inflate, fuller than they have in months. And the obsessive loss I felt for months after the retreat fades away.

"Are you working?"

Her hand shifts in mine as she traces her fingers along mine, over my palm, on the lines of my wrist. Tingles dance up my forearm, up my bicep, and spread across my chest. My eyes roll shut as her simple touch swallows me whole.

How can you miss someone who was never yours?

"Three days a week. And only mornings."

I want more than just a dinner with her. Need more. "What would you say to a day together and dinner?"

Her smile brightens. "Sounds wonderful. I work Monday, Wednesday and Thursday."

Considering it's Friday, I'm half tempted to spend every day I can with her. Like we did last year. Would she be open to the idea? Other than my gigs, I am free to do as I please.

Suppose we should start with one day first.

"Are you free Sunday?"

She bites her bottom lip and I follow the movement with my eyes. "Yes," she whispers.

I take a deep breath, hold it a beat then release. "Can I have your number?" Her eyes widen then relax. "To coordinate tomorrow. I don't know what to do around here."

Madeline waves Benny over. When he reaches us, she asks, "Do you have a pen?"

"Certainly, miss." Benny smiles and hands her a pen before walking off.

She frees her hand from mine, grabs a clean napkin from the stack, clicks the pen and scribbles. When she finishes, she lays the pen on the bar, folds the napkin and lays it in my hand. The folded square weighs me down and lifts me up simultaneously.

I tuck the precious paper in my pocket and take her hand again. "Thank you. Promise not to abuse it."

Her soft laughter floats through the air. I replay and stash it in my memory. "Wouldn't bother me if you did," she admits.

Wait, what? I don't follow up her comment, but plan to ask more later.

We finish our drinks and I pin a twenty under my

glass for Benny. I rise from the stool and proffer my hand to Madeline. Without hesitation, she takes it.

I guide us through the restaurant toward the doors. "Did you valet?" We step outside and Madeline shivers.

"No. I rode here with Phillip and Sylvia." I narrow my eyes. "My brother and his girlfriend."

She shivers again. Without thinking, I step closer and wrap her in my arms. For a split second, she tenses. But the moment she melts into me, I breathe deeper and revel in the feel of her so close.

"Do you need a ride? I have a rental."

Madeline fists my shirt and rests her cheek on my chest. I lay my chin on her crown and she sighs. "I'll request an Uber."

"You sure?" I don't want to let her go yet.

She shakes her head. "No, but I probably should."

I lean back enough to look her in the eye. "If that's what you want. But I don't mind. Up to you." I brush loose strands from her face. Trail a finger down her temple, her cheek, her jawline. I follow the movement with my eyes and stop when I reach her lips.

Her hands clutch my forearms as she licks her lips. "Not what I want," she mutters. My eyes dart up to hers. "But what I should do. Tonight, anyway."

Is she having trouble resisting temptation too? Or am I reading her wrong?

In the two weeks spent with Madeline, I interpreted her every word and gesture with accuracy. But life has shaped us differently in our time apart. And my perception may not be what it once was around her. It may be more biased now; filled with false ideas of how I envisioned her in my head while apart.

I frame her face, lean in and kiss her forehead. Her warm breath paints my throat and I fight the urge to keep my lips on her skin. "Okay," I say when I pull away.

I step back enough for her to pluck her phone from her purse and schedule the ride. Done, she steps back into me and fists my shirt with her free hand.

"I missed you," she croaks out against my chest. "So much."

My arm around her waist tightens as I lift the other and stroke her hair. "Me too." My response dry and scratchy. "But I'm glad we found each other again."

Until her ride arrives, we stay like this. Off to the side and in each other's arms. I inhale her sweet apple scent and marvel at how perfectly she molds to me. Seeing her again, touching her again, is something I never thought I'd have.

Fate must have plans for us. Or so I would like to believe.

The Uber driver arrives and we reluctantly pull apart. I cup her cheek, lean forward and kiss her forehead again. I don't miss her quiet whimper as I break our connection.

She gets in the back seat of the car, her hand still in mine. I give a quick squeeze then release her hand. "Talk to you tomorrow."

"Tomorrow," she squeaks out then closes the door.

I step back to the curb and watch as the car drives off.

When the taillights disappear, I wander back inside to collect my things. Guitar secure in the case, I sling my backpack over a shoulder and leave.

As I drive back to the hotel, I stare less at the sidewalks and storefronts. No longer a need to search the sea of faces. Because tonight, I found her again. Madeline. The woman who I'd often wondered over the last year might be a figment of my imagination.

Each time I questioned her existence, I stared at the painting in my house. The very same painting I take with me each time I travel. Her painting.

She is here. She is real. And I have no idea how I will ever leave her. How I will wrap up this tour then go home when it all ends.

For now, I will take it one day at a time. And tomorrow, I have work to do.

FIFTEEN

Madeline

"Crap. Donation. Crap. Crap."

For whatever reason, I choose to spend Saturday cleaning my closet. But that was after I woke at five in the morning and deep cleaned the living room. Followed by the kitchen, dining and spare rooms. Not like I have an overabundance of stuff or that I have anyone to clean up after.

Not like Fletcher will show up unannounced. He doesn't even know where I live.

At the back of the closet, I take a box off the top shelf and carry it to the bed. The unfamiliar box is unmarked with a thin layer of dust on top. I unfold the box flaps and gasp when the contents come into view.

"Oh, Christopher." A tear spills down my cheek.

Inside the box is a collection of cards and trinkets and random things I thought I'd lost over the years. Birthday and anniversary cards bundled together with thin cord. Photos of us from college and early postcollege. A swimsuit and shirt I searched weeks for and wrecked our first apartment to never find. Notes and letters I wrote him. Fortune cookie fortunes I gave him because I loved the sentiment. Homemade CD compilations I made, that he played until the disk scratched.

"Never let go of anything that meant something." I hear the words as if he were over my shoulder.

I pull out each item with the care it deserves. Sift through the memories and weep over a man lost too soon. Once I sift through it all, I contemplate what to do next. Do I keep it? The pictures, letters, and notes—definitely. But what about all the other pieces? I pick up the swimsuit and shirt, laugh a moment, then toss them in the donation pile.

Staring at the small pieces of history, I decide today is not the day to sort it all out. So, I gently return everything to the box, secure the flaps and stash it where I found it. And for a beat, I stand at the far end of my closet, just beneath the box.

"I miss you, Chris."

"Miss you, too, sweetheart." Pressure builds in my chest. An ache that has dimmed with time, but I know will never disappear. *"But I'm always here. Always will be."*

Tears flow down my cheeks with ease. Tears for a lost love and tears for a lost life. "I'm scared."

Warmth surrounds me. *"I know you are. It's okay to be scared. And it's okay to move on."*

I choke on the sentiment. Choke on the idea of moving past a future I wanted desperately, but will never have. Not with the man I expected to. "What if I can't let go? What if I forget you?"

"Maddie, you know in your heart neither is true. You also know you need to live life."

So many people have said the same words over the last year and a half. Live life. Haven't I? No, not truly. Although I get out more now than I did months ago, I am just existing.

"It's okay to love him, Maddie."

This rips the chord and lets my tears flow freely. I crawl up the bed and hug the pillow. Let the tears pour without shame. Soak the pillow that once belonged to Chris, but no longer smells of him, which brings on a new wave of tears. One by one, pieces of him fade away.

I startle awake when my phone chimes with an incoming text. How long was I out? I grab the phone from the bedside table, see a text notification from Fletcher and note I slept more than an hour.

Fletcher: Hey. How are you?

His short text makes me smile. Like he doesn't know what to say but wants to check in. We have never been very vocal. Our quiet communication more comfortable than with any other person.

Madeline: Good. Been cleaning 🌚

Fletcher: Have you been to the winery?

The winery that is less than an hour away? The winery that has been there longer than I have lived here?

Madeline: No. Which is funny because I love wine.

Fletcher: Want to go tomorrow? Tour the grounds and sample wine.

Madeline: Sounds wonderful. I'd love to.

The text bubble dances then disappears, over and over. Before his text comes through, I half expect it to be a mile long. But it isn't.

Fletcher: Can I pick you up?

I love and hate how such a simple question made him hesitant and uncomfortable.

Madeline: Yes.

I text him my address and he says for me to be ready by ten in the morning. Smiling at the screen, I press down on his response then tap the heart icon. Then I snap my head up and slap a hand to my mouth.

"Oh my god," I mumble into my palm. "Oh my god." I drop my hand and stare at nothing. "I have a date. With Fletcher."

Not sure why this surprises me, but it does. In a good way.

Unlike the blind date my brother set me up with last night, I have no jitters about a date with Fletcher. Okay, not *no* jitters. But I rather enjoy the posse of fireflies swirling beneath my breastbone. How they brighten the darker regions of my heart.

I bolt off the bed and dash into my closet. Bite the tip of my thumb as I stare at too many options on hangers. Then I rip shirts and dresses down and toss them on the bed. Skirts and pants next. What do you wear to a vineyard? Is it casual or dressy? From what I have heard, you spend part of the tour outside.

Casual. Casual seems the way to go.

I shove several pieces aside and spend the next hour trying on clothes and staring at myself in the mirror. My inner critic waves away this top and those pants and an occasional dress. But after several looks, I narrow it down to three. Yet, I can't decide.

So, I take the easy way out. I number each outfit, jot the numbers on paper, toss them in a cup and pick one blindly. Outfit two for the win!

After everything is back in its rightful place, I finish my cleaning spree and order takeout.

Being alone almost two years, one would think you grow accustomed to change. And in some instances, you do. It's nice to come and go as I please. To make spur-of-the-moment decisions without concern over someone else's feelings or plans. Or to spend an entire day in bed without being called grumpy or lazy.

But solitude isn't all sunshine and flowery meadows.

Cooking for one isn't easy. Not when food is sold for couples and families. And sitting at a dining table for four alone seems pointless. Sure, you can eat whatever you want. Under or overeat. But there is something odd about eating alone when you had someone with you for a decade.

Hence, takeout.

I miss the after-work conversations while we cook or eat—discussing our time apart. I miss having another person in my space—the way we ebb and flow with each other. And I miss the cuddles. The late movie nights on the couch shrouded in darkness. Giggles under the comforter. Fingers in my hair and on my skin.

Intimacy. God, do I miss intimacy.

Not just physical touch from a man, but all the parts that lead up to it. The banter and teasing. The laughter and mental foreplay.

The two weeks with Fletcher at the retreat felt like a form of foreplay. The lead up to something more. But, at the time, I wasn't ready for anything more. Not mentally or emotionally, anyway.

Our last night at the retreat, I desperately wanted to kiss him. Have his lips warm on mine. To feel something other than heartache for just a moment. To feel *desirable* again. To feel like a woman. Whole and strong and wanted.

But it was too soon. Chris wasn't a memory in my head. He still felt real. Tangible. I still smelled his cologne in the air and felt his fingers on my skin.

And letting anything else happen between me and Fletcher felt... *wrong*.

That was a year ago. Although feelings for Chris remain rooted deep in my bones, a lot changes in one year.

Chris will always own a piece of my heart. Will always own part of my soul. I will never forget him, our life together or the thirteen years we shared.

But I don't want to live the rest of my life alone. I don't want to miss out on the possibility of more.

Once dinner is delivered, I park in front of the television and choose a sappy movie to watch. One that makes me ugly cry every time I watch it.

"Tomorrow, everything changes."

Where the hell did confident Maddie go?

Fletcher will be here in thirty minutes and I look like a murder victim. My hair disheveled no matter how much I brush it or add product. The purple undertones beneath my eyes visible through the layers of makeup. Lips so chapped, even gloss won't hide the peeling skin. The slow fading handprint near my collarbone from where I obviously slept on my hand for hours during the night. And this dress… it is all kinds of wrong.

Gah!

Hot mess—party of one. Can't remember the last time I was such a disaster.

"Take a breath," I coach my reflection. "Just take a breath. It's Fletcher."

Yeah, brain. It's just Fletcher. The man I almost kissed. The man I have dreamed of kissing.

After a few cleansing breaths, I take a mental step back and have a light-bulb moment. I grab the brush and a hair tie, and finagle my hair into a presentable high ponytail, securing any flyaways with bobby pins. Next, I rethink my makeup. Rather than add more layers beneath my eyes, I opt for a smoky look with subtle liner. Add a pop of pink gloss to disguise my dry lips and done.

One last look in the mirror has me more confident than an hour ago. *Thank god.* Only one thing looks out of place.

I reach up and press my palm to Chris's wedding band over my heart. Fist it and close my eyes.

"It's time, sweetheart." The backs of my eyes sting. *"Love lives in the heart. Not material possessions."*

I tip my head, stare at the ceiling and blink back the tears threatening to spill. Swallow past the swell in my throat. Take a deep breath and level my gaze with the mirror.

With slow, shaky hands, I reach for the clasp at the nape of my neck and unhook the necklace. I lower my hands and bite the inside of my cheek until the sting is all I feel. My eyes glaze over, but I refuse to cry. Chris wouldn't want me to.

I fasten the necklace and place it in the small box inside my dresser top drawer. Stow it away, secure with my wedding rings.

One more deep breath. I grab a tissue from the box and blot the tears at the corners of my eyes.

"No more tears, Maddie," I tell myself. "You've shed enough to last a lifetime." Perhaps more than one lifetime.

The doorbell rings and snaps me from the sadness. I exit my room and stroll to the door on wobbly legs. Grab the handle and twist. Open the door and meet Fletcher's eyes.

And then I breathe for the first time in almost two years.

SIXTEEN

Fletcher

MADELINE OPENS the front door and all breath evaporates from my lungs.

From the first time I laid eyes on Madeline, I thought she was beautiful. The magnetic warmth in her soft brown eyes. Unopened invitation of her slender yet plump lips. Her petite frame—fuller now than the frail woman I met a year ago.

Yet, those qualities are not the ones to call out to me most.

Madeline holds an air of natural elegance. A classic undertone in a modern world. Someone who loves simplicity and tradition and sentiment, but is willing to step out of her comfort zone. An old soul with a giving heart.

"You look incredible," I manage to say after standing quiet too long.

She looks more than incredible. In a soft yellow dress with thin shoulder straps and the skirt to her knees, Madeline brightens the already sunny day. Hair secured in a ponytail, a few wayward strands tickle her temples, jaw and where her shoulder meets her neck on the left.

As my eyes trail her neck down to the ribbed material covering her bust, I note the necklace she wore two nights ago—the necklace carrying a large silver band—is absent.

Did she remove the necklace because it bears promise to another man? A man I know absolutely nothing about, but have a long list of questions to ask on who he is and what happened. Or did she remove the necklace because she wanted to? Does she feel now is the right time? I know nothing of losing loved ones. Of losing a best friend, partner and lover. But I don't imagine the loss being easy by any means.

"Thank you. Please, come in. I just need to grab my things."

Madeline steps back and allows me to step inside. I close the door and stand in the foyer as Madeline walks toward the living room straight ahead. She disappears from view and I take a minute to take in the small section of her home.

Cedar planks the floor. Off to the right, open doors display a room I imagine is for guests and an office with a simple dark wood desk and two full bookshelves. Just outside the rooms is a bathroom. The walls soft gray with white baseboards and crown molding.

Taking a step left then one forward, light greets me when my eyes land on her living room. Large glass French doors with windows as tall on either side open up to the backyard. A couch and love seat form an L shape with a small side table between them and a lighted ceiling fan overhead. A television mounted to the wall opposite the couch with a fireplace beneath and a rustic hearth. Paintings and photographs and ornate mirrors decorate the walls.

Then I stumble back and stop breathing.

My eyes land on the wall leading toward the living room. A wall I didn't easily see until I shuffled a little more left. A wall where my painting of Madeline hangs with gallery lights illuminating the canvas.

Footsteps clap against the hardwood and I shuffle back to the right. Madeline rounds the corner with a bright smile and the previously wayward strands tucked into her ponytail.

"Sorry about that," she says. "I switched purses and couldn't find my keys."

"No need to apologize." I swallow down the urge to ask why my painting is the only highlighted art in the house. "You have a beautiful home. At least the parts I see."

Rouge paints Madeline's cheeks and adds a new layer of natural beauty. "Thank you. I'll give you a tour later."

"I'd like that."

We exit the front and Madeline locks up. Without thought, my hand rests on her low back as I guide her to the car. Briefly, I consider removing my hand. But seeing as she doesn't shy away from the gesture, I leave my hand in place until she gets in the car.

With the car started, I open the navigation and select the address for the winery. Shortly after we leave her neighborhood, the navigation leads us south on the 101. The area is a mix of residential, commercial and tall trees with large green canopies.

The ride is filled with the comfortable silence I have only ever shared with Madeline. Quiet music plays in the background. Madeline stares through dark lenses out the windshield and passenger window as if she hasn't visited this part of the city.

Off the highway, I drive us through Santa Rosa, eyes on the road and the passing scenery. In the city, it looks much like most I have traveled to in the northern part of the state. A nice change of pace from the busy life in Los Angeles.

I park at the winery, exit and walk around the passenger door to escort Madeline out. As we step away from the car, Madeline takes my hand in hers as if the action is second nature. The unmistakable energy I always feel at her touch heats my fingers, my palm, and winds its way up my arm.

"Thank you for bringing me here." Madeline peers up at me through her lenses.

I smile down at her. "Glad you could join me."

We walk up a brick-paved walkway and under a white canopy. Wine barrels with bold purple flowers rest at the base of each canopy post. A stone bench off to the right of the entrance. Brilliant red flowers in terra-cotta pots sit on either side of the glass double entry doors.

Inside, a vineyard employee greets us and I inform her of our reservation. After verifying the reservation on her computer, she guides us through another door, out on to a patio with seating, hands us tickets and indicates the tour will begin shortly.

"Wow," Madeline says as the employee wanders back inside. "This place is extraordinary. How have I not visited any of the vineyards nearby?" The question more to herself than to me.

I give her hand a slight squeeze. "Glad you haven't visited. Then we get to see and enjoy it for the first time together."

We sit at an open table with a red umbrella overhead and wait for the tour to start. The patio is lined with tall, lush trees, wine barrels with a colorful mix of small flowers, grassy plants, flowering vines climbing up the outside of the building and a breathtaking view of acres of grapevines.

The tour doesn't start for at least ten minutes. Much as I enjoy silence with Madeline, I want to ask her questions off the long list in my head. Instead of jumping into a full-on assault of Q and A, I decide to start small.

I stare down at our joined hands as my thumb strokes small circles near the web of her hand. The fact that she doesn't shy away from my touch does mind boggling things to my psyche.

"How have you been?" I peer up from our hands and meet her gaze. "It's a loaded question, I know. You seem different, though. Better than last year."

Our eyes hold for three breaths before her body relaxes and a muted sigh leaves her lips. "Things are good. Better. Sorry if I came across as strange or mopey last year. It's just…" She trails off as her eyes drop to my lips, blinks a couple times then meets my eyes once more.

"Please don't feel obligated to share anything you aren't ready to." I twist to face her at an angle. "If or when you want to share, I will listen. If that time never comes, that's okay too. You're allowed to be sad and not share why with the world."

Glassiness coats her earthy irises as they dart between mine. Her tongue darts out and sweeps across her lips before she tucks them between her teeth a moment. After a hard swallow and a deep breath, she blinks away the threat of tears as a soft smile perks up the corners of her mouth.

"I seem to be thanking you a lot, Fletcher. But it feels as if I haven't thanked you enough."

A small voice in the back of my mind wants to speak up and say she never needs to thank me for anything. That if she ever needs me, day or night, I will be there. The same voice also begs to ask what made her so sad. What stole her smile and silenced her heart.

But it isn't my place to ask such questions. In the

future, if Madeline wants to share that piece of her life with me, she will do so when she is ready.

I lift a hand and lightly brush my knuckles from her temple to the angle of her jaw. "Only say the words if you need to. I see gratitude in your eyes and a smile. And that's enough for me."

Madeline opens her mouth to say something in response, but gets cut off by the vineyard tour guide stepping outside and instructing us what today entails.

Soon, we join three other couples as the tour begins. Madeline and I walk hand in hand past rows of grapevines as the guide details the history of the vineyard. A sweet, fruity earth scent fills the air as we pass each row. The guide tells us the vineyard owns three different valleys and grows different grapes at each for a variety of wines.

Next on the tour is a visit to the production facility. Most of the facility isn't visible to guests, but the guide details the process of vine to bottle. Then we wander to a different outdoor seating area. Some guests leave at this point, while we and one other couple remain.

"If you'll have a seat, we'll have samples for you momentarily," the guide states.

"Samples?"

I nod. "When I set the reservation, I thought it was pointless to visit without sampling the product. If we enjoy them, I may buy a bottle or two before we leave."

Madeline picks at her thumbnail with her index finger.

Nips at the corner of her lower lip with her teeth. And I can't help but wonder if I did something wrong.

"Is that okay with you?" I ask. I don't want Madeline to ever feel obligated to do something that makes her uncomfortable.

After a moment, her shoulders soften and she nods. "Yes." Her voice almost inaudible. "It's just… since… I don't often drink when not home or at a place I'm not leaving."

Since… Was alcohol involved with whatever happened in her past? With whatever had her grieving?

"Madeline." I take both her hands in mine. "We don't have to do the tasting if you don't want to. No hard feelings, I promise."

Staff members walk out of a small building thirty feet from us. Some carrying stemware, others with bottles of wine, and two with cheese samples. Much as I would love to sample both the wine and cheese, I would decline if the situation makes Madeline uneasy.

"No" —she squeezes my hands— "it's okay."

"Are you sure?" I ask before glasses are set down in front of us.

"Positive. But thank you for checking with me."

The next hour is spent sampling five different wines. Tasting them with and without cheese, a variety of fresh fruit and homemade rustic bread. When the official tour and tasting are done, we are told of some small seated areas within the vineyard we can sit at, if we care to stay longer.

We locate two wooden Adirondack chairs under tall, shady trees and sit. Staring at rows of grapes, Madeline's hand in mine, we enjoy the quiet and spark occasional conversation until the sun shifts more west and cooler air surrounds us.

I rise from the chair and hold out my hand. "Let's get dinner."

Leaving the vineyard, I drive us back toward Madeline's house. I exit the highway when the navigation indicates and pull into the restaurant parking lot a couple miles up the street.

Madeline peers out the window at the building then back to me. "Fletcher, this doesn't look like a restaurant. More like a resort."

"From what I saw online, it's both. But you don't have to stay at the resort to eat in the restaurant. I checked when making reservations."

We exit the car at valet, walk under a vine-covered pergola and enter through the door held open for us. I provide the hostess with our reservation, then she walks us through the main dining room and out on to an enclosed outdoor table for two. Our seats close together face another vineyard and garden; the sun starting to descend on the horizon.

Once seated, the hostess hands us menus and states our server will be with us momentarily. For a moment, we both stare out at the rows of grapevines and breathe. Every breath I take with Madeline furnishes my soul with a new level of solace. A peace I never knew existed until she walked into my life.

"Uh, Fletcher?"

I shift to look at Madeline, who stares wide-eyed at the menu. "Everything okay?"

She sets the menu down and leans toward me. "This place is crazy expensive," she whispers.

Without looking at the menu, I already know the prices are higher than typical restaurants nearby. I am also aware I paid more than this to tour the vineyard and do the wine and cheese tasting. But I have no plans to share said information. I would much rather enjoy a wonderful evening with the woman who has been bewitching me for the last year.

"Don't worry about the price." She twists enough to meet my gaze; her brows knit together as her warm irises search mine. "Please, Madeline. I promise our next meal can be your choosing. Let us enjoy this place together."

Yes, I all but told her we will spend another evening together before I leave. Not that I would force Madeline to do anything she doesn't want to. But after our time together last year, instinct tells me she wants to spend time with me just as much as I do with her.

Leaning back into her chair, she inhales deep through her nose, picks up the menu and exhales through the faintest part of her lips. "Fine," she says with soft resignation. "My choice next." Her eyes narrow on me. "The next time you choose, though, just pick a normal restaurant." I open my mouth to answer, but she cuts me off with her hand up. "You don't need to impress me, Fletcher. I do like nice things, but I prefer your company over fancy atmosphere and high-priced meals."

I take her hand, bring it to my lips and kiss her knuckles in turn. "You have my word."

After studying the menu, we elect to share an appetizer and order lesser-priced options. Over dinner, we talk about normal life stuff. Madeline tells me about work and how she enjoys being back, but wishes it fulfilled her as it once did. I tell her about songwriting and music and the tour. That when I leave the Santa Rosa area, I will be on the road another three months.

I don't miss the way her eyes and lips downturn at this news. Or how her body appears to weep like a willow tree.

God, how I wish this was the tail end of the tour. That I would return home to touch base with Jonathan, tie up a few loose ends in the studio and return to Madeline for a well-deserved, extended vacation. Spend time together and get to know each other in the real world.

Unfortunately, the rest of the tour will be spread across Northern and mid-California—too far to easily visit her on off days. The last stop of the tour is scheduled in Los Angeles.

When our plates are empty, we both agree to skip dessert at the restaurant. After I pay the bill, we meander toward the exit and wait at valet for the car. It isn't long before the distance between the restaurant and her house vanishes.

"Would you like to come in?" Madeline asks as I turn the car onto her street. "For coffee or tea."

"I'd love to."

Once parked, I help her out of the car and she leads the way inside. As we walk past the painting on the wall, I can't help but speak up.

"It's lovely to see your painting again."

Back to me, Madeline fusses with the coffee maker, adding a filter, grounds and water before pressing start. When she turns to face me, an endearing half smile tugs up the corner of her mouth.

"*Your* painting is one of a few things that makes me smile each day. Do you still have mine?"

"Are you joking?" Her eyes widen briefly. "Of course, I have it. Matter of fact, I take it with me when I travel."

Madeline fetches mugs from the cabinet and sets them on the counter. "No you don't," she says with a layer of incredulity.

"I'll show you. This week, when we see each other again, I'll show you."

She clutches at her bare chest, probably out of habit, then drops her hand when realization strikes. "No need. I believe you. Just seems odd that you'd bring it along." The coffee maker beeps and she fills each mug. "Why *do* you bring it with you?"

She sets a mug in front of me, followed by a small container of sugar and a carton of half-and-half from the fridge. I add a dash of sugar and cream, then watch as she adds only cream; enough to make her coffee look more like tea and creamer.

"More than one reason," I say then sip my coffee. "I love how it makes me feel." Madeline nods but focuses on her mug as if it may disappear if she looks away. "And I've been hoping it'd be a good luck charm."

She perks up and brings her eyes to mine. "Good luck charm?"

I nod, slow and subtle, set my mug down and step closer to her. "I've been looking for you. Nothing creepy, like stalking. More like looking for you in stores and on sidewalks in each city I visit. I thought maybe having your painting nearby would bring me luck."

"Do you think it worked?" Her voice barely above a whisper.

I grab the mug from her hands and set it on the counter. Take one more step, brush my knuckles down the side of her face and along her jaw.

"Took longer than expected, but yes," I say, inches from her lips.

Her breath hitches as the space between us slowly evaporates. Before my mind overthinks what is happening, I tip her head back and press my lips softly to hers.

Warmth spreads over my lips and across my skin as our mouths meet. Several erratic heartbeats pass before either of us moves or takes a breath. And after all the hints of Madeline's past, I let her guide the kiss. Direct it down the path she wishes to take. Because if I lead this kiss, I may scare her off.

A hand lands on my hip, then the other. Fingers flex and grip as they decide to press forward or push away.

And then her lips move. Without rushing and with purpose, she kisses me as if my lips will wake her from a deep slumber. The kiss isn't sultry or carnal. Just two sets of lips tasting one another. Getting acquainted with one another.

My hand at her chin traces her jaw and gently wraps around the back of her neck. The other hand reaches forward, rests on her lower back and draws her impossibly closer. Heat radiates between us and a thin layer of sweat slicks my skin.

Not losing control with Madeline takes more effort than originally suspected. Her body pressed to mine… lips dancing with mine… the occasional moan escapes her throat as the intensity of the kiss builds. It all becomes too much.

The second I let myself get carried away, the second I lick the seam of her lips, Madeline breaks the kiss. She doesn't step back, but does add space between our mouths.

"Sorry," I say in a whispered rush.

Eyes closed, Madeline shakes her head. "Please don't apologize." Iridescent brown eyes lock with my greens. "If anyone should apologize, it should be me."

As her eyes study mine, I try to read between the lines. See or hear or somehow comprehend her unspoken words. I have assumptions about why she was so sad when we met last year and why she wore a man's wedding band around her neck.

Assumptions don't equal truth. The only person who can provide me with truth is Madeline. And she must give it in her own time and of her own accord.

"Why do you say that? You've done nothing wrong."

Her head falls forward and rests near my heart. I hug her close and kiss the crown of her head. As if we have done it hundreds of times, we slowly rock in place.

"I want to," she whispers into my chest. "It's just…"

"Shh. I promise, it's okay. When you're ready to share, I'll be here. But only when you're ready. Please don't feel pressured." I kiss her hair. "And when you're ready for other things…" Madeline leans back enough to look me in the eye. "I can wait as long as you need. Okay?"

"Yes." The corners of her mouth perk up as she nods.

"I should get going. You have work tomorrow."

Madeline walks me to the door. We stand in the open frame—me rocking back on my heels and her picking her cuticles. I bite my cheek to resist laughing at how nervous we seem.

"Will you have dinner with me tomorrow?"

My eyes widen in surprise and delight. "I would love to."

"Do you mind if I cook?" She picks at her cuticles harder. If I don't answer soon, she may hurt herself.

"Not at all. Haven't had a home-cooked meal in a while. Sounds perfect." My heart swells and rattles my ribcage when she smiles.

"Is five good?"

"Perfect." I step forward, frame her face and kiss her forehead. The small hiccup in her breathing doesn't go unnoticed. "See you tomorrow. Good night, Madeline."

"Good night, Fletcher."

At the end of her street, I sit at the stop sign longer than necessary. No one pulls up behind me to interrupt. And for a moment, I stare out the window and delight in the tingle still on my lips. Rejoice in the kiss I may have taken too soon, but wasn't denied.

Madeline may not be one-hundred-percent ready for things to grow between us, but I wasn't lying when I said I would wait. For Madeline, I would wait a lifetime.

SEVENTEEN

Madeline

How does an eight-hour shift feel weeks long? Easy. When you would rather be somewhere else—*with someone else*—time deviates the path normally traveled. The second hand moves slower, ticks louder. Each passing hour laughs at you. Mocks as you fumble to occupy your time with repetitive tasks. And no matter what you do, no matter how many items you check off your list, the minute hand seems to never move.

When the doctor locks the front door for lunch, I sag into the desk chair. Office lunchtime signals the end of my workday. Most days, I loiter and finish up menial tasks. Hang around a bit and relay the day to Lewis, who works the front desk the hours I don't.

But today, I have plans that deserve my attention more.

I sign off the computer, shoulder my purse and fetch my insulated lunch bag. Before leaving, I survey the desk one last time. Double-check the note I wrote for Lewis. With everything in order, I say goodbye to the staff and head out the back door.

Car started, I slip on my sunglasses, buckle my belt and press the call button on the steering wheel. A double beep echoes through the speakers before Siri asks what I need.

"Call Nadia."

"Calling Nadia."

I pull out of the parking space and exit the lot. The phone rings and, after the third, my closest friend since college answers.

"Hey, stranger." Nadia may be my closest friend, but it isn't odd if we go weeks without catching up. More often than not, we talk or visit weekly. "What's up?"

"I saw him again."

Two weeks has passed since Nadia and I last spoke. With her schedule, catching up when one of us wasn't working seemed an impossible feat. So, she has yet to learn about the ridiculous blind date set up by Phillip. A date worth keeping to myself... if not the sole reason Fletcher and I connected again.

"When you say him, you mean *him*?"

Although our time at the retreat was short lived, each day spent with Fletcher stitched itself in my head and heart. When I returned from the retreat, several weeks passed before I relayed any information Fletcher-related. My conflicted feelings layered me with fresh guilt. Family and friends saw me sad daily for months. It wasn't until Nadia forced my truths from me that I spoke of Fletcher. Only to her.

"Yes." I wring the steering wheel. "Phillip set me up on a blind date. He and Syl were there. And no, I don't want to talk about the date. But Fletcher was playing at the restaurant."

"For now, I'll ignore the fact I knew nothing about this blind date until today." She pauses, the background noise on the other end of the line quiets. "Sorry. Just finished a class. Back to the good stuff. Fletcher was at the restaurant?"

I guide the car through the city toward the grocery store. "Yes. He's on tour and the restaurant is one of his stops."

"How did seeing him feel after so long?"

Like coming home again. Like every moment we shared a year ago was a precursor of what is yet to come.

"Wonderful and surprising and a guilt-trip." I huff out a breath. "Nadia, what kind of wife am I? Finding solace and happiness with another man. A man who seems more my other half than Chris ever was."

The backs of my eyes burn. The familiar swell of sorrow and shame builds in my throat.

"Oh, honey. No one doubts you loved Chris. Or that

you still do. But after almost two years, no one would begrudge you finding happiness with someone else."

I steer the car into the grocery lot, locate a spot and throw the gear into park. For a moment, I hang my head and let the emotions consume me.

"Nadia, it feels as if I'm cheating on Chris. That I'm shaming or tarnishing his memory and what we shared."

"Do you honestly believe anyone will think that if you move on? His family or yours?" She pauses to let her words sink in. "No, they never would. Everyone, including Chris's family, has given you their blessing to move past the tragedy. To be happy."

I bite my tongue because what she says is true and I have no valid rebuttal. "I'm scared," I whisper the truth weighing me down.

"Wish I could hug you right now. Fear is natural. Especially after everything that happened. But don't let fear rule your life, Maddie. Don't let it hold you prisoner and keep you from something else great."

Is that what I am doing? Punishing myself. Denying myself the opportunity to experience joy, and possibly love. Maybe.

"I spent the day with him yesterday." I swallow and whisper the next part. "He kissed me."

"Really?" Nadia practically squeals through the line. "Did you happen to kiss him back?"

I chuckle and swipe a single tear from my cheek. "Yes, but nothing more than lips."

"Tongue can be overrated sometimes. How was it?"

My mind drifts back to last night. To Fletcher in my home, in my space. The brush of his knuckles along my cheek. The trail of fire and sparks I felt for hours after he left.

"Better than imaginable."

"Eek!" My hands slap over my ears at Nadia's high-pitched cry. "I'm so freaking happy for you. When are you seeing him again?"

Although she can't see me, I wince. Because I know my answer will result in another ear-piercing noise.

"Tonight," I say with hesitation, hands at my ears.

"Are you serious?"

"Yes."

"Is he taking you out again?"

"No," I answer quickly. "He spent a lot of money yesterday. I insisted on dinner at the house." The line goes silent for far too long, but the call hasn't disconnected. "Hello?"

"I'm here. Just needed a minute to register what you said."

"That I'm cooking?"

"Mmhm." On the other end, she takes a deep breath. Then continues on the exhale. "Maddie, you never cook. For anyone. Not even Chris."

I search countless times I have been in the kitchen. Sure, cooking has never been my forte, but I have made food before. Haven't I? Since Chris, everything I ate came from the freezer section or takeout/delivery. With Chris, he did most of the cooking. Not that I didn't want to. He enjoyed being in the kitchen and, on occasion, I helped out.

But I never planned and cooked dinner of my own accord, from start to finish. Not like I am tonight.

I close my eyes and cover them with my hands. "Oh, god."

"Stop it. Right now. You're doing nothing wrong. Sharing something new with another man doesn't make you a horrible person. It makes you human." She pauses a beat. "Answer me this, without second-guessing. Does Fletcher make you happy?"

"Yes," I answer without hesitation.

"That's all the answer you need. Don't overthink it. Do what feels right for you. The rest will flow naturally."

"I should go. Groceries are calling my name."

"Go. I expect to hear from you sooner rather than later."

"Love you."

"Love you, too, Maddie."

What was I thinking?

The last time I cooked for more than one person was ages ago. I don't count the time I helped at the retreat because I wasn't the person in charge of the whole operation. If I really put brainpower behind it, the last time I prepared a meal—from preplanning to the final execution—was more than two years ago. A dinner party, I think.

So why did I put myself in this position? And why did I give myself only a few hours to pull this off? At least I had the smarts to buy dessert already made. Well, all the components are made—assembly required.

I pop the casserole dish in the oven, set the timer then clean up the monstrosity of a mess that is my kitchen. Dishwasher loaded and counters cleaned, I wash and cut fruit to pair with the almond cake and coconut whip.

Did I mention it is meatless Monday? Yet another reason to stress myself out. Considering Fletcher ate a hefty steak last night, who knows if he will enjoy my meatless spin on a classic favorite.

Once all the berries and apples are sliced, I half an orange and squeeze the juice over top, give it a stir and pop it in the fridge.

With everything caught up, I dash to my room, yank my clothes off in the process, and riffle through my closet. One by one, I shove the hangers from left to right.

"Nope. Nope. Nope." *Ugh!* Why is this so flipping difficult? Not like we are going out in public or to another fancy restaurant. Besides, Fletcher has seen me in "normal" clothes. Has seen me down and dismal and when I didn't care if I looked acceptable or far from it.

So, why is it so important now? Why am I making such a major effort to impress this man? Dress me in tattered clothes and he would still look at me as if no other woman existed.

That in mind, I stop fumbling through my wardrobe. Instead, I pluck a blue V-neck from the hanger and swap my slacks for dark denim. I leave my hair down, but brush out the tangles from the day.

As I exit the bedroom, the timer buzzes. I take the food out of the oven and set it on a trivet to cool. With minutes left until Fletcher arrives, I grab placemats, napkins, and silverware to set the table. The moment I set the second placemat down, queasiness erupts beneath my diaphragm. Ravages every cell and nerve ending. Causes my hands to tremble and makes it difficult to swallow.

"It's okay, sweetheart."

I look up from the spot at the table. The spot where Chris always sat. "How can it be okay?" I choke out.

"We will always love each other. And there is nothing wrong with you loving another."

Tipping my head back, I blink back the tears threatening to fall. Swallow, again and again, to dislodge the building emotion. Clutch at my chest then drop my hand when I don't grab hold of the wedding band I removed yesterday.

"I'm scared, Chris," I whisper into the room.

"I know you are, sweetheart. Scared is normal." Heat grazes my cheek and I close my eyes briefly. *"You have my permission to move on."*

Dropping my gaze, I stare down at the place setting. "What if I love him more?" My eyes squint tightly. "What if I forget you?" There, out in the open, is my biggest fear. The singular thought that terrifies me more than anything. Forgetting my best friend, my husband.

"You won't. Not you. But it's okay if someone else makes you smile and laugh and love. Please be happy. For me."

Before I respond, the doorbell rings and the image of Chris disappears. "I'll do my best," I whisper on my way to the door.

EIGHTEEN

Fletcher

NOT SURE WHAT voodoo Madeline did in the kitchen, but she certainly sold me on meatless Monday. Who knew shepherd's pie could be a) meatless and b) so damn good? But I have a newfound appreciation for the dish.

"I'll get dessert if you'd like to sit on the couch. Thought about watching a movie. If you're good with that."

Not sure why, but I love the bumbling, antsy side of Madeline. The way she clenches and straightens her fingers every other second. The slight bounce from right to left and back again as she awaits my response. This side is such a contrast to her sullen, silent side.

"Sounds wonderful."

I head to the living room, which is open to the kitchen

and dining area, and sit on the couch facing the television. While I wait for Madeline, I survey the room. Rake my eyes over the two tall bookshelves filled with hundreds of paperbacks and hardcovers. Take in the small chaise chair near the window with a throw blanket folded and draped at the foot and a book resting on top.

I picture Madeline lounging in that chair, the sun shining through the tall windows and glass doors, reading a book on the chaise. I also picture her falling asleep in the same spot, worn out from the day and too tired to move. Then, I picture scooping her from the chaise, cradling her in my arms and carrying her to bed. Kissing her forehead before wishing her good night.

Imagining Madeline in moments such as this is not difficult. After two weeks with her a year ago, I dreamed of her nightly. Daydreamt of her while writing and composing. What it would be like to hold her close every day. Press my lips to hers. Share a life with her.

To be hers.

The thought of her consumed me. Still consumes me. But in the same way a flower consumes the sun. Slow and constant and as if it would fail to exist without it.

"Here you go," Madeline interrupts my introspection. "My spin on strawberry shortcake."

She hands me a small bowl filled with cubed cake, mixed berries, apple, fresh cream and a sprig of mint. As she takes a seat beside me, I stare at the dessert that resembles art more than something to eat. Most people would just toss it all in the bowl and not give a second thought to display.

Madeline isn't most people. She adds love to everything she touches. Everything.

"Everything okay?" Worry laces her words. Her gaze searing my profile.

I shift to face her and unintentionally press my shin to her leg when I settle. A familiar bout of nervous energy stirs in my belly at the contact. Jitteriness I only feel with Madeline. An addicting buzz I hope never faces.

"Yes. Just admiring your artwork."

Her cheeks pink immediately, and I discover a new love and appreciation for the color. Then, her tongue darts out and dampens her lips before she tucks them between her teeth.

I don't want to appear the creeper, but can't look away from her lips. Lips I tasted less than twenty-four hours ago. Lips I hope to taste again. Soon.

As if privy to my internal battle, Madeline releases her lips. Spell semi-broken, I lift my eyes to hers and read her unspoken thoughts. We haven't known each other long, but Madeline and I connect on an inexplicable level. From day one, she captivated me. Not just as a muse, but something much deeper and profound. Oddly, in Madeline's presence, I feel more myself.

"Someone once told me you eat with your eyes first." The pink on her cheeks darkens. "The saying stuck with me. So, I try to make food visually appealing.'

"Mission accomplished." The corners of my lips inch up. "What movie are we watching?"

She gives a slight shake of her head and blinks a few times. "Didn't know what you like, so I picked *Meet Joe Black*. Thought it was kind of neutral."

Not too much romance, but enough to keep you rooting for love to win. "Good choice."

Madeline cues up the movie then dims the lights as I shift to face the television. In a blink, the intimacy level goes from fifty to a hundred.

Night after night at the retreat, Madeline and I sat by the bonfire. We held hands and shared quiet conversations. I will never forget any of those moments and the affection that bloomed inside me for this woman. But none of those nights compare to this one here.

In the privacy of her home, not a soul nearby to interrupt us, I become hyperaware of all things Madeline. The rhythm of her breathing. Her knee pressed against my thigh as she sits cross-legged. How she spears cake and fruit and dips it in the cream with each bite.

Thank goodness I have seen this movie. Because sitting in the dark next to this woman… it is impossible to take my eyes off her.

Not a quarter into the movie and both our bowls sit on the coffee table. I stop ogling Madeline like a creep and start focusing on the movie. Until Madeline rests her cheek on my bicep and I stop breathing.

"Is this okay?" she asks, voice timid and eyes on mine.

I swallow and nod. "Yeah. You comfortable?"

She wiggles closer and snuggles into my side. I lift my arm, wrap it around her shoulders and hug her to me. She inhales deeply before her body melts to mine on the exhale. Laying my cheek on her crown, I close my eyes and memorize the way Madeline feels in my embrace. Warm and soft and perfect. Inhale her sweet apple scent and let it stir up memories from last year.

The movie plays on and it isn't until close to the end that I hear Madeline's quiet snores. With slow moves, I shift so that her head leans more into my side and doesn't slump forward. When the credits roll up the screen, I finagle us and scoop her into my arms.

For a moment, I let the light from the screen highlight her profile as I watch her sleep in my arms. Then, with an arm under her neck and knees, I rise from the couch and pad across the room to the open door I assume leads to her bedroom. In the short distance, she curls into my chest and clutches my shirt.

Gingerly, I lay her on the bed and shimmy the comforter to cover her. She draws the bedding to her chin, but doesn't open her eyes. For several beats, I breathe in how peaceful she looks. How beautiful she is, inside and out.

Before tiptoeing out of the room, I bend down and press my lips to her forehead. Close my eyes and take one last pull of her apple scent.

I force my lips from her skin and straighten my spine. "Good night, my beautiful Madeline," I whisper.

When I turn to leave, a hand grabs mine and stops me. "Fletcher." Her voice thick with sleep.

I peer over my shoulder. "Go back to sleep. I'll see you tomorrow."

She sits up and pulls me to her. "It's late. You…" Her free hand fists the comforter. "You can stay."

I sit on the edge of the bed and hold her sleepy gaze. Her offer could be interpreted countless ways. Platonic or not. The couch, guest room or beside her. In her groggy state, she may not be thinking clearly. She may wake in the morning, see me in her house and freak out. That is the last thing I want.

"Madeline…" I pause to find the right words. "You're tired. I don't want to impose."

Her hand finds my cheek, then the other. I close my eyes and lean into her touch. Bask in the tingling sensation her thumbs leave as they stroke my cheeks. Shudder when the bed shifts slightly and her breath delicately paints my lips.

"Fletcher, look at me." I open my eyes and swallow at our nearness. "Please. Stay."

I turn my head and kiss her palm. "Okay." I nod and kiss her palm again. "Where?" With Madeline, I will never assume her line of thinking. Never make decisions based on what I think she may want.

Yet, more often than not, Madeline surprises me.

She draws back the comforter on the opposite side of the bed and pats the sheets. "Will you hold me?"

Forever.

"Yes. Let me go turn off the TV." I kiss her forehead. "Be right back."

In the living room, I take a brief moment to gather my wits. To remind myself that everything moves at her pace. Remind myself that Madeline inviting me into her home, into her bed—although innocent—is monumental and should be handled as such.

I turn off the television then visit the bathroom. With no other possible distractions, I walk back to the bedroom, peel my shirt and socks off and crawl into bed beside her. In my absence, Madeline stripped off her jeans and top, replacing them with a long sleep shirt.

Once I settle, she rolls onto her side so she faces me and curls into my chest. Her fingers brush my pecs as her breath paints the base of my throat. I wrap her in my arms and kiss her crown.

"Sweet dreams, Madeline."

Her lips press to the hollow of my throat. "Thank you for staying. Good night."

Ten breaths later, Madeline's body relaxes as she falls asleep in my arms. I lie awake a bit longer—not because I can't sleep, but because I don't want to. Not yet. Whether ten minutes or an hour, I want to remember this moment. The way my heart races as I hold this beautiful, precious woman in my arms.

A woman I spent months searching for, town after town. A woman who could have moved on or forgotten about me over the last year, but didn't. A woman I never want to let go of. Not tonight or tomorrow. Not ever.

NINETEEN

Madeline

EXISTING in the same space as Fletcher for the last few days has been nothing short of a dream.

When I woke Tuesday morning in his arms, I never wanted to leave the bed. More than an hour passed before he opened his eyes. But while he slept, I studied the man I grew more fond of with each passing day. In this state, I had free rein to admire him in my own way.

Fletcher didn't come off as someone who lived in the thick of beach and outdoor life. His fair complexion a juxtaposition to days spent in the sun. Thick, shoulder-length locks framed his face as he lay on his side. How my fingers itched to run through his hair. Without his glasses, his brows were broad, but neat with the arch more lateral than center. Golden brown lashes fanned out above each cheek. His slender nose widened slightly at his nostrils. Stubble lined the sharp angles of his jaw and above his lips, adding a touch of rugged to his exterior. And his lips… looking at them made me lick mine. Soft and warm and more inviting than any lips I had known.

When Fletcher woke Tuesday morning and caught me surveying his every feature, he didn't tease or deliver a crude one-liner. Instead, he smiled, kissed my forehead and said good morning.

That was three mornings ago. Since Tuesday, we have spent every available minute together. Visits to local museums, walks in the park, dinners out and at the house, and more movies on the couch. Tuesday and Wednesday night, Fletcher returned to his hotel. But last night, I asked him to stay again.

After waking in his arms Tuesday morning, I wanted the comfort and security his arms provided. A solace I hadn't felt in far too long. Fletcher was more than happy to oblige.

When I woke, Fletcher had mimicked my actions from Tuesday morning. Except he swept my hair from my face, leaned in and kissed my cheek, the corner of his lips at the cusp of mine. God, I wanted him to shift a little to the right. To press his lips to mine again.

But he was being a gentleman. Patiently waiting for me to make the next move or give him permission to do the same. The words sat on the tip of my tongue. The urge to step closer grew stronger with each minute we were together.

And the fact that he'd slept in my bed twice and not crossed any lines made me want to step over every line drawn.

"What time do you need to be at the restaurant?"

Tonight and tomorrow night are the last two days Fletcher performs in Santa Rosa. Sunday afternoon, he is scheduled to leave for Sacramento. Although it isn't far from here, between his schedule and mine, there won't be time for us to see each other. After Sacramento, he tours some smaller cities between here and Los Angeles until he arrives home. In three months.

Needless to say, we make every second count. After Sunday morning, we won't see each other until the tour ends. Unless he gets extended time away. As it stands now, he is booked to play four nights a week in the other cities.

"Five. I don't go on until six, but need to make sure everything is set beforehand."

I nod, sag deeper into the couch and sip my coffee. Heat sears my cheeks as he watches me. For a beat, I bask in the warmth and intensity. No one has looked at me the way Fletcher does. Not even Chris.

I set my mug on the table and turn to face him. "What would you like to do today?"

The day is still young. He still has to return to the hotel and change before tonight. But we still have hours until then. I want to make each minute of the time we have left count. Make them memorable and everlasting.

"Would you be upset if I said nothing? If I just wanted

to sit here and talk, would that be okay? Maybe watch a movie or read a book with you."

In some respects, his response feels very Fletcher-like. Simplistic. Comfortable. Perfect. It says, *all I want to do is spend time with you.* Distracting ourselves with dressing and driving and venturing into the world steals our time. And I love how he wants every minute to count too.

"I'd really like that."

We spend the next several hours learning more about each other. My previous assumptions that Fletcher enjoys a simple life are validated—comfortable cotton or linen shirts, jeans or cargo shorts, and a trusty pair of Chucks or Vans. I always knew the tattoo on his inner left wrist was musical, but today I learn it's a bass clef. Although he doesn't play bass now, he played bass guitar in high school and in a band he formed with friends.

Fletcher tells me about his love for roasted garlic, green beans, and homemade macaroni and cheese. I share my obsession with avocados, cashew butter, and all forms of potatoes. He also prefers tea to coffee, but drinks both.

Without going into detail, he tells me about his stepfather—who is also his manager and producer—and stepsister. He and Jonathan, his stepfather, have a more solid relationship than he and his biological father.

I talk very little about my family—not because I don't love them, I do. There are too many layers to unfold and we need more than half a day for me to unravel them.

"I want to ask you something, but I'm scared," he confesses, then nibbles at his lower lip.

What on earth would Fletcher be scared to ask? Not that we have fully exposed ourselves, but this is the most open I have been in years.

"You can ask me anything." And I mean it.

He takes a sip of water then returns the glass to the table. May be a play of lighting, but Fletcher appears to be sweating.

"The ring you used to wear around your neck… who did it belong to?"

Now I understand his reluctance to ask. No doubt he has assumptions about Chris's wedding band. If I saw a ring close to someone's heart, I would want to know the story behind it too.

Since his passing, countless people have asked about Chris. How he died. If I was with him when it happened. Why I didn't get hurt. The questions were endless. Some straightforward and less painful to answer. Others had me tight-lipped and on the verge of tears.

No one meant offense when they asked. By nature, humans are curious creatures. We want to know how something works or came to be. Why bad things happen to good people. What the ripple effect is.

Honestly, it surprises me Fletcher hasn't asked more questions before now. What is more surprising? Telling Fletcher what happened doesn't put me on high alert or make me sweat or clench my stomach.

"It was Chris's ring." I rest a hand on his knee and swallow. "My husband."

Neither of us speaks for a moment. His eyes that

remind me of the tree canopy on the hiking trails at the retreat hold mine. Glass over slightly as they seek more clues. But the subtle redness rimming his eyes tells me he has assumptions. Assumptions he doesn't want to speak aloud in case they hold no merit.

But they do.

"Chris passed away the December before the retreat."

For the first time—outside of therapy sessions—I spoke the most painful words to ever leave my lips. Before now, anytime I considered speaking of Chris's passing, a searing knife pierced my heart. My stomach would flip and wrench. The urge to run to the closest toilet was inevitable.

Somehow, with Fletcher, none of those sensations occur. Somehow, Fletcher quells the pain and sorrow I assumed would always exist. Granted, it will never fade completely. But what if it fizzles? What if, after a while, it doesn't hurt as much?

Fletcher wraps my hand with his and squeezes. "I don't know what to say, Madeline. The word sorry doesn't seem remotely fitting."

"You don't have to say anything. Believe me, I've heard and seen every term of sympathy. That you want to find the right words means more."

In a blink, I am in his arms. Awkwardly, he hugs me to his frame with a gentle ferocity. An embrace loaded with protection and love and healing energy. An embrace that says apologies would never fill the cracks in my heart.

But what if there is another way to mend the fractures?

Without second thought, I crawl into his lap and wrap my arms around his neck. Hug him so close, space is a foreign concept. His arms drop to my waist and hold me tight. Thumbs slowly stroking up and down, up and down near my sides.

"If you don't want to talk about it anymore, I'll understand." He buries his nose between my neck and shoulder then inhales deep as he hugs me tighter. "But if you do, I'll listen."

Why can't more people think this way? Most people can't wait to ask for all the details of my husband's death. Some overly insistent people never let up—they just find a new way to ask every time we talk or see one another. As if being privy to someone's passing satiates some strange need in them.

But not Fletcher. He leaves the choice up to me— whether or not I want to and when.

I toy with the length of his hair at the nape of his neck. Breathe in his clean cedar scent. Close my eyes and mold myself to him. Get lost in the idea of the relationship—the bond—we share becoming more.

"Not today, but another time in the future," I whisper.

His arms tighten briefly then relax before his hand strokes my hair. "Whatever you want, Madeline." Warm lips press to the bend of my shoulder. "Anything for you."

We sit wrapped in each other until Fletcher has to leave. I absorb every stroke and caress on my skin as if it were the last. Relish every moment wrapped in his arms and every kiss to my head.

I won't see Fletcher tonight after his show. Tomorrow morning, he plans to check out of the hotel, come over before his last performance in Santa Rosa, then stay with me until he leaves Sunday. The fact that he leaves in less than two days hasn't hit me yet. Or him. Until the exact moment, I am all too happy in the bubble we created.

"Thank you."

When Fletcher leaves to finish his tour, I will buck up the courage and figure out how to tell him what happened to Chris. To an outsider, explaining how someone died isn't as difficult. Law enforcement, medical professionals and media personnel do it regularly. They aren't necessarily numb to violence or death; they just know how to compartmentalize it. They didn't know the person, weren't close to them, didn't laugh or smile in their presence. So, not feeling the pain or loss is simpler for them.

Fletcher lifts his head, glances to the right and groans. "I don't want to leave. Not right now." His hand traces up and down my spine as he kisses the curve of my neck again.

God, I love it when he kisses me there.

"Wish you didn't have to, either." I lean back enough to tuck his wayward strands behind his ears and capture his serene irises. "But we'll see each other tomorrow."

My gaze drops to his lips. Lips I want on mine again. Our first kiss took me by surprise, in a good way. Yes, almost two years have passed since I kissed anyone intimately. I didn't expect kissing another man to come without challenges. Not after kissing the same man for almost thirteen years.

The fire that erupted inside me when our lips met… it shocked me the most.

When our eyes meet again, the corners of his lips and eyes turn up slightly. He knows what I am thinking. Knows that our kiss is at the forefront of my thoughts. As much as I want Fletcher to kiss me again, I don't think he will. After breaking our only kiss and learning about Chris, Fletcher will wait for me to make the next move. Fletcher is that type of man.

Reluctantly, I slip off Fletcher's lap and occupy a cooler section of couch space. He brushes his knuckles down my cheek, kisses my forehead then rises from the couch.

I draw my knees up and rest my chin on them while he shuffles around to gather his belongings. He doesn't have much here—a pair of lounge pants, a plain cotton T-shirt, his toothbrush, and a phone charger. Everything else sits alone in his hotel room.

"See you in the morning," he says before kissing my forehead at the front door. Each time his lips touch my skin, my knees start to buckle.

"Have a great performance." I fight the urge to reach out and yank him back inside. "I'll make brunch tomorrow."

"I look forward to it." His knuckles graze my cheek one last time, then he spins and walks off.

I wave him off and wait outside until I no longer see his rental car. Then I spend several hours in bed, inhaling his scent on the sheets and searching brunch ideas online. I want to make the last of our time together as memorable as possible. That is, until we see each other again.

Then the perfect idea strikes. I rush to the closet and slip a dress from the hanger. Ditching my pajamas for the dress, I step into the bathroom and stare at my reflection. *Fletcher will love this idea,* I tell myself. I brush the tangles from my hair and apply a light coat of makeup.

After stepping into a pair of heels, I fetch my purse and head for the garage. Less than a minute later, I am on the road. Steering the car to the one place I want to be. With Fletcher. Although I have to share him with the audience, I want as much time with Fletcher as possible.

As an added bonus, I get to listen to him play. Listen as he croons beautiful lyrics. Lyrics he wrote about me.

TWENTY

Fletcher

MY LAST PERFORMANCE wraps up in Santa Rosa.

Madeline watching me from the bar most of the evening was an unexpected surprise. I wish she would have stayed until the end. But when she yawned for the third time in less than five minutes, I smiled as she slipped off the stool and waved goodbye.

Although happy the night went by quickly, I hate how fast time moves since finding Madeline. Yes, I will see her sooner rather than later. But that also means I leave Santa Rosa in less than twenty-four-hours.

Ugh!

Being on tour started out as the best idea. Traveling the state to share the music Madeline inspired and to hopefully find her. Lucky for me, both came true. Now, this leg of the tour is over. Tomorrow, I have to pack up and drive two hours east. Away from her. Away from where I want to be.

On our off days, we could try to meet in the middle and spend time together. But with my tour dates scattered in the upcoming weeks, we would exhaust ourselves with driving and lack of sleep. As badly as I want to see and spend time with Madeline, the next three months will be packed with phone calls, texts, and hopefully FaceTime chats.

"Got everything?" Benny asks as I approach the bar, guitar case and duffel slung over my shoulders.

"Think so. If I forgot anything, you guys know where to find me."

"Water for the road?"

"That'd be great, Benny. Thanks."

He fills a paper cup with ice and water, pops a lid on and hands it to me with a straw. "See you next time around." His hand extends across the bar and I take it. "Enjoy the tour."

I offer him a smile then tip my head. "Thanks, Benny."

Darting out of the restaurant, I hop in the car and drive to Madeline's place. Just after ten, I hope to have some time with her tonight before we crash.

No matter how exhausted I am tomorrow, I plan to wake early and spend as much time with her as I can before leaving. It isn't long before I park in the driveway and all but sprint for the door.

Seconds after I knock, Madeline opens the door with

a smile on her face and a blanket around her shoulders and arms. My first thought is *I should be the one wrapped around her*. My second... *I'd love to come home to her every day.*

"Hungry?" she asks as I shut the door.

"A little." We wander into the kitchen and she goes straight to the fridge. "Maybe just a snack," I suggest. She holds up a bag of baby carrots and a tub of hummus. "Perfect."

We settle on the couch after I kick off my shoes. She picks a random movie on Hulu, rests her cheek on my arm and crunches carrots with hummus. Although our eyes focus on the television, I don't think either of us pays attention. Well, I'm not.

It isn't long before her soft snores fill the air. I gently prop her on the sofa arm, put the food away then shut off the television. Scooping her in my arms, I walk to the bedroom and manage to pull back the covers before she stirs.

"Need to use the bathroom," she mumbles as I set her on the bed.

I kiss her forehead. "Okay. Be right back."

While she uses the en suite, I use the bathroom in the main part of the house. I make it back to the bed before her, slip under the covers and pull back her side while I wait. When the door opens and she steps out, I stop breathing.

The length of her bare legs glimmers in the faint light. A cotton shirt ends at the curve of her butt. Her wavy locks tousled and free. And her lower lip is trapped between her teeth.

Someone help me find the strength to remain a gentleman.

Tonight is not the first time I've slept in bed with Madeline. Our relationship somewhere between friendship and lovers, I've held her in my arms all night. Felt her skin against mine in places. Knew she wore nothing more than a shirt and panties to bed.

But she always made it under the covers before me. Always put on pajama pants before leaving the bed in the morning. Not once have I seen her like this. Seen her so intimately. Madeline in a cotton undershirt and boy shorts is more intimate than any piece of skimpy lingerie.

And so help me, I need my erection to taper off before she molds her body to mine.

She crawls into the bed, flips the covers over herself and snuggles my frame. "Hope you don't mind that I borrowed your shirt," she says, voice thick with sleep.

I wrap her in my arms and pray to whoever listens. *Please keep me in line. Please don't let my physical self make asshole decisions.*

"Not at all. I'll leave some when I go."

I kiss her forehead and hug her closer. Her arm snakes around my waist a beat before her hand traces up my spine and settles between my shoulder blades. Breath hot on the hollow of my throat. Leg resting between mine.

"I'll miss you," she whispers and her lips graze the top of my sternum. "When you're gone."

"Me too." I stroke and kiss her hair. Close my eyes and

imagine not having to leave tomorrow. But waking in the morning and staying with her until she asks me to go.

Hope she never asks me to go.

"Go to sleep, sweet Madeline. Dream of beautiful things."

I wake to a chaste kiss on my throat and Madeline's hand leisurely roaming my spine. If I thought morning wood was bad during the year of her absence, her delicate touch amplifies it a hundredfold.

Borderline self-conscious over my obvious erection, my mind babbles dozens of questions within seconds.

Does she think it is my normal morning wood? That I am still asleep, possibly dreaming. Or does she realize this is my response to her touch? That *she* sparks this part of me, this hunger. That this isn't just some normal bodily function or the result of a fantasy. Other women or situations have aroused me, but Madeline has a different effect on me altogether.

The sensible side of me wants to say good morning and let her know I woke up. The irrational side of me wants to lie here and revel in her exploration of my body.

A little longer. Maybe a minute or two.

She kisses my throat again as her hand drifts up the

side of my torso. Before I stop myself, a groan rumbles in my chest. Madeline freezes for two breaths then resumes her steady caress.

"Didn't mean to wake you," she whispers the words like a kiss on my skin. "Sorry."

I kiss her crown, her forehead, her temple, then meet her gaze. "Don't apologize. Was enjoying your touch, if you hadn't noticed."

Pink tinges her cheeks as she swallows. "I… I did notice. Wasn't sure if that was, uh, normal or a side effect of me."

Madeline and I have never brought up age. It has never been relevant. Still isn't. With what I know about her life and level of maturity, I would guess she is older, but not by much. If based solely on her appearance, my guess would be that we are close in age, maybe a year or two off.

With that in mind, I smile internally at her timid nature. The flush on her cheeks. How she stumbles over her words. Do I make her nervous? Has she always been so shy about physical intimacy? Is this because I am the first man she has been close to since her husband passed?

I bring a hand to her cheek and stroke my thumb over her soft skin. *God, I want to kiss her.* "Both," I rasp out. "But if it makes you uncomfortable…" I glance down between us momentarily. "You can stop."

Her eyes search mine before she gives a subtle shake of her head. "It doesn't make me uncomfortable. Does it make *you* uncomfortable? Me touching you."

"Never." My thumb strokes her cheek. "As I said, I was enjoying it."

Fingers drift down my side, to my back, up my spine. I roll my eyes closed as my breathing spikes. Focus on nothing but her fingers as they trace my skin. On her breath as it heats my flesh. On her body as she shifts beside me, inching closer, jittery with nerves.

"Fletcher?" My name on her tongue is quiet and apprehensive.

My eyes open and home in on hers. "Yeah?"

"I feel silly asking this." She clamps down on her lips a moment.

"Don't be embarrassed," I say as I tuck hair behind her ear. "Ask me anything."

Her soft brown eyes dart between mine before she takes a deep breath. "Can I kiss you?"

I love and hate that she asked. From our first kiss, she should know I want nothing more than to kiss her.

I trace a finger over her eyebrow, along her temple and across her cheek. "You never have to ask."

"After last time… since I stopped…wasn't sure if…"

"Madeline." I lift her chin slightly so her eyes stay on mine. "I never want you uncomfortable. If you're overwhelmed, we stop. Just because you ended our last kiss doesn't mean I never want to kiss you again. Quite the opposite. But we go at your pace. Seeing as I kissed you without permission last time, I didn't want to do that again."

She stays silent a moment. Digests every word and the meaning behind them. "Thank you."

Before I open my mouth to tell her she doesn't need to apologize, her lips press to mine. Chaste and sweet and soul-stirring. Our legs weave and tangle into some new sailor's knot—one I hope never unravels. My fingers trail up her spine and thread the hair at the base of her skull. She hugs me closer as her lips move faster and her body trembles in my arms.

The idea of this moment ending tortures me. But I take everything she gives without complaint. That is until she licks my lower lip and sucks it between hers.

I gasp then feel her tongue stroke mine. Fire and a year's worth of yearning detonate in my chest. I roll her onto her back, position myself between her legs, press my weight into her and kiss her as if the opportunity won't come again.

Sweet moans spill from her lips and slide down my throat. Nails graze on either side of my spine. Her body rippling like waves. I consume every whimper, relish the sting in my flesh and savor the way we move together. So in sync. So perfectly in tune with one another.

And before we go any further, before we take the next step—a step she may not be ready for yet—I break the kiss. Hover a breath above her and smile lazily.

"Why'd you stop?" She pants the words out.

"I would love nothing more than to spend my last day here, in this bed, with you." I drop a chaste kiss on her lips. "But I wanted to serve you breakfast in bed. Maybe cuddle and watch a movie."

She forces her head deeper into the pillow and presses two fingers to her lips. "Am I a bad kisser?"

This makes me chuckle and I shake my head. "No. God, no. But if we keep that up, things may go further than either of us is ready for. And I'd much rather wait until I return. When I have more time. When *we* have more time."

The cutest huff blows hair off her face. "Fine." She pushes out her bottom lip then rolls her eyes. "What's for breakfast?"

God, I will miss her.

The willpower necessary to leave her in bed and go cook is tremendous, but somehow I manage. Cooking breakfast seemed a good idea when I thought of it. Executing breakfast… that is more of a challenge since I bought nothing and have no idea what Madeline keeps on hand.

I rummage through the fridge and pantry then pull out the ingredients for Florentine egg white omelets, sausage, fresh fruit and toast. In a matter of minutes, the house smells of maple, cheese and bread. My stomach growls and I pat it. *Soon.*

Once everything is plated, I brew coffee and search for something to carry it all. When I walk back in the bedroom, Madeline slaps a hand to her mouth and snickers.

"I have a small tray." She looks at my makeshift tray —

aka the sheet pan—and giggles harder. "Should've told you where I hide it. Sorry."

"No worries. This makes it more memorable."

Her eyes leave the tray and meet mine. A softness set at the corner of her eyes. A slight upward curve of her lips. She swallows then blinks several times as her eyes glaze over.

"Fletcher…" she whispers; voice thick with emotion. "I'd never forget this moment. Or any other with you."

Why? Why do I have to leave?

Oh, right. Because I committed to a tour in the hopes of this very moment happening. Problem is, I didn't think to give myself time in between each leg of the tour. I didn't consider I'd want time after each leg of the tour, on the off chance I did find her.

But I suppose my lack of preparation has its upsides. None of my other stops have idle time at the end. And once the tour ends, I have weeks of free time. Time I plan to spend with Madeline, if she will have me.

"Glad to hear." I crawl back into bed and kiss her cheek. "Now, let's eat before it gets cold."

TWENTY ONE

Madeline

THE MINUTES LEADING up to Fletcher leaving have been insufferable. Minutes zooming by faster than seconds. Obviously, we know his departure is inevitable. Still, the moment looms like a gray storm cloud.

Breakfast in bed is followed up by hours in each other's arms. Nestled between his legs, he hugs me close, occasionally kissing my hair and cheek. Peaceful moments with no words shared. Other moments, neither of us silent as we share more about ourselves. Nothing too in depth, but small snippets each of us will remember while apart.

Fletcher tells me about friends back home. A couple from high school that he catches up with from time to time. She is a physical therapist and he is a firefighter.

They married a few years ago, but have just started talking about children.

Children.

Once upon a time, I thought about children with Chris. I voice as much to Fletcher. Not that I couldn't *still* have children. Conceiving at thirty-seven isn't impossible or unheard of, but I worry about the risks. Not only the risks weigh on my mind, though. You actually have to *have* sex—or go through several steps with sperm donation—to conceive. Sex—let alone conception—won't happen anytime soon.

"Is there a reason you and Chris never got pregnant?"

"Early on, we wanted to wait. Both of us were in college and had a mountain of student loans. We thought it'd be smart to settle into our careers and be more financially comfortable before having children. Then, he started traveling more for work. It wasn't an obscene amount of time away, but he didn't want me to feel like a single parent when that wasn't the case. Time got away and then…"

Fletcher strokes my hair then kisses my shoulder. "If children were still possible, is that something you'd want?"

I neither love nor hate children. That should be my answer. But the truth is much more complex than that.

When Chris passed, I was relieved we didn't have a child. Not because I didn't love him or wouldn't love to have a piece of him still in my life. My reason was more about seeing Chris reflected in a mini version of us each day and having to explain to him or her why their daddy never came home. It would be glimpsing features and habits Chris once had in a child and not knowing how I would react.

Would I have been a good parent? Being a single parent is hard. Very hard. Especially with young children. Or would I have sunk into the same depression? Ignored not only myself, but also someone who depended on me? Honestly, every instinct in me says it would have been the latter. Which is why I am glad we didn't have children.

But do I want children now? If the opportunity were to arise, would I take that step?

"I don't know. After everything, that's something I'd have to think on." I take a deep breath. "What about you? Do you want children?"

He gives a noncommittal shrug. "I've not really thought about it either. My longest relationship fell apart as we grew more into ourselves. She didn't think me being a musician would lead to a happy life—for her or us. We were both young and having too much fun to think about children. My relationships since never got far enough to have conversations about serious topics." He kisses the top of my head. "But if everything fell into place and *felt* right, it would be surreal to create life with someone I loved."

I swear to god my ovaries just exploded.

Isn't it funny how one conversation can change your entire way of thinking? How I never gave specific thought to procreation before now. Yet, here I am, thinking about what it would be like to have a mini version of me—or Fletcher.

Gah! I barely know this man. Truly.

We spent two weeks together a year ago. Have spent the past week together. Yes, we have shared intimate details about ourselves, our past. Our time in my bed has been PG, borderline PG-13. We have cooked for each other, shared silence and hugs and the most amazing kisses.

Intimacy with Fletcher isn't the same as with others. Yes, the physicality is there. But in small touches or light kisses or thoughtful gestures. Do I want more physical intimacy with Fletcher? God, yes. Will I rush either of us to reach that moment? No. Although my hormones scream at me to fist his shirt and take what I want, common sense tells me to have patience. That all good things happen in their own time. The pace of any relationship is not written in stone, and ours will unfold as it is meant to.

"Did I scare you?" He kisses my shoulder. "You haven't taken a breath in too long."

Oops. I take in a lungful of air and relax into him.

"Sorry, and no. You didn't scare me." I twist to face him. "Just never thought of it that way." I glance at the clock on the bedside table and groan.

"What?"

I drop my forehead to his chest. "You have to go soon."

He hugs me closer and kisses the top of my head. "I'll miss you. So much."

I shift in his lap so I straddle him and wrap my arms around his neck. "Me too."

We sit like this until Fletcher can't wait any longer. He peppers me with kisses before he rises from the bed, changes clothes and gathers his belongings. I exit the bathroom after changing to find a small stack of neatly folded shirts on the bed. Shirts he is leaving for me.

Not hearing him in the house, I assume he is putting stuff in the car. So, I locate a small brown bag and add two tokens for him. I fold the flap of the paper bag and hand it to him when he reenters.

"For you. But you can't open it until you're gone."

He narrows his eyes. "What is it?"

"You'll see. Guess you could say it's my version of the shirts."

A groan peals from his throat as he pulls me into his arms. "Wish I didn't have to go."

"Same." I lean back enough to see his face. "Be safe and we'll see each other soon."

He nods, steps back and walks to the front door with his hand in mine. Under the canopy of the front porch, Fletcher stops in his tracks, spins to face me and cups my cheeks.

"I'll call when I get there." My eyes glaze over as I nod. "And we'll talk all the time."

"Okay," I choke out, emotion expanding in my throat.

I push up on my tiptoes as Fletcher leans down and

our lips collide in the middle. The kiss is joy and sorrow. Deep affection and loss. I don't want you to go and I will see you soon. It is torturous and pure bliss.

Tears roll down my cheeks, slow and without pace. Fletcher breaks the kiss, swipes the tears away then kisses the trails they left behind.

"I like you, Madeline Reynolds. More than admissible." Warm lips press to my forehead. "More than imaginable."

Before I respond, he drops his hands from my cheeks, pivots and walks to the car. The engine roars to life seconds before he backs out. He lifts a hand and waves as he drives off. I return the gesture with tears staining my cheeks and an unrelenting pain beneath my breastbone.

At least this time, we said our goodbyes.

TWENTY TWO

Madeline

YESTERDAY, I arrived home from work to a bouquet on my doorstep. But not just any bouquet. Blue and white anemones.

During one of our first nights of conversation, Fletcher nonchalantly asked my favorite flower. *"Blue anemone,"* I had told him. For days, I expected to see flowers when he arrived at the house. No one asks what your favorite flower is without purpose. Or so I thought. But Fletcher never appeared with flowers during his stay.

Instead, he waited until his absence. A small gesture to show I was on his mind while we were apart. The simple note with the arrangement—*I'm blue without you.* I giggled, sighed and melted on the spot reading the small card.

Off work today, no deliveries have mysteriously

appeared on my doorstep. But when the mail arrives, I gasp at the envelope wedged between bills and junk.

Mindlessly wandering back inside, I deposit the rest of the mail on the kitchen counter. My fingers trace the scrawl, study the loops and flow of Fletcher's penmanship. My eyes follow the movement before I slowly peel open the envelope in my hands. Tucked inside are two unlined, thick pages filled with more of Fletcher's artsy handwriting. Before reading a word, I lift the pages to my nose and inhale. Catch an inkling of Fletcher's fresh cedar scent and sigh. Hug it close to my chest as I walk to the couch and prepare to read his words.

Dearest Madeline,

I just hung up the phone with you after arriving in Sacramento. It's only been hours since I held you in my arms, but I miss you like crazy. The next three months will be torture, but phone calls and FaceTime will make our time apart easier.

Thank you for the photo and your pillowcase. At first, I thought the pillowcase was an odd gift. Until I brought it to my nose and smelled you on the cotton. Needless to say, I have stowed it in a sealable bag to not lose the scent of you. And your picture, it will be with me wherever I go.

There are so many things I want to say, but I'll wait until I wrap my arms around you again.

Yours always,
Fletcher

I read the letter again and again. Hug it to my chest and let my imagination run wild. *There are so many things I want to say, but I'll wait until I wrap my arms around you again.* The idea of voicing how I feel about Fletcher to him makes me weak in the knees. Has my stomach in knots and heart beating viciously.

Without question, I like Fletcher. *A lot.* But the last man I gave my heart to, he left far too soon. Yes, I am aware losing Chris was not my fault. But the weight of his loss still sits heavy on my shoulders. A large part of me fears losing Fletcher, too. I fear opening my heart again, just to have some cruel twist of fate pummel it with more tragedy.

Then I hear what my therapist repeated several times over the last twenty months.

"Life will never be free of pain or sadness or disappointment. But you still need to live. You need to get up each day and look for a positive. Just one. And one day, you'll see many. One day, you'll be less sad. One day, it won't hurt as much."

Today's positive: Fletcher wrote me a letter. I wouldn't exactly call it a love letter, but he wrote it with intense feelings. Affection. Heart. When was the last time I received a handwritten letter? In the mail, at that.

There is something to be said about receiving words from the heart on unique sheets of paper. The thought and time and care that went into the words. Taking those words and bringing them to life on the page. Sealing them away and sending them out into the world, to the person who provoked the emotions.

Writing and receiving letters — "I like you" letters — is an old tradition I welcome with open arms.

"It's nice to see you smile." Chris's voice echoes in the room.

"Never thought I would again."

"I did. Seeing your smile makes me happy. It'd be a shame for no one else to see it, too."

Twisting in my seat, I peer over my shoulder and glance at a photo on the wall. Tucked in an ornate silver frame, Chris and I stare at the photographer with bright, ear-to-ear smiles. Chris in a sharp black suit, white dress shirt and thin black tie; a simple boutonniere pinned to the jacket breast pocket. Me in floor-length white satin and lace; a bouquet of red roses in one hand, my other on Chris's chest.

I recall our wedding day with such clarity. More now than when Chris was alive. Pine and frankincense permeated the nave of the church. Red carpet a soft cushion against my heels as I strode down the aisle. Sounds of the wedding march infinitely louder and poignant as it resonated with the acoustics in the room. And the man at the end of the aisle...

God, Chris stole my breath on our wedding day. With the most dazzling smile and extra bounce in his stance.

"I thought we'd have forever," I whisper, seeing him plain as day in front of me.

The ghost of his hand caresses my cheek and I close my eyes, wishing for the warmth I once felt with his touch. The tender caress any time his knuckles grazed my cheek. But it never comes. Not anymore.

"Me too. You can still have your forever. With him."

My eyes open, vision blurred by the tears threatening to fall. My chin wobbles as I open my mouth to speak. "It doesn't seem fair."

"Life isn't meant to be fair or easy. Life will always be full of obstacles and challenges. It's how we overcome them that defines us. Whether we choose to wallow or rise above or both, it's all part of the journey."

Even now, almost two years later, Chris still lifts me up. Gives me the pep talk I need to hear. Although I am the only one who hears him, his words help. They give me clarity in the fog.

Do I have some form of psychosis?

The first time I mentioned to my therapist Chris talked to me, she wanted to prescribe medication "to help provide relief." Hearing or seeing loved ones who have passed is not unusual. Many pass it off as old memories replaying in a time of mourning. But when the mourning period ends—not sure who determines the time frame someone returns to "normal" after loss—so should any visuals and voices.

Guess I am still mourning. Because I see and speak with Chris somewhat regularly.

Yes, I know he isn't *actually* here. Thankfully, I know the difference between reality and fantasy. Fantasy Chris, as I see it, helps me come to terms with reality. Speaking with and seeing him is my method of coping. Of moving forward without the future I once expected.

Is it unhealthy to "interact" with my deceased husband? Probably, but it is how I make it one day to the next.

Except when Fletcher is present.

I never expected someone like Fletcher to walk into my life. A gentle force that makes me question much of my life. A beacon in my darkest moments and continual light on better days. Our time together is extraordinary without effort. After Chris, I never imagined myself with another man. But Fletcher... he changes everything.

I stare down at the letter in my hands. Rub my thumb over the grainy handmade paper. Read the last line of the letter again and again. *There are so many things I want to say, but I'll wait until I wrap my arms around you again.* Tip my head back and blink over and over.

We have only spent three weeks together over the last year. *Three weeks.* And yet, it feels as if I have known Fletcher an eternity. As if a part of me came back to life finding him. A piece of my soul from another lifetime locking back in place.

To think I would have never met Fletcher had I not had a reason to go to the retreat. I would not have met Fletcher if Chris had not passed.

Overall, this revelation unnerves me the most.

TWENTY THREE

Fletcher

EXHAUSTED IS the understatement of the year. My last show in Santa Cruz wrapped yesterday evening. Two more stops over the next two and a half weeks before my final performance in Los Angeles.

Then, a well-deserved vacation. The countdown is on and I am eager to spend several days with Madeline.

I fetch my clothes from the dryer in the hotel's laundromat. Back in the room, I fold and pack up my belongings before hitting the road. Then I sit at the small dinette table in the room with a small stack of blank papers and a pen poised to write.

Since leaving Madeline nine weeks ago, I send regular reminders to let her know she is constantly in my thoughts. Flowers, postcards from each city, letters.

Although we have spoken on the phone several times and done a handful of FaceTime chats, I want her to have something tangible. Something she can hold in her hands, brush with her fingertips, hold to her nose and breathe in. Odd as it may sound, I want her to have pieces of me when I can't physically be at her side.

Madeline is the type of woman to appreciate small tokens, to enjoy the nostalgia of handwritten notes and physical photographs. And I swear to give her several in our lifetime.

Dearest Madeline,

I leave Santa Cruz as soon as this letter goes to the post office. Not sure if you've visited Santa Cruz, but it's a fun, artsy town. I think you'd like it very much. Everyone is friendly and laid back. At every turn, art paints the town in brilliant pigments. Music is abundant and diverse. The people are equally eclectic and welcoming. Maybe one day in the future, we can visit together.

Only two more stops on the tour before I'm back in LA.

And if you'll still have me, I'd love nothing more than to spend time with you when the tour ends. I know we've talked about it several times, but I'll keep asking. I never want you to feel pressured—by me or what we have.

Counting down the days until I see you again.

Yours always,
Fletcher

On the face of the envelope, I write Madeline's address and my return address information. Folding the pages, I slip them in the envelope, lick the flap and seal it. I take my wallet from my back pocket, dig out the stamps I purchased when I wrote the first letter and add one to the envelope.

Three more stamps. Three more letters. Then, I will see her again.

Going through the room one last time, I double-check I packed everything. I hook the duffel over my shoulder, tuck Madeline's painting under my arm and roll the carry-on suitcase behind me out the door. After stowing everything in the rental, I check out with the hotel reception then drive off.

I deposit the letter to Madeline in the post office drop box then head for the highway. A few miles out of town, I press a button on the steering wheel and the sound system beeps.

"Call Madeline."

"Calling Madeline," the robotic female voice responds.

The phone rings twice before Madeline's voice floats through the car. "Hey, you," she says. I picture the smile on her face as she holds the phone to her ear. "On the road?"

With each city I leave, I call Madeline once on the road. Call it a new habit. One I don't plan to let go.

"Yeah. Left Santa Cruz minutes ago."

"Fresno next?"

"Mmhm." I flip on the blinker and shift lanes. "A week there, then a week and a half in Santa Barbara before LA."

"Almost done," she says wistfully. I don't miss her slight sigh at the end.

Being apart from Madeline is a new form of torment. Without a doubt, when we see each other again, I will take the first full breath in months. My heart will find its rhythm again. But at least this isn't like our time apart after the retreat. Now, we have daily contact in some fashion. This tour would be agony without speaking or texting with Madeline each day.

We talk over an hour as I navigate across the state and farther south. She updates me on work since our last conversation. Then tells me she had dinner with her parents, brother, and his girlfriend last night and it was less awkward than prior visits.

In a prior conversation, Madeline told me she hadn't been as close to her family after her husband passed. Not because she didn't love them. More along the lines of seeing them so happy and in love caused her pain. Physical and emotional hurt at the idea of not having what they had so easily. Before she and I met, she said she felt betrayed by the universe. Not understanding why someone so good would be taken away—not just from her, but his family and the world too.

I understood why she felt this way. Cheated out of a life.

The selfish part of me bit my tongue and kept my mouth shut. Didn't voice how losing one love opened up the possibility for us. Because saying such a thing aloud would make me the villain. And that is not who I am or ever want to be. Not with Madeline. Not ever.

Life or fate may have dealt her a painful hand, but I wouldn't have her if it didn't. Without the loss of Chris, Madeline and I would walk different paths. I weep and rejoice in equal measure at how our lives came together.

I exit from the highway and drive a short distance until several restaurants and gas stations come into view.

"Stopping to stretch my legs, grab a bite and gas up. I'll call when I get to the hotel?"

I phrase it as a question, always wanting to leave the option open for Madeline. By no means am I a stage-five clinger, but I do want as much of her in my life as possible. But I never want her to feel obligated or pressured to reciprocate. Ever.

"Yes. I have some errands to run, but should be home by then."

"Talk to you later."

"Drive safe."

"Always." I bite my cheek to stop myself from saying the words on the tip of my tongue. Words I have said to only one other woman; and those feelings were minuscule compared to what I harbor for Madeline. "Bye."

"Bye."

The call disconnects as I park in front of a fast-food chicken place. I drop my forehead to the steering wheel and groan. Bang my head a few times then stop before I walk into the restaurant with a red bump on my forehead. Take a few deep, methodical breaths.

How is it that everything with Madeline comes effortlessly?

We exist without complication. Share a natural harmony, whether near or far. When together, everything not important fades to the background. When together, nothing but each other matters.

Hence my impulse to say those three words to her. Three words. Eight letters. Ten characters. When strung together, they mean more than any other sentiment.

But saying them aloud—and not face to face—scares the hell out of me. Not because I don't mean them. *God, do I mean them.* The fear lies in the possibility of rejection.

I don't want to say the words and stress her into responding. It is no secret we both have immense feelings for one another. The constant need to see and touch each other isn't one-sided. What if she isn't ready to hear such proclamations, though?

What if I say those three little words and scare her away?

Worst of all, what if I say those three words and she doesn't feel the same?

A pit forms beneath my diaphragm and the desire to eat goes out the window. *Deep breath. In and out.*

This is Madeline I think of. Without her saying a word, I *know* how she feels. Maybe she won't be ready to say the words, but she feels what I do. The fact is undeniable.

But I must wait. Pull up my big boy pants, take a deep breath and practice patience with every cell in my body. If there is one thing I learned over the last fourteen months, it is that Madeline requires and deserves patience. My patience as well as her own.

So, this is me. Exuding patience. Biting my tongue and waiting for the right moment. The moment to tell her I love her.

TWENTY FOUR

Madeline

FLETCHER WRAPPED up his final performance two nights ago. Every minute since, I have been on pins and needles. Picking my cuticles as I guess when I will see him again.

Over the last three months, Fletcher proclaimed, no less than a hundred times, that he would see me once the tour ended. Now that it has, I have no clue how much time will pass before he arrives at my doorstep. Between the weekly flower deliveries, more than a dozen letters, a new postcard when he arrived in each city, text messages and calls, I never once felt lonely with his absence.

After having Fletcher in my bed the week he was here, sleeping the last three months alone has been challenging. His scent faded sooner than anticipated from the shirts he left behind and the pillowcase he slept on. It irked me to no end to not wash the sheets on the same day as usual after he left. But the need to bask in his clean cedar scent as long as possible overrode the routine without effort.

It wasn't just his scent I missed, though. Also the heat of him next to me on the couch and under the sheets. His arm wrapped around me as we slept, holding me impossibly close most of the night. How he kissed the crown of my head when he woke each morning. How we had lain in bed for hours, in each other's arms, while we chatted about life or said nothing at all.

Needless to say, I miss Fletcher. Terribly.

Through the front window, I see the mail carrier walking toward the house. I step outside as she walks up, and she hands me a thin stack of envelopes.

"Thank you," I say and she responds in kind.

As I shut the front door, I shuffle through the stack and see a new letter from Fletcher. Returning to my spot on the couch, I toss the other mail on the coffee table and gingerly open the letter.

Dearest Madeline,

The tour is finally over! God, it feels like years have passed since we last touched. I hope to remedy that soon.

On the road, I came across so many unique places. At each one, I asked if it would be a place you would enjoy too. Presumptuous of me, but I would love to take you to all of them one day. Maybe take a small road trip, visit places new to you or me, and experience them with you.

Don't think I asked before, but are you more of an indoor or outdoor woman? In my eyes, I see you loving both equally and for different reasons.

Maybe I will learn the answer soon. Sooner than expected.

Yours always,
Fletcher

The last line makes my brows pinch at the middle. Does this mean I will see him in the next day or so? Really hope so.

I rise from the couch, walk to the bedroom, and enter the walk-in closet. Near the door, on the shelf over my tops, I pick up a box and carry it to the bed. The square box plain on the outside—white with black outlined flowers and vines. Something pretty I stumbled across in the craft store when looking for fall decor. It caught my eye and was in my cart in an instant.

Removing the lid, I stare down at the stack of letters and postcards Fletcher has sent. Eight postcards and today's letter is number twenty. I also dried a flower from each arrangement he sent and have them safely tucked in a small box inside the bigger box, along with the floral delivery cards. A dozen dried flowers—most of them blue or white anemone, but there's also a baby red rose, pink peony, and white lisianthus.

Prior to these, it is hard to pinpoint the last time I received flowers. The arrangements when Chris passed definitely don't count. I mean flowers given to show affection; a simple I love you. Not to say Chris never gave me flowers—he did. But it had been years and only on special occasions—birthdays, anniversaries, or celebrating other milestones. But not often and not on a day without an observance in mind.

Chris loved me fiercely. He just had his own way of showing that love. It wasn't wrong or right; it was simply his way. I never felt unloved by Chris.

As I stow the letter in the box, my phone pings in my pocket. Closing the lid, I stash the box back in its place in the closet. I take my phone from my pocket and unlock it to see a text from Fletcher.

Fletcher: Go outside.

What kind of message is, *Go outside*? No hey or hello. Just a directive. Weird. Maybe he sent another delivery?

Madeline: Okay. But so you know, that is the strangest text ever.

Not sure what I am walking out to see, I slip on a pair of flats and a cardigan. Fall has definitely made itself known in the northern part of the state, but I love the change. The warm-colored leaves and cooler tempera-tures. More opportunities to wear cable-knit sweaters, jeans, and boots. Not to mention lighting the fireplace in the living room or sitting by the fire bowl outside.

I shuffle toward the front door and suck in a breath as I turn the knob, unsure what I will find on the other side.

The patio comes into view, but everything looks as it does every time I step out the door. I look left toward the small bench and table. Nothing different. So, I step out more and close the door behind me. Walk down the small path toward the double driveway, which is partially blocked by the exterior garage wall.

Right, left, right… more of the driveway comes in to view. I spot the back of a black SUV in the farthest spot of the driveway. Wrapping my sweater tighter around my torso, I slow my steps and inch forward to peer around the corner with caution. But all uncertainty goes out the window when I take in the whole scene.

I gasp and throw a hand over my mouth as my eyes glaze over.

Fletcher. He's here.

I dash across the driveway and hurl myself at him. In an instant, he opens his arms and hugs me to him with a soft chuckle. My arms circle his neck and bring him impossibly closer.

"Good surprise?" he whispers in my ear.

I lean back enough for our eyes to click. "Best surprise. Why didn't you say anything? I could've made us dinner and made myself a little more presentable."

He lifts a hand from my waist and tucks locks of hair behind my ear, his eyes following the motion. "One, you look beautiful. Two, I stopped for dinner supplies. And three, I figured the surprise would be welcome." The last comes across as a statement, but his eyes silently ask if his spontaneous arrival is acceptable.

"Are you kidding?" I drop my cheek to his pec. "More than welcome. Always."

Fletcher hugs me tighter before he straightens his spine. "Let me grab some things from the back seat and we can head inside."

Stepping back, I release Fletcher and watch as he retrieves two canvas bags from the car. I lead us inside and go to the kitchen, ready to see what he brought for dinner.

First item he pulls from the bags is a small bundle of flowers wrapped in brown paper. Blush garden roses, small budded white roses, eucalyptus and thistle. He steps into me, places a kiss on my forehead, then hands them over.

"They aren't your favorite, but hope you love them the same."

I bring the bundle to my nose and inhale. The perfume sweet and musky and piney. On the exhale, my entire body melts. They may not be the flower I love most, but I am learning to love many new things when it comes to Fletcher.

"They're perfect."

I fetch a vase from the cabinet, add water and arrange

the flowers. Setting them at the heart of the dining table, I turn back to see what else Fletcher brought.

On the counter, I survey a medley of ingredients. Fresh green beans, acorn squash, onion, lemons, garlic, pearled couscous, and two butcher-wrapped packages. A small tub of fresh-cut fruit and a mini chocolate frosted cake have me salivating for dessert before dinner. There is also a handful of small bags with sprigs of fresh herbs. Fletcher unwraps the butcher paper to reveal shrimp and scallops.

Well now, didn't he go all out.

"What can I help with?" I ask, not sure if he wants to cook solo.

He stares at the ingredients spread across the counter, his lips puckered in thought. "Maybe the vegetables." Fletcher proceeds to tell me how to chop the squash and snap the ends from the beans.

As I get to work on the vegetables, he pulls out pans and pots before starting the couscous. Every once in a while, I peer at him from the corner of my eye. Watch how he moves with ease around the kitchen. Watch as he makes us dinner as if he has done it thousands of times.

I keep my eye on him and fall a little harder with each move he makes. If he keeps it up, I may never let him leave.

TWENTY FIVE

Fletcher

STARTING each morning with Madeline in my arms gives me life.

With my unexpected arrival three days ago, I had no clue how she would react. I didn't think it would freak her out, but I was mentally prepared to stay in a hotel if it did. As predicted, she was beyond excited to see me.

We spent the last two days lounging about and catching up on lost time. Chatting over the phone and through FaceTime helped with our time apart, but it was nothing compared to being with her in person. In less than seventy-two hours, we have fallen into a comfortable routine.

This morning, though, Madeline works. Which leaves me close to seven hours of alone time. Not such a bad thing, but I don't know how comfortable she is leaving me in her home alone. I have plenty of things to entertain myself with — guitar, books, movies. I would be willing to run to the grocery store too. After several months of travel, I am quite content doing nothing or simple, day-to-day life chores.

Madeline exits the bathroom in navy scrubs and half her hair secured in a clip. She fidgets with an earring as she peers up and locks onto my eyes. Three breaths pass before either of us blinks.

I still lie in bed, only in a pair of boxer briefs. Will she want me to leave while she works? Maybe I should have gotten dressed on the off chance I need to leave.

Seeing Madeline in the morning distracts my train of thought.

Without shame, I rake my eyes down her frame before coming back up to lock on the brown irises I missed so much in the last three months. How the hell can a set of scrubs be sexy? I have no clue, but Madeline pulls off the allure without effort.

"Do you have time for breakfast?" I ask.

"Yeah." She nods then glances at her watch. "About thirty minutes until I need to leave."

I bolt out of bed and slip on lounge pants. "Any requests?"

We head for the kitchen and I whip out a pan. "Eggs and toast are good. I don't like to eat too much this early."

I get to work on breakfast while she packs up items for lunch and snacks. In no time, I portion eggs on a plate with slices of buttered toast. We sit at the dining table and eat breakfast in comfortable silence. I watch in fascination as she scoops the scrambled egg onto her fork then plops it on her toast before eating it. Cute habit.

"What will you do today?" she asks after swallowing her bite.

"Didn't have set plans." I set my fork down and look up at her. "Do you want me to leave while you're gone?"

She chews the last of her breakfast and waves me off. "Don't be silly." Her eyes lock on mine. "I trust you, Fletcher." The statement speaks volumes. "But if you plan to leave, I'll need to give you the code for the door lock."

"Okay, yeah. I may peruse the city and do a little shopping while you're out."

The wood legs of her chair scuffle on the hardwood. She takes her plate to the sink, rinses it and puts it in the dishwasher. Then tears the bottom of the grocery list off the fridge, grabs a pen and writes.

"Here." She hands me the paper. "It's the code for the front door lock. That way, you don't feel obligated to stay here or out while I'm gone." She wanders off to the bedroom, only to return seconds later. "Here's the spare key. In case the keypad is finnicky." As if no big deal, she places the silver key in my palm.

Feels as if I have been handed the crown jewels. I tuck the code and key in my pocket and the impact hits me with unbelievable force. My heart beats viciously behind my ribcage as my skin breaks out in a light sweat.

"Wish I didn't have to go" —she steps into me— "but work calls."

We exchange an all too brief kiss and then she heads to the garage. A moment later, she drives off.

What just happened, it felt so *normal.* Waking up with her alarm, sharing breakfast, chaste kisses and daily goodbyes.

I have never had a life like this. In my three-year relationship with Tricia, we never reached the cohabitation phase. For me, the desire to exist in the same space as her never crossed my mind. Maybe because we were so young and were still paving our way. Perhaps it was our different levels of maturity. Tricia liked to party. A lot. And me, I enjoyed a good time, but didn't feel the need to get sloshed every night of the week and act like a teenager. Seeing as Tricia was my longest relationship and she never took my music—or life, in general—seriously, we went our separate ways.

So, living in the same space with someone I have deep affection for is a new adventure. Not sure if it is only me that feels this way, but it seems as if Madeline and I are on the path to cohabitation.

Most of all, the notion doesn't scare me one bit.

Madeline strolls through the front door shortly before two. From my spot on the couch, I take her in head to toe as she shuffles through the door with her phone pinned between her shoulder and ear. She appears slightly miffed —over what, I have no idea.

"Yeah, Mom. Sounds good." She reaches up to hold the phone and meets my gaze. "Friday at six. See you then."

She disconnects the call, puffs out a breath and a few wayward strands float off her cheeks before landing back in place. Isn't it funny that even as adults, our parents can still get to us. Not necessarily in a bad way, it is just the nature of the parent-child relationship.

"Everything okay?" I ask, marking the page of the book I started before placing it on the table.

"Yes. No. I don't know." She sets her purse and lunch tote on the kitchen island, along with the mail. "Mom called as I was leaving work to check in. And it slipped that I have company." Her eyes dart to mine. "Not that I'm trying to hide you from anyone," she rushes out.

I stroll over, wrap her in my arms and press my lips to hers. "It's okay. We're still very new, so I have no expectations one way or the other. We go at your pace. I never want to hide you away, but I won't make you uncomfortable either."

She sags in my arms. "Thank you."

"So what did she say that has you flustered?"

After a deep inhale, she relays the call. "Mom wants us over for dinner on Friday." She leans back and peers up from under her lashes. "I told her who you are, but nothing else."

I brush my knuckles over her cheek. "Hey, it'll be okay. People love me."

"Not worried about them not liking you." Her cheeks pink.

"Then what *are* you worried about?"

She buries her face in my chest. "What if they think I'm being disrespectful to Chris's memory? What if they think I got over him too soon? That I'm moving on too quickly."

I shift and grasp her chin between my thumb and forefinger, lifting her gaze so our eyes lock. "Hey. One, you're a grown woman. You have every right to make your own decisions. Regardless of the opinions of others. Two, didn't your family push you to go to the retreat? That was their way of helping you move forward. I doubt they meant for you to find another connection at the retreat. But I don't believe they'd ever want you to remain alone the rest of your life. Not when you have so much left to give."

Glassy brown irises dart between my greens. Not as if she doesn't believe me, but more like she wants the thought in writing and may be able to extract it from within me.

"Are you okay having dinner with my family? Or is this all a little too soon?" she asks, voice so soft the words almost fade with the sunlight.

I press a chaste kiss to her lips. "Not too soon. I'd be honored to meet them." The corners of her mouth curve up in a small smile. "Now, on to more pressing matters." Madeline inches back as her brows scrunch in the middle. "I did a little shopping today and I need help deciding what to make for dinner."

She chuckles and play slaps my chest. "Oh, I think we can figure it out."

As Madeline saunters off to the bedroom to change, I swallow down every natural instinct to follow her footsteps. I bite the inside of my cheek and stifle a moan as my mind drifts to places harder to ignore the more time I spend with her.

In the short time we have known each other, Madeline has become more of a permanent fixture in my heart and mind. With each passing day, the urge to say more, to *do* more, to *be* more, expands faster than the universe.

Now, Madeline's parents want to meet me at dinner on Friday. What has me most curious is what title Madeline dubbed me while on the phone with her mother.

Titles and status have yet to be discussed, but does Madeline consider me her boyfriend? 'Cause I sure as hell would love to be. And so much more.

TWENTY
SIX

Madeline

IF I DON'T STOP SWEATING, I will need to change. Again.

Never once have I been this nervous about having dinner with my family. Not when I first introduced Chris or the guys I briefly dated before him. Not when I almost failed a midterm at college. And not when Mom and Dad wanted to have "the talk" when I entered middle school, knowing I couldn't leave the dinner table until excused.

Now, though… Tonight is all those previous occasions thrown in a mixing bowl, blended well, and sprinkled with extra tension.

Fletcher steps into me and wraps his arms around my waist. I jump at the contact then sag against his frame, returning to my dilemma of which earrings to wear. Diamond studs or silver hoops? Both small and simplistic.

Choosing which pair to wear has never been this daunting.

"Hey." He presses a light kiss to my shoulder. "Everything okay?"

All it takes is the simple press of Fletcher's lips to my skin and the anxiety from moments ago withers away. Still baffles me how he soothes me with such ease.

"Yes. No." I huff out a breath. "I don't know."

He shifts so we are face to face. "Talk to me."

The constant up and down is a nonstop trampoline bounce in my gut. Calm and collected while down, excited and hysterical when up. Can't say I recall feeling this back and forth with Chris and my emotions. It isn't necessarily a bad thing, just new. And I haven't quite mastered how to handle it.

"Is it weird that I'm nervous about dinner?"

Fletcher bends at the knee until level with my line of sight. "Do you think it's too soon for them to meet me? Because we can skip dinner, if that's the case. Or is it because you're introducing another man to your family?" He asks the last question quieter as his hands rub up and down my biceps.

"Mostly the latter." I hold his gaze. "But a little of the former." I bite my bottom lip. "How soon is too soon? I have no freaking clue." My stomach does another flip. Inhaling deep, I exhale loudly with a slight shake of my head. "God, I feel like a teen all over again. Scared to do or say the wrong thing with my parents. Why?"

The question is meant to be rhetorical, but I doubt Fletcher will leave it unanswered.

"Madeline, it's okay to be nervous or uncomfortable or whatever else you're feeling. There's no manual to relationships. Nothing to tell us how to move on after certain experiences. We have to guide ourselves the best way we know how. And sometimes…" He pauses to make sure I pay attention, that I listen to what he says next. "We wing it. Fly by the seat of our pants and go with what our heart tells us. Live in the moment and not let society dictate what we do." Warm, calloused fingertips swipe hair from my cheek and send the most delicious shiver down my spine. "I'm nervous too." My eyes widen at his admission. Since we started getting ready, Fletcher appeared so at ease. "But only because I like you. A lot."

Soft lips press to mine, sending every skittish nerve and jittery muscle to the wayside. When the kiss breaks, Fletcher drops his forehead so we are nose to nose.

Moments like this—when he quells every worry and I am putty in his hands—have me on the verge. Those three little words scoot closer to the tip of my tongue. Stand on the edge of the cliff, ready to dive headfirst. The intense emotion there, yet I fight expressing the deep affection I obviously feel for Fletcher.

I don't worry about those three words being spoken aloud. Nor do I worry he won't reciprocate. My fear runs much deeper. It chills my blood and turns my veins to ice.

What if I say those words aloud, tell Fletcher I love him, and then I lose him? Whether by choice or accident.

"I like you a lot too." My palm grazes the scruff on his jaw and my eyes follow the movement. "So much."

He plants one last chaste kiss to my lips. "Before we veer off and forget we have plans, we should go."

I take his hand and guide us toward the door. "Smart man."

Fletcher parks behind Phillip's car in the driveway. For a beat, I stare up at the house my parents bought after my brother and I moved out. Downsizing from four bedrooms to two, they lost half the square footage and practically live in a tiny home. But not really. The small space works for them, though, and that is what matters.

Through the windshield, I stare at the pale-blue house with dark-brown shutters. Try to peek through the sheer white curtains to see what my parents, Phillip and Sylvia are up to. Unfortunately, no one is in the living room. So, I have no clue what we are walking in on.

With the simple lack of information, a new layer of perspiration blankets my skin.

Quit freaking out! Jesus. I have never been this on edge in my life. *Because Fletcher is different, and you know it.*

"Ready?" Fletcher's soft tenor breaks my mini meltdown as he takes my hand. "We're early, so if you need more time, we have it."

I peer down at our clasped hands then meet his sunny, forest-colored irises. In two breaths, my erratic mindset simmers down and my skin dries. With simple words and touch, Fletcher melts away all anxiety. Blankets me with comfort and security and love.

Love?

Yes, love. Although neither of us has voiced the word aloud, no use in denying it.

Interestingly enough, the older I get, the less I worry over things once considered most important—material possessions and societal perceptions. While those I took for granted slip into the foreground—expressing how I feel and spending time with someone I love.

I have no need to flaunt Fletcher to everyone we know, to cling to his arm and bat my lashes at women who look our way. There is no need to mark territory or beg for his attention. We have evolved past such mediocre flashes of ownership.

Without voicing it, we both know where we stand. Fletcher orchestrated his tour in the hopes of finding me. If that doesn't say *"I'm with her"* in every way imaginable, I don't know what does. And with my past—details I haven't shared with anyone except Fletcher—Fletcher is fully aware where my heart lies.

I take a deep breath, squeeze his hand then release it. "Let's head inside."

A burst of warm air and laughter greets us as we stroll

inside, hand in hand. At first, no one notices our arrival. We stow our coats and my purse on the hooks in the foyer then meander toward the kitchen, where all the chatter bounces off the walls.

"Maddie Mae," Mom greets us as we come into view. "Didn't hear you come in. Sneak."

Fletcher leans in, his lips at my ear. "Maddie Mae?"

I don't miss how the room goes absolutely silent and all eyes swing our direction. "Family nickname," I whisper back.

The brightest smile steals Mom's expression. Dad, Phillip, and Sylvia follow suit.

"Wasn't purposely quiet, Mom." I breathe deep, hold it a beat, then relax my shoulders on the exhale. "Everyone, this is Fletcher." His thumb lightly strokes the top of my hand. "Fletcher, this is my mother, Jeannie, my father, Robert, and my brother and his girlfriend, Phillip and Sylvia."

The kitchen roars back to life as everyone exchanges greetings and handshakes. In less than a minute, Fletcher charms my family. Mom plasters on her best high school teacher smile. Dad holds his best electrical contractor stance. Phillip asks what type of car Fletcher drives—ever the salesman—while Sylvia smiles and shakes her head.

Everyone migrates to the dining room, where the four-seater table has been converted to six. Mom sets the roasted sweet potatoes, balsamic Brussel sprouts and homemade rolls on the table while Dad carries out the rosemary and citrus pork tenderloin.

One truth about my and Phillip's childhood, we always had delicious meals. Neither of my parents were masters in the kitchen, but they learned much from our grandparents, cookbooks and cooking shows. Dad loved—loves—home-cooked meals and Mom loved experimenting with what ingredients we had on hand. A win-win for all.

"Fletcher, do you have Thanksgiving plans with your family?"

"Mom!" My cheeks feel the heat of a hundred suns.

Fletcher softly chuckles at my side. "It's okay." He sets his palm on my thigh and my body heats for a wholly new reason. "No, Jeannie. Since I wrapped up my tour last week, I'm taking time to myself. When I'm not on tour, I see them often. My stepfather is my manager, so Mom stops by the studio almost daily."

"Well, that's nice. How long is your stay with us?" she asks as if this is normal conversation. As if Fletcher stays "with us" regularly.

I sip my wine as Fletcher chews his food. Fletcher's "Madeline Radar" must have gone off, because his thumb languidly strokes my leg. An automatic need to calm the irrationality brewing in my head at the idea of him leaving.

"Haven't set a leave date yet."

God, I want to look him in the eye and ask what he means. But that would stir up a whole new round of questions for my family to ask—me and him. No one at this table is clueless to the connection I share with Fletcher. If they are, I will gladly take them to the optometrist. I may be biased, and we may not have defined *us* yet, but our relationship must be obvious. Right?

"Oh, well I hope to see more of you while you're here," Mom says with a little too much enthusiasm.

A thick fog of embarrassment swallows me whole. This is so much worse than when I was a teen. Listening to my mother all but beg for Fletcher to stay.

Do I want him to stay for an extended period of time? Yes, without a doubt. But our relationship isn't at the stage of making such colossal decisions. Or is it?

Why *isn't* there a manual for relationships?

Dinner ends, dishes are cleared from the table, then Mom emerges with her infamous apple, pear, and cranberry cobbler. Dad delivers the bowls, spoons, and fresh whipped cream. And thank goodness, the table goes silent while we all moan over the last course.

The rest of the night goes smoother. We stay after dessert for coffee and tea. Phillip and Sylvia at the center of attention as we all chat. Shortly thereafter, we gather our belongings and prepare to leave.

On our way out, Dad pulls me in for a fierce hug. Stronger than any previous hugs we have shared. "Does he make you happy, sweetheart?" he whisper-asks and I nod. "Then follow your heart. Everything else will fall into place."

"But—"

"No buts. Chris would want you happy. *We* want you happy. The rest can be sorted later."

At thirty-seven, I didn't expect to still be receiving

advice from my father. But here we are, and I wouldn't have it any other way.

"Thanks, Daddy. Love you."

He breaks the hug and leans back to look me in the eye. "Love you too, sweetheart."

We wave to everyone as we back out of the driveway. Once Fletcher steers us out of the neighborhood, I buck up the courage to ask his opinion.

"So… how was meeting the parents?"

He turns down the already quiet music and chuckles. "They're about as quirky as any other parents, including mine. But they mean well. And it's obvious they love you. A lot."

"Was it awkward?"

Taking my hand in his, he lifts it to his lips and kisses my knuckles. "Surprisingly, no." He glances at me from the corner of his eye. "With you, everything feels… *right*."

My heart kicks into fifth gear as I stop breathing. Not because his words frighten me. The exact opposite, actually.

Deep down, rooted in my marrow, I feel more at ease than ever. More at home. With Fletcher. The thought of forgetting Chris still scares me. But in Fletcher's arms, I have a sneaky suspicion he will keep me safe and guard my heart. Forever.

I study his profile in the dimly lit car and take a deep breath. "It does feel right."

TWENTY SEVEN

Fletcher

I REPEAT Madeline's words for the hundredth time in my head. *"It does feel right."*

Did she actually admit her feelings aloud?

Yes, Madeline and I have been on this odd roller-coaster journey for a while. For the most part, the ride has coasted somewhat level with the occasional upward climb. And I am one-hundred-percent okay with our pace. Taking this slow—discovering more about each other, learning what we love and loathe—has been the best adventure. The gradual journey makes it easier to fall harder for her.

But is she ready for more?

She said it feels right for her too. In my opinion, there

are only so many ways to read into that statement. And not a single version sounds ill fated.

I park the car in the driveway and we head into the house. Neither of us has spoken up since our most recent confession. As always, the silence hasn't been uncomfortable. But I wonder if her mind is recycling the last words I said to her too.

We kick off our shoes. Madeline hangs her purse on the back of the bedroom door then sets her phone on the charger while I empty my pockets.

As she saunters around the bed, a new jitteriness blooms in my chest. I study her eyes, her lips, the arch of her brows. Her expression flaunts several tells, but I don't jump to conclusions. I will never assume when it comes to Madeline.

"Tired?"

The hint of hunger in her gaze is far from tired. But if Madeline wants more, if the way she licks her lips is any indication, I need to hear the words from her mouth.

With a subtle shake of her head, she answers, "No."

She steps into me, glides her palms up my chest and laces her fingers behind my neck. I swallow and hope it keeps me from outright panting. Then she tugs the hair tie free, drops it to the floor and combs her fingers through my hair.

A moan spills from my lips a beat before she pushes up on her tiptoes and presses her lips to mine. My arms snake around her waist to hug her closer. To feel every inch of her pressed to my frame. The perfect fit.

Her tongue drags over my bottom lip and I open without hesitation. Adrenaline pumps through my veins at the intensity of our kiss. Tongues tangled, bodies magnetized, fingers clenched.

This isn't our first kiss, but it outshines all its predecessors.

Madeline drops her hands to my abdomen, curls her fingers into fists and pulls me impossibly closer as she walks backward. A slave to her touch, I follow her footsteps. Don't question where her head is. I simply let her guide us and whatever happens.

Until she lowers herself to the mattress and tugs me down with her.

All too soon, our lips break apart. Our panting echoes in the silence. Our eyes lock on one another in the dim light.

"Madeline…"

Unsure where she plans on taking this, I don't expand. Right here, right now, she needs to take the lead. Guide us down whatever path she wants us to follow. If left to me, I may choose something she isn't ready for.

A hand cups my cheek. Slow strokes of her thumb follow. I lean into her touch. Revel in every intimate touch she bestows me with. Touches not given so easily or frivolously. Touches I never take for granted.

"I want to, Fletcher." She leans closer and kisses me chastely.

My eyes roll closed as my heart stretches my ribcage. I lick my lips then open my eyes and tilt my head slightly.

"You'll need to be a little more specific." Her brows twitch. "Madeline, I don't—no, can't—assume with you. So you need to tell me what it is you want."

Over the short time we have been together, I have learned a lot about Madeline. But we have barely scratched the surface. I feel as if I have always known her, but there is still so much left to discover. One being her bedroom habits. Not in a perverted sense. More along the lines of her tells. Knowing when she wants to be held or just kissed versus sex.

Every instinct I own says she wants the latter. Unfortunately, testosterone may be attributing to my instincts more than usual. So hearing what she wants from her lips is essential.

"Fletcher…" She lifts her free hand and frames my face. "Make love to me."

My lips crash to hers. I have craved this moment far too long, but refuse to rush it. Madeline means more to me than some quickie or random hookup.

I break the kiss, reach for the back collar of my shirt and tug it over my head. As I toss it to the floor, the tips of her fingers graze the planes of my abs. I shiver under her caress, cup her cheeks and bring my lips back to hers. The kiss grows more intense, deeper, as her hands trail down my body, fingers dancing along the waistband of my pants.

With slow precision, my hands drift down her neck and traipse over her shoulders. Wander lower, graze the outer swell of her breasts and edges of her abdomen. At the bottom hem of her shirt, I slip a finger beneath the fabric and lightly brush my knuckles over her belly.

The kiss breaks briefly as she sucks in a breath. I use the temporary interlude to grab the hem of her shirt and lift up. I toss the fabric to the floor and rake my eyes over her skin. Subtle curves accentuated by her lightly sun-kissed skin. Creamy lace hugs her breasts.

I swallow and fight my barbaric compulsion to strip her bare and take her fast. Because the more Madeline I get, the more I lose my resolve. The more my gentlemanly tendencies attempt to fly out the window.

I trace a knuckle over her cheek, down the column of her throat, along her collarbone. "Beautiful," I whisper before bringing my lips back to hers.

Fingers roam my chest, my abs, my back with leisure. Memorizing this new piece of me. One she has seen but hasn't navigated as a lover. I trail my lips along her jaw, stop at her ear and suck the lobe briefly before sweeping my lips and tongue down her neck. At the curve where her shoulder meets her neck, I worship her. Leave fevered kisses on her flesh. Lick her soft skin. Gently nip and follow it with another kiss. Then repeat the same on the opposite side.

She claws at my back, my neck, my hair. Head tipped back, she gasps for breath.

Then her hands drop to the front of my pants. Her deft fingers undo the button and slide the zipper to the base. My pants slide down my thighs, fall to the floor, and I kick them aside. Following her lead, I unfasten her pants and she wiggles out of them.

For a beat, we simply take each other in. Me in my briefs and her in a matching lacy set that makes my mouth water. Her eyes drag over my body, pausing a beat when she lands on my erection. I have never been a boastful man, but the way Madeline regards me in this moment, I want to be.

When her eyes meet mine again, I slip my fingers beneath the waistband of my briefs and push them down. Madeline swallows, but holds my gaze as she reaches around and unhooks her bra. The strapless material falls away and I drop my eyes to take her in. Her small breasts perfect and round; nipples pale pink and pert.

She scoots back on the mattress, pushes the bedding down toward the foot and peels off her panties. This more brazen Madeline turns me on as much as subdued Madeline. Seeing this new side of her, it calls out to a more feral side of me. One I never knew existed.

I crawl onto the bed, climb up and over her. Settle between her legs and lightly press my weight into her. Rest my forearms on either side of her face. Lock eyes with her and absorb every facet of this moment. The enormity of what this means. For Madeline, for me—for us.

What we are about to do… it's a big deal. For both of us. Since the first day I laid eyes on Madeline, I sensed this connection between us. Something absent to the naked eye. An invisible force or magnetism slowly bringing us together. A bond that will be forever linked by this moment.

Shit. I mentally slap my forehead.

"Uh, Madeline. I don't have a condom."

Her expression remains unfazed by the news as she reaches for my cheek. "It's okay. I'm on birth control." My brows pinch a moment. "I've been on it years for other reasons."

Another slap. How stupid of me to forget not all women take birth control to prevent pregnancy. "I promise I'm clean. Was tested after my last partner."

She lifts her head off the pillow and gives me a brief kiss. "I trust you, Fletcher."

All in all, we have spent close to a month together. Although we were in constant contact, I don't count the three months I was away on tour as spent together. Those days felt like we were still learning how to navigate us.

It feels as if I have known Madeline all my life, though. Voicing her trust in me—ultimate trust—amplifies every emotion she stirs in my veins. It builds and expands, ready to rip at the seams and spill over the edge.

I toy with a strand of her hair then drop my lips to hers. Her arms circle my torso as we get lost in the kiss.

Her legs shift, hips rock up into mine. Fever licks my skin. Tingling spreads from my limbs to the center of my chest. My heart pound, pound, pounds against my sternum. Pressure builds in my groin—thicker, heavier—as Madeline slicks my cock with her arousal.

Unable to resist waiting any longer, I shift my weight

above her. Line myself up with her entrance. Then rest my forehead on hers.

"You're sure?"

I have to ask one last time. Have to know that she wants this as much as I do. Because once we cross this boundary, there is no going back. Every moment after this moves us forward, to a future I would love more than anything.

Her eyes dart between mine as she nods. "Never been more sure." She kisses me with an unparallel tenderness then meets my eyes again. "I love you, Fletcher."

The room wobbles a moment. My ears fill with white noise as my heart bounces in my ribcage. Every ounce of oxygen gets sucked from my lungs at her confession. A proclamation I have had on the tip of my tongue, but resisted voicing so as not to scare her.

But now...

"I love you, too," I whisper against her lips. Then, with our eyes locked, I rock my hips forward and we gasp in unison.

If this is love, I never plan to let go.

TWENTY EIGHT

Madeline

CHEEK PRESSED TO HIS CHEST, leg draped over his, I listen to the vicious tempo of Fletcher's heart as we catch our breaths. His fingers draw lazy lines up and down my spine. Lips press tender kisses to my crown.

This blip in time couldn't be more perfect.

Almost two years passed since the last time I had sex. Two years. Part of me had been scared I wouldn't remember what to do. The possibility of me freaking out and shutting down had entered my cacophonous thoughts. Or the off chance I would stumble like a first timer and leave Fletcher unsatisfied and uninterested.

All that went out the window when he rocked his hips forward. When his mouth took mine and he consumed every part of me. When we connected physically, nothing else existed.

At one point, tears stung the back of my eyes and begged for release. Not from pain or something Fletcher had done wrong. The urge to cry was rooted in my marrow. Hidden and locked away until the time arrived to set it free. A place Fletcher unlocked in my soul.

Making love with Fletcher opened the floodgates to a range of emotions I wasn't quite prepared to experience. Love, levity and tranquility. Lust and excitement. Vitality, purpose and hope. But with the positives also came the negatives. Guilt and shame. Fear and uncertainty. All of it hit me in one fell swoop. Knocked me breathless and made me dizzy as my soul wept.

I wept for what once was and what will be.

"Can practically hear the cogs turning. What has you so deep in thought?" Fletcher kisses my hair.

I twist to peer up at him. The backs of my eyes sting. My throat swells as saliva floods my mouth and I swallow. But I fight the tears that threaten to fall. I cried enough tears for two lifetimes.

I never want to hide anything from Fletcher. In life, I learned far too early there is no time for petty nonsense or keeping secrets. No time for skirting the truth to soften the blow. Time is a fleeting concept measured by the tick of a second hand. The older we get, the faster time passes. If time has taught me anything, it would be to treasure every tick of the clock. Because you never know when it will be the last.

"Just thinking over the last hour. The feelings it stirred up."

Fletcher tucks fallen locks of hair behind my ear. "Do you want to share? You don't have to, but I'll always listen if you do."

Inching up the bed and his body, I press my lips to his. His arms curl around my waist and hug me tighter to his chest.

"It's confusing." His brows pinch in the middle. "The emotions, not anything else."

"How so?"

I take a deep breath and sort out how to translate my feelings into words. Easier said than done.

"First and foremost, making love with you is incredible. Life altering kind of incredible." A cute half smile tugs up the corner of Fletcher's mouth. "I didn't expect to feel this surge of love and satisfaction so easily. To be so consumed with everything I hold in my heart for you. For it to expand and swallow me whole at the same time."

"And this confuses you?"

I tuck my lips between my teeth for three, two, one. "No." I shake my head. "The guilt and shame afterward confuse me. I know we aren't doing anything wrong. Deep down, I know this. Yet, they hit me like a wall."

Dropping my head to the pillow, I bury my face at the crook of his neck. His fingers leisurely swipe up and down my spine; soothing me.

"Can't say I know anyone who has been through what you have, but I'm sure what you're feeling isn't out of the ordinary. You and Chris had more than a decade together. And you lost him to unfortunate circumstances. History like that doesn't vanish. I'd think it odd if you hadn't felt some form of disarray."

Why is Fletcher so perfect? No matter what I say, no matter what happens, he always seems to have the right words or notable solution.

"There was something else," I mumble against his skin.

"Tell me." His voice barely above a whisper.

Tears sting my eyes with harsher intensity. The swell in my throat doubles, triples. A tremor moves through my body like a tidal wave. Although it terrifies me to speak the words aloud, let alone look him in the eye when I say them, I lift up on my forearms and meet his gaze.

"I'm scared. So very scared." The first tear rolls down my cheek and drops on Fletcher.

His eyes glaze over as they search mine. "Why?"

I close my eyes and buck up the courage to speak of the horror that now resides in my mind, that infiltrates my heart. *You can do this, Madeline. You need to tell him. He needs to know.*

Opening my eyes, I let the tears flow freely as I speak. "What if I lose you too?" I sniffle and Fletcher swipes the tears from my cheeks. "I love you. I'm *in love* with you. And it would destroy me if I lost you. There's no way I'd survive."

"Hey." He frames my face. "Hey." My unfocused eyes go to his. "You won't lose me. Promise."

I laugh without humor. "Fletcher, you can't make such

bold promises. Not when we don't always hold control of our destiny."

"True." I jerk my chin back and blink at his admission. "But what if *I'm* your destiny. No disrespect to Chris or what you shared together. But what if everything happened to lead you to me? If destiny truly holds power over us, wouldn't it redirect us every time we veered off course? Maybe we both needed to experience happiness and hardship before fate tightened our string. To prepare us for the bond that exists between us. Tell me…" He swipes a thumb over my cheek, his eyes following the movement before returning to mine. "On that first day at the retreat, did you feel it? Our connection?"

Before laying eyes on Fletcher, I felt our bond. A high-intensity vibration in the air. An undeniable force that lured me from the get-go. At first, I didn't know what the hum was. But the more time I spent with Fletcher, the more I felt it, and the stronger it became. Much as it confounded me and I tried to fight it, the connection was —is—undeniable.

"Yes, I felt it."

"Terms like *soul mate* and *the one* get thrown around too much. The bond we share, Madeline… I felt empty after the retreat. Hollow. Weak. Like part of me was missing." I nod because I felt the same. But I didn't know if it was because of Chris or Fletcher. "When Jonathan set up my state tour, I told him I wanted most of the stops up north. I had no idea where you lived, but my gut told me you weren't far from the retreat. And I wasn't wrong. When I saw you in the restaurant, time stood still. And when it kicked back in, the world righted itself again. Because I'd found you."

Dopamine floods my veins and undiluted love seeps from my pores. If only it could vanquish the haunting terror.

"How do I get past the fear of losing you too?"

"Time. And telling me when those thoughts creep in. Like all things, you need time to mend the wounds in your heart." He presses a soft kiss to my lips. "I have no plans to leave. For as long as you'll have me, I'm yours. Always."

What if I want you forever?

Is that selfish? To want to keep Fletcher in my life for good. To never let him go. Yes, it is selfish. The most selfish I have been. But after what happened to Chris, how can I not be selfish? How can I not want to keep Fletcher close?

Then clarity slaps me. How *can* I keep him?

Fletcher has a life away from me and the bubble we created. Not just a home and family and friends, but also his career. Everything he knows exists somewhere else. Hundreds of miles away. In a place I am not.

"How?" I croak out.

He tilts his head, narrows his eyes and studies my face a beat. "How what?"

"How can you be mine?" The crinkles on his forehead deepen. "You live on the opposite end of the state. With family and friends nearby. Your studio…" I pause and take a deep breath as my vision blurs. "So, how?"

In a heartbeat, Fletcher has me on my back. His breath hot on my lips as his sparkly green irises lock with my muted browns.

"Madeline." My name a litany on his tongue. "From the moment we existed in the same space, I became yours. Everything else is semantics. Music can be made anywhere. My family and friends wouldn't fault me for moving away. Although I returned from the retreat musically inspired, I was a mess. They don't know the details, but know I met a woman."

"Fletcher," I whisper, shocked. My hand grazes his cheek and he melts at my touch.

"We may have only spent two weeks together, but those fourteen days brought me back to life. Opened me in a way I never knew was possible. I won't let that slip away. I won't lose you. Now or ever." His rich green irises shimmer with his confession. "Without a doubt, I'd move for you. For us." He toys with hair near my temple, his eyes following the action before meeting mine again. "I love you, Madeline. I love you deeply."

The space between our lips vanishes. Fletcher kisses me with unexpected fervor. Love spills from his heart through his lips and fuses with my soul. I tighten my hold on him and match his intensity as we lose ourselves in each other.

If his words hold truth, I never plan to let Fletcher go.

TWENTY NINE

Fletcher

TIME FLIES when you fall in love. Madly in love.

Aside from her short morning shifts a few days a week, Madeline and I spend no time apart. And each minute is pure bliss. While she works, I do the same. Setting up in the spare room or on the back porch if the weather is nice, I work on new songs. I add more songs to what will be my next album. A second album with Madeline as my muse.

The stovetop timer beeps and I shut it off. "Can you take that out, please?" Madeline shouts from the bedroom.

"Got it."

I open the oven door and get hit with a wall of cinnamon-coated apples. Retrieving the pie with potholders, I set the pie on the trivet to cool. Also on the counter are large casserole dishes of garlic mashed potatoes and homemade macaroni and cheese with a bread-crumb topping. Both of which I want to devour, but have to wait until dinner. Well, more like linner—that weird time between lunch and dinner that everyone seems to eat at on Thanksgiving.

Over the last few weeks, Madeline and I have fallen into an easy routine. Naturally slipping into coupledom. Breakfasts in bed, walks in the park, movie nights, and cooking dinner together. All of it so normal and perfect and domestic. With Madeline, I wouldn't want life any other way.

I wander toward the bedroom and stop in the doorway when I see Madeline.

Facing away from me, she steps into a pale rose dress and shimmies it up her body. She slips her arms into the three-quarter sleeves and adjusts the shoulders. I swallow as I take in the loose, open back while the rest of the dress hugs her curves and stops just below the knee.

She spins around and I bite the inside of my cheek. How can one woman be demure and provocative in the same breath?

I step up to her, hold her at arm's length and take it all in. "Stunning."

She waves me off as her cheeks pink. "I still need to fix my hair."

"Either way, you're gorgeous."

"Thank you." She slips on a pair of nude ballet flats, kisses my cheek then waltzes into the en suite bathroom.

Back in the living room, I plop down on the couch and

pick up the book I've been reading. A sweet romance from Madeline's bookshelf. Romance isn't my typical go-to—I am more of a mystery/thriller type—but Madeline's shelf has more romance than anything else. Figured it may be smart to see why women love these books so much. So far, the storyline has me hooked. Great love story, great laughs and a small whodunit vibe.

As I reach the end of the chapter, Madeline exits the bedroom and owns all my attention. Each day, I discover a new reason to fall further in love. Today, her natural beauty steals the spotlight. I witnessed her morning routine. Watched as she applied makeup to her eyes, cheeks and lips. But what I love is how she still looks herself when done. The makeup light and neutral and enough to highlight her already magnificent features. Nothing bold or over the top. Simple and classic and flawless.

I set the book on the side table, rise from the couch and step into Madeline. Wrapping her in my arms, I kiss her forehead. "Love that we get to share today together."

Holiday gatherings with my family have been wonky since my younger stepsister started college. Between Mom's nonstop schedule as a day care provider, my and Jonathan's unpredictable timetable with tours and albums, and Ann's calendar full with college and work, holidays grow more lackluster. Maybe once Ann graduates college, holidays will have more potential with my family. We all see each other whenever possible, but there is no consistency.

So, celebrating Thanksgiving with Madeline and her family is a wonderful change. One I want to repeat countless times in the future and on other holidays.

"Me too." She smiles up at me, and her brown irises twinkle and warm my insides.

We pack up the pie, mashed potatoes, and macaroni and cheese, slip on coats and leave the house. Classical music plays in the background as we drive to Madeline's parents' home. Tonight's guest list will be the same as our last visit, and I more than love the smaller gathering versus some of the larger ones Mom and Jonathan have hosted—many of which include more business guests than personal.

Madeline twists in the passenger seat, hands fidgeting in her lap. "There's something I want to ask, but don't want you to freak out."

Reaching across the console, I take her hand and peek at her briefly. "Ask me anything, Madeline." I lift her hand to my lips and kiss her knuckles.

We reach a stoplight and I face her. Teeth nibble on the lower left corner of her lips. Her free hand toys with the strap of her purse. And she has difficulty holding my gaze. Close as we have gotten, seeing her this nervous has my stomach in knots.

"Would it be weird if..." She pauses, eyes dropping to her lap.

"Madeline, whatever it is, don't be scared." Her hesitancy has me dizzy and my mind going in countless directions.

Inhaling deep, she lifts her chin and we lock eyes. "Would it be outlandish if I asked you to move?" Her lips form a tight line then relax. "If I asked you to move in with me?"

The light turns green and I hate that I have to focus on the road. All I want is to look her in the eye and answer her question. A question that took more bravery to ask than comprehendible.

Of course, every traffic light we approach stays green. And the next thirteen minutes age me thirteen years as we drive in silence.

Soon as the car is in park, I unbuckle the seat belt, face Madeline and cradle her hands. "Please don't take my silence as a declination. Just wanted to look you in the eye when I answered." Her eyes dart between mine as she nods. "Madeline, I would love nothing more." The brightest smile lights her face and skyrockets my pulse. "But before we make such a hasty decision, I need to know where your head is at. That this isn't a spur-of-the-moment choice. Or one made out of fear."

Slowly, her smile falls away as her brows pinch in confusion. And I mentally berate myself for making her feel conflicted or that I don't want this as much as she does. That I make her question my feelings. More than anything, I would love to spend every minute with Madeline in my arms.

But moving in together is a major step. This decision should be hard and not taken lightly. For either of us.

Although the pain she harbors for her husband has

lessened, she still holds on to it. Wouldn't surprise—or bother—me if it never fades completely. Losing someone you love should never be simple. You don't wipe your hands clean of them because someone new appears. The heart doesn't work that way.

Us cohabitating would be a dream. To wake up next to her each morning. Hold and kiss her during any time of the day. Make love to her nightly before we fall asleep in each other's arms. To build a life and evolve together. I would love nothing more. But understanding what prompted her to ask matters.

"No, not spur of the moment. I've actually thought about it a lot. A lot, a lot. Since you got here, in fact."

I breathe easier with this insight. Her asking me to move in not an impulse. Knowing she mulled over the idea quite a bit before voicing it. Which means, hopefully, she looked at both sides of the coin. Not that I think either of us will regret me moving in after the fact, but living together is one of several major steps in a relationship.

A smile tugs up the corner of my mouth. "I've thought about it too. But…" I lean in and kiss her chastely. "Let me marinate on it a little more before I answer." A shadow falls over her beautiful features and I hate how she may feel a slight sense of rejection. No way I will ever reject this woman. Not in this lifetime or the next. "Hey." I bring a hand to her chin and lift so we are eye to eye. "I'm not saying no. Just asking to mull over the idea a little longer."

"Okay." Her single word soft and timid.

"Promise I won't make you wait long. Couldn't bear seeing you tortured." I kiss her again, this time with more zeal. "I love you, Madeline. More than comprehensible."

The last time I experienced a family setting such as this was after Mom and Jonathan married. Ann was in her last year of elementary school and I was a high school senior. Our first official Thanksgiving as a family was the best I'd had to date. The years prior, Mom and I had gone to her parents' house. Much as I love them, they were a bit stuck up. So, we spent little time with my maternal grandparents.

Our first Thanksgiving as a family included more smiles, laughter and love than any memory I had of my birth father. Mom and Jonathan dated less than a year before marrying. Only, I learned of their relationship after Jonathan proposed—three months before the wedding. For weeks, I stalked Jonathan on the internet. Looked for every possible skeleton or indication he was shady. All I found was article after article of praise for his work in the music industry. Which I appreciated more with my love for guitar and lack of a father who cared.

"Fletcher." Chair legs groan against the tile as Robert scoots back and pats his belly. "You watch football?"

"On occasion. Not enough to have a favorite team."

Picking up his plate, he takes it to the kitchen sink and rinses it before adding it to the full dishwasher. "Game starts soon, if you'd like to watch with Phillip and me."

One by one, everyone starts carrying dishes and left-overs into the kitchen. "Might watch a bit, sure."

Madeline and I help Jeannie portion leftovers into containers for care packages. Jeannie starts on dish-washing while Madeline warms the apple pie we brought and the pumpkin from Phillip and Sylvia.

I go into lost puppy mode as I follow Madeline. Help her fetch dessert plates and forks while she gets out fresh whipped cream and cinnamon.

From the corner of my eye, I watch her. Stare at the slight pout only I seem to notice. A pout I, no doubt, created. I tap her hip with my leg and she peeks up.

"You okay?" I mouth.

A gentle smile lifts the corners of her mouth and she nods. *Fibber.*

I tip my head to the side then walk off in the hopes she understands to follow. Down the hall, I step into the bath-room, but don't shut the door. She follows, steps in the tiny space and I close the door behind us.

"Fletcher, what are you —"

I cut her off, my mouth on hers in a flash. At first, she stiffens in shock. A breath later, her frame melts and lips devour. My arms snake around her waist as her fingers lace behind my neck. She tugs me closer and mewls when our tongues tangle together. I deepen the kiss, swallow her passionate cries, grip her waist tighter with one hand as the other traces up her spine.

God, this dress is dangerous. So tempting to shimmy it up and take her on the counter.

Then, I snap out of my lusty haze and break the kiss. Wouldn't take much to convince Madeline to follow through. She may be a lady—classy and semi-reserved—but the more time I spend with her, the more outgoing and spontaneous she becomes. Deep down, this side of her always existed, but got tucked away after Chris passed. Now, it stirs back to life.

Best not to take advantage of the moment. Especially in the bathroom of her parents' home.

"Yes," I whisper, dropping my forehead to hers.

She tilts her head, her forehead bunching beneath mine. "Yes?" Inching back, she narrows her eyes, unsure of why I said yes.

"Yes." I press a brief kiss to her lips. "I'll move in."

Her eyes widen and back straightens. Her lips curl up at the corners as a radiant glow blooms on her skin. "Really?" A touch of honey glints in her warm brown eyes and it soothes my soul.

"Absolutely." I hug her with more strength and drop my lips to her ear. "My answer was already yes. Just needed to know you were certain." She tips her head back. "I love you." I tuck loose strands behind her ear. "Never doubt that."

Our lips meet, the kiss slow and heady. A promise

solidifying the bond between us. Forever etched on our hearts. A forever I only want with her.

"I love you, too." She steps back. "Now, let's go eat pie before someone walks in here."

I laugh and stumble in her wake. Madeline Reynolds. My woman. My heart. My forever.

THIRTY

Madeline

Tomorrow is the day.

When I asked Fletcher to move in, I psyched myself up for all the possible outcomes. Rejection and doubt took up the most space until he answered. The possibility of him saying no haunted every breath and heartbeat.

But, to my surprise, Fletcher said yes. Much sooner than expected.

His resolute yes set off a chain reaction. The gray cloud looming overhead at his delayed response evaporated. In its place, sunshine took up residence. An intense energy flitted through my fingers, my toes, my limbs. On a slow trek to the epicenter; converging at my heart and setting my soul on fire.

For the first time in almost two years, I took a breath.

A real breath. The type that doesn't just fill your lungs and oxygenate your blood. No, the breath that invigorates you. Gives you purpose. Makes you look forward to tomorrow and all the days that follow.

God, it had been so long since I felt whole. Felt more myself and less of a shell. And I owe it all to Fletcher. Not only did he bring me back from never-ending darkness and depression, he also proved love is possible again.

There will always be a piece of my heart reserved for Chris. Chris was my first real love. Someone I shared a life with for more than a decade. No matter how much time passes, Chris will always linger—in my heart and memories.

And Fletcher is the type of man who takes no offense. He has a past, as do I. We pay homage to and respect those pieces of ourselves. Without them, we wouldn't be where we are now. We wouldn't be together.

From the couch, I peek over at Fletcher as he paces the back porch. Phone to his ear, he laughs and chats with Jonathan. Since he said yes ten days ago, he has spent hours on the phone. Most of the calls to Jonathan and his mother, Frances.

Sharing the news with my family went smoother than expected. Fletcher's family had been more taken aback than anything. His family knew of me, that we met at the retreat and Fletcher returned to my side when the tour ended. But the seriousness of our relationship hadn't been previously spoken of—to either of our families. Needless to say, everyone interjected how fast-tracked our relationship has been thus far. But after several conversations, they have come to accept our decision.

"You aren't moving too fast."

I peer over to the framed pictures between the living room and foyer. Beside the framed photo of our wedding day, Chris stands tall with his gentle, bright smile.

Slipping the bookmark in place, I set my paperback on the table and rise from the couch. Feet padding across the room, I stop in front of the frame.

"After losing so much…" I glide the tip of my finger over Chris in the photo. "I don't want to miss anything else."

"He's a good man, Maddie. I approve. No matter what, he'll take care of you and give you the love you deserve."

I smile at this. Fletcher is a good man. As good a man as Chris was. Fletcher cradles my heart with gentle hands, provides me with what I need, yet allows me space to persevere on my own. He holds my hand with such tenderness, kisses me as if no other woman exists and bestows me with more love than imaginable.

"Thank you." Not that I needed Chris's reassurance but knowing he would approve of Fletcher is pivotal. Had Chris and Fletcher met, they would have been friends. "I know he will."

"Who are you talking to?"

Every muscle in me freezes; and it has nothing to do with the draft from Fletcher reentering the house.

Heat crawls up my neck and blooms on my cheeks. *God, this is embarrassing.* Will Fletcher lace me in a straitjacket if I speak the truth? It isn't every day you explain to someone you love that you speak to and see your deceased husband. That you have full-blown conversations with him, ask his opinion and somewhat take his advice. Technically speaking, they are what I *think* Chris's opinions and advice would be. As many years as we had together, I knew Chris better than anyone.

I spin around and face Fletcher. His eyes drop to my hands, maybe in search of a phone to explain my random chatter. When he discovers me empty-handed, his brow furrows before our eyes meet.

"Erm…" I fiddle with the front hem of my shirt. "We should probably sit down."

We shuffle across the room and plop down on the sofa. His constant gaze sears my skin as I toy with my shirt and refuse to look up from my lap. Mortification adds a fresh layer of heat to my cheeks as I gather my thoughts.

"Whatever it is, Madeline, you don't have to worry." Fletcher lays a hand over mine, stops my fidgeting fingers and curls his fingers with mine in reassurance.

I exhale heavily then laugh without humor. His sparkling green irises provide a level of tranquility as I open my mouth to spill my truth. *Here goes nothing… or everything.*

"Chris. I was talking to Chris."

Clamping down on my lips, my eyes dart between his in search of a reaction. I expect to see his eyes widen, for his jaw to go slack, and for him to lean away. To be appalled at the woman he claims to love. To rise from the couch, dart in the bedroom, pack his bag, and drive away.

But this is Fletcher, and he never does what I expect.

Instead, his grip tightens, eyes glaze over and he scoots closer. Releasing my hand, he frames my face, holds my stare and presses a chaste kiss to my lips.

"You won't scare me off that easily, you know." I audibly exhale then take a deep breath. "Madeline, I'm fully aware I'll always share you with Chris. Nothing will change that, and there's nothing wrong with it. He was taken from you, which is vastly different from you going separate ways. All I ask is one thing."

Fear has no place in my heart with Fletcher. Will I do things he deems strange? Sure, and vice versa. But I have never been more comfortable with anyone, and we are still figuring us and each other out. Strange will happen. With those quirky nuances, though, comes love and respect and loyalty. A new contentment floods our veins, rules our hearts and makes our lives full. Those odd pieces of each other are what makes our love better, stronger, everlasting.

"What's that?"

"Share some of those conversations with me too. We may be new at this, at us, but I want to be there for you. I want to help you work through whatever has you over-thinking." Knuckles graze from the angle of my jaw to my chin. "I want to be the one you lean on." He drops his lips to mine and I lean on him, melt against him, and forget anything else exists.

When the kiss breaks, I stare into Fletcher's forest green eyes. See every ounce of love this man has for me. Know that I have nothing to fear as long as he stands at my side.

Taking a deep breath, I prepare to be more vulnerable than ever. Prepare to tell him what only my family and close friends know. Tell him how I lost Chris.

His brows pinch at the middle. "Sure. Is everything okay?"

We sit on the couch and I inhale deeply. *You can do this, Madeline. Let Fletcher carry some of the weight.* I take Fletcher's hands in mine, take another deep breath, and speak on the exhale.

"It was late and we'd just left our favorite restaurant in the city." I pause and Fletcher squeezes my hands; his quiet way of telling me to take my time, that he isn't going anywhere. "I'd fumbled with my jacket as we stepped outside. Snow was expected overnight and we wanted to get home before the weather shifted." I pinch my eyes tightly as pain lances my heart. "I was so concerned about my coat, I never saw the man approach us."

Fletcher strokes the backs of my hands with his thumbs. "There's no rush. Take your time."

My watery eyes meet Fletcher's and all I see is love. Love and patience and tenderness. Whatever I did to deserve this man, I will forever be grateful.

"The gun glinted under the streetlight. The man shifted it back and forth between the two of us as he demanded our wallets and jewelry." A tear slips from my eye and I make no move to wipe it away. "We were so jittery, so scared, but somehow managed to hand over our wallets." I tip my head back, swallow, then meet Fletcher's gaze. "When we refused to hand over what little jewelry we wore, the man waved the gun. I think he intended just to frighten us. Then the gun went off."

The bang of the gun doesn't haunt my dreams as often as it once did. Not since finding Fletcher. But every now and then, it rings so loudly in my head. Stirs up every second of that horrible night.

"Soon as the shot was fired, the man fled." Tears spill down my cheeks more evenly and steadily now. "I didn't know Chris had been shot. Not right away. My adrenaline was through the roof. It wasn't until he fell into me that I saw the blood on his shirt." Emotion clogs my throat, but I continue forward. "By the time the ambulance arrived, he stopped breathing."

Before I say another word, Fletcher wraps me in his arms. Hugs me close. Whispers how sorry he is. How he wishes he could take the pain away. How much he loves me and will do his best to keep me and my heart safe.

We pull apart and Fletcher wipes the tears from my cheeks. "You know you can always talk to me about Chris?" I nod. Fletcher presses his lips to my forehead. "I love you, Madeline. Always."

The backs of my eyes sting for a new reason. "I love you too." I take a deep breath. "Thank you."

"For what?"

My cheeks tighten as I smile. "For being you. For loving me."

He sweeps a lock of hair off my face and tucks it behind my ear. "Loving you is the easiest thing I've ever done. I'm just happy we found each other."

Although it wasn't under the happiest of circumstances, meeting Fletcher was fate. A way to heal my heart and put me back on my destined path. I love Chris. I always will. But Fletcher... he is irreplaceable.

With us driving to Los Angeles tomorrow, dining out seemed the best option. No messes to clean up and no leftovers to worry about.

I took the next week off work to help. Most of tomorrow will be spent driving and meeting Fletcher's family. If all goes according to plan, we should arrive in Los Angeles around four. After introductions, we plan to go out for dinner then stay at Fletcher's house and start packing the next morning.

From our conversations, Fletcher doesn't seem to be someone with an overabundance of *stuff*. With the house paid off, he plans to keep it for when we visit his family. The furniture will stay behind while we pack small items, keepsakes and necessities.

"Want dessert?"

I arch a brow at Fletcher. "Is that a serious question? Who declines dessert? Not me, that's for sure."

He chuckles, plucks the dessert menu from the table and skims the options. "Chocolate or no?"

Holding my hands out in front of me, palms up, I weigh the possibility. "Yes," I answer after a beat.

When the server clears the table, Fletcher orders us chocolate lava cake to share. Once the server is out of earshot, I narrow my eyes at him.

"Hope you're ready for me to eat more than my share of dessert."

Leaning across the table, lips kicked up in a smirk, he shakes his head on a laugh. "What if I want more than a taste?" I swallow as my cheeks heat. "Guess I'll have more dessert when we get home."

Dear lord. Soon as dessert hits the table, it's going down the hatch. Because dessert at home already sounds much more delicious.

Fletcher laughs at how fast I eat the small chocolate confection. I shrug him off and rush the server for the bill. Once he settles the bill, we dash for the car.

Five minutes into the twenty-three minute commute and I am ready to add rocket fuel to the gas tank. We haven't made it a mile yet and have already hit two red lights. Every time I tap my fingers or bounce my knee, Fletcher laughs from the driver's seat.

"You crack me up. Quit thinking about how long the

drive is. Find something on the radio to distract us until we're home."

Every time Fletcher says home and means my house, I sigh internally. I love how easily our lives have come together. How, without effort, we slip into this place. Slip into us.

The light turns green as I flip through the radio stations. Fletcher eases into the intersection as I peek up and out the driver's side window. Headlights blind me as they come at us. Quickly; far too quickly.

I brace myself as I grab the handle over the door and fist Fletcher's arm as a scream spills from my lips. "Fletcher! Look—"

THIRTY ONE

Fletcher

PAIN. All I feel is pain. Stabbing, burning, excruciating pain. A pain so fierce, it steals my breath and slows my heart. *Pain*. Then… the world goes black.

THIRTY TWO

Madeline

Flashes of red and yellow, white and blue fill my fuzzy vision. Metal creaks to my left and right. The scent of gasoline and smoke waft up my nose. And heat like I have never experienced blankets me head to toe.

"Stay awake, Maddie. Don't close your eyes."

"Chris?"

I shake my head, confused. What the hell is happening? Where am I?

Chris frames my face, his inches away as his blue eyes sear. *"Maddie! Stay awake. Help is here. It's not your time, baby."*

"I'm so tired, Chris."

"I know, baby. But you need to fight."

"So tired of fighting." With heavy eyes, I drift into a

black sea of nothingness. Bask in the darkness, the quiet. The peace.

Blunt force hits my chest. Pounds my sternum, over and over and over. Voices call out, say my name and break up the silence. They sound so far away, but I hear them. Burning inflates my lungs as ice floods my veins.

"Ma'am." *Whoosh, whoosh, whoosh.* "Madeline Reynolds. Can you hear me?"

Stabbing pain digs into my back, my spine, my skull. Warmth replaces the chill in my bloodstream. A shiver erupts across my skin and I jerk against something hard. The pounding on my chest ceases as something foreign brushes my cheek.

"She's breathing," a voice says. "Madeline Reynolds, can you hear me?"

What the hell is happening? Who is this person?

"Maddie, open your eyes, baby."

Cracking my eyes, I squint as the bright lights come into view. Sandpaper coats my throat as I breathe. Hot moisture slicks my hair and cheek as I reach for the throbbing point on my scalp.

My arm gets redirected. "You're safe, Ms. Reynolds. Try to stay still."

"What happened?" I croak out, not recognizing my own voice.

My body lifts from the ground and I land on something hard, flat, and cold before getting strapped in place. Hard plastic wraps around my neck, then I get hoisted up.

"You and Mr. Lockwood were in a car accident. Do you know what day it is?"

Mr. Lockwood? Who—

"Fletcher!" I choke out as fire rips up my throat. I try to reach for my neck to quell the burn, but can't move my arms.

"Ma'am, please stop fighting against the gurney straps. We still need to assess your injuries." The man's voice stern yet placating.

"Fletcher!" I yell with more gusto, but my voice cracks.

An EMT wheels me closer to the flashing lights and my heart goes into hyperdrive. The backs of my eyes burn as tears flood my vision of the night sky. The frigid winter air is a thousand knives piercing my lungs with each breath in. My muscles seizing at the lack of response from Fletcher.

"Where is he? Where's Fletcher? Is he okay?"

Hot tears spill down my temples as a sob rips from my throat. I squeeze my eyes shut as my breaths come in quick, short bursts. Each one faster than the previous. A new pressure wraps my midsection. An endless constriction of my heart as it batters my ribcage and screams for release.

Lights blind me as I am wheeled into an ambulance. Antiseptic and bleach and a hint of metal waft up my nostrils. The EMT jumps in with another before the doors slam shut and someone bangs on the back.

"Please," I whisper. "Tell me Fletcher is okay."

His expression softens as he stares down. "Mr. Lockwood suffered severe injuries. We were able to resuscitate him, but he's currently unconscious."

No. No, no, no.

I close my eyes and let the tears flow freely. Let the pain that has nothing to do with my injuries take hold. Consume and swallow me whole. A soul-searing pain much different than when I lost Chris. An ache threatening to rip away the love around my heart and crush the organ into a million shards.

This cannot be happening. Not again.

Please, whoever is listening. I can't lose him. Not Fletcher. After everything I have endured, I can't lose him too. I won't survive. Not without Fletcher, alive and in my arms. I need him. And he needs me too. Please don't let me lose him. I love him. Fletcher is my forever.

THIRTY THREE

Fletcher

Endless night shrouded in eternal agony.

Every direction in black, empty, hollow. No sights, no sounds, no smells. No indication of where I am, where I have been or what has happened. No semblance of life or meaning. Just… darkness. A darkness that never ends.

I dig deep in my memories. Hunt for the reason as to why I am here. And where *here* is. A knife in my temple twists as I search for answers. I reach for the unrelenting source, but can't move my limbs. Can't *feel* my limbs. My eyes drift down my body, but I come up empty. No body. No… anything.

What the hell is going on? Where the hell am I?

"Hey, man," an unfamiliar voice says.

"Hello?"

Off in the distance, the darkness fades slightly. The faint outline of a figure steps closer, disrupting the void. The closer they get, the more I narrow my eyes to make out who it is. Soft light hovers like an aura and glows far too bright.

Feet away, I start to make out his features. Short in stature; I stand a full head taller. Young, but lines at the corners of his blue eyes age him with years of love and laughter. Trimmed, clean-cut blond hair and a welcoming smile highlight his face. I glance down his white button-down and black slacks, stopping at the red stain on his shirt.

How odd.

He stops in front of me and I avert my eyes from his injury. A hand juts out and hangs between us, waiting for me to take it.

"Fletcher, right?" I narrow my eyes at this stranger. How does he know my name? "Chris. Nice to meet you."

Holy. Shit. Am I dead?

"No, you're not dead," he answers my unspoken question. "Coma, actually. That's why I'm here."

I lift my hand, no longer finding the task impossible, and give his a shake. "I don't understand."

"Yeah, it's weird for me too. But from what I gather, someone is looking out for our girl."

"Our girl?"

"Maddie. Madeline."

Damnit.

An odd whoosh flutters near my heart, but it doesn't

feel the same. Like an echo of an organ that isn't in the same place as I am. I clutch my chest and curl my fingers into a ball.

"Is she okay? How the hell do I get out of here? How do I get back to her?"

I bend at the waist as sheer panic floods my mind, but doesn't impact my physical self. At least not wherever this place is. Is this purgatory? Am I on the brink of death? Whatever this place is, it feels as if I am just a stream of consciousness verses in a physical location.

"She has injuries, but she's safe and healing. You, on the other hand, need assistance. Which is why I must be here. Leaving this place isn't as easy as waking up. There's more to it."

I straighten my spine and look at the man who once owned every piece of Madeline's heart. A heart that belongs to him still, but is now shared with the love she has for me. A love I refuse to let go of.

"What does that mean?"

He wanders into the darkness and I follow. Out of nowhere, a bench appears and we sit. Silence stretches between us for an immeasurable amount of time. But the quiet feels vaguely familiar; close to the peace I feel with Madeline.

How odd.

"Odd indeed." Chris leans back and peers in my direction. "To get back to Madeline, you need to heal. Unfortunately, healing takes time. But waking up isn't just about physical wounds closing."

I mimic his position and hold his gaze. "Not sure I follow."

Chris looks out into the darkness as if a lake or trees or life exists in front of his eyes. "Have you ever heard of people having miraculous recoveries? A person who is told they'll never walk again, but their determination eventually wins and they prove everyone wrong." His eyes meet mine again. "You haven't suffered such an injury, but you'll have lifelong scars."

"Hate to sound like a broken record—maybe this place has me in a fog—but I don't get what you're saying."

Chris rises from the bench and takes a step away. "Mind over matter, man." Another step. "You have to *will* yourself awake. See past the empty. Feel more than the pain. Think beyond yourself." Another step. "Use Madeline as motivation. Picture yourself waking up and seeing her again, touching her."

I stand and start to follow, but he slowly fades into the black. "How?"

"Love. Use your love for Madeline as fuel and wake up. Fill your thoughts with nothing but the love you have for her, so you can return."

Chris disappears and I am once again alone in the silence.

"Use your love for her as fuel and wake up."

I close my eyes and imagine every molecule of emotion I feel for Madeline. In my imagination, this cluster of emotion—love and adoration, pride and rapture—glows bright red. Bold and crimson and potent. Her beacon, summoning me forward. I stumble blindly toward the light, let every ounce of love I harbor for Madeline consume me, and step through.

Next time I open my eyes, I pray Madeline is in my arms.

THIRTY FOUR

Madeline

Th-THUMP. Thump. Th-thump. Thump.

Curled into Fletcher's side, I rest my ear to his chest and listen to his heartbeat, making sure the machine next to the bed is accurate. Not that I don't trust the electrodes and tubes connected to his body. More that I need to hear the actual organ working with my own ear. To feel the chambers of his heart contract seventy times a minute. Observe his lungs as they inflate with each inhalation. Keep a hand or cheek on his skin to maintain our connection and feel his heat.

"Have you eaten?"

I peer over at the man entering the room. A man I had only heard about until two weeks ago. Jonathan North.

His wife, and Fletcher's mom, Frances, clings to his arm as they both rake their eyes over me on Fletcher's bed.

"No, but I'm fine," I whisper.

Two and a half weeks ago, on December fifth—really starting to hate December—a drunk driver ran a red light at fifty-plus miles per hour. The truck smashed into the rear driver's side door of Fletcher's SUV. Had the truck hit six inches closer to the front of the vehicle, Fletcher would not have survived. Nor would I. The unbelted drunk driver was ejected from the vehicle and died at the scene.

After my hysterics in the emergency room, I coerced the hospital staff to put me in the same room as Fletcher. Our beds as close as possible without disrupting the nurses and doctors from doing their job.

The day after we were admitted, my family arrived and showered me with tears, love, and support. Two days later, Fletcher's family did the same. If my family wasn't in the room, his was. On occasion, everyone was here.

After a week of physical healing, the doctor released me from care. But I haven't left the hospital. And I refuse to leave unless I walk out the door with Fletcher—alive and well.

Mom and Sylvia have brought me changes of clothes, helped me clean up and given me their shoulder when the tears won't stop. Majority of the time, though, a dull numbness crowds my mind. I refuse to be positive or negative until more happens.

Most of my time is spent right here. In this very spot.

On Fletcher's hospital bed, curled into his side, carefully avoiding the lines and tubes. I listen to his even breathing and thumping heart while I wait for him to open his eyes. To wake up and come back to me.

The doctors and nurses have assured me, time and again, Fletcher will wake up. All his vital signs indicate he will recover. Each time I repeat questions, they give me an endearing smile and remind me he sustained severe injuries and his body just needs time to recuperate.

More or less, Fletcher coming back to me is a waiting game. A game based on time and patience. A game I am sick of playing.

"Well, I need a bite. While I'm in the cafeteria, I'll grab you something too," Frances says before she exits the room.

Once Fletcher's mother leaves, Jonathan steps up to the bedside. Unconditional love softens his features as he stares down at his stepson. They may not share the same genetics, but Jonathan loves Fletcher as his own.

"How is he today?" His words scrape the air as his eyes glass over.

"No change. The doctor says all his vitals are good and the last scans came back perfect too. Now, we wait. Doc said it could be hours or weeks. His mind is the only thing holding him back."

Out of nowhere, Jonathan chuckles. The low, throaty sound disrupts the heart monitor noises. He lays a hand on Fletcher's shoulder and leans in. "Now is not the time to be stubborn, son. Not with so many people waiting to see you. Not with so many people here who love you."

In the time I have known Fletcher, not once has he been bullheaded. If anything, I would be the one filling those shoes in our relationship. Although, Fletcher softens the points on my bull horns. Makes me less fiery—outside the bedroom, of course. Brings out my best qualities and drives me to push forward, even on my worst days.

Laying my head on his pec, I rest a hand over his heart. "I miss you, Fletcher," I whisper. "I need you to come back to me. Please." I close my eyes and focus on the rhythm of his heartbeat.

Th-thump. Thump. Th-thump. Thump.

Then I fall asleep in the same place I have slept since I was allowed to leave my own hospital bed; at Fletcher's side.

Something bumps my leg and I shift out of its way. Another bump. I moan into the darkness, crack my eyes open and squint at the faint fluorescent light shining down on the bed. Antiseptic and artificial lemon blend with a hint of Fletcher's cedar smell that fades a little each day.

I narrow my eyes toward the foot of the bed and see no one. *Weird.* As I snuggle back into Fletcher's side, I feel it again. This time, a soft groan rumbles in Fletcher's chest after.

Lifting my head, I peer down and gasp as Fletcher looks up. His breathtaking green eyes dull and bloodshot.

I bring a hand to his cheek, stroke my thumb over the thicker beard I have grown accustomed to seeing these past weeks. He leans into my touch, closes his eyes and takes a deep breath. Ever so slowly, I drop down and place a gentle kiss on his lips.

He moans as his fingers brush against my thigh. "Madeline." My name hoarse on his tongue as he locks me with his gaze.

I kiss him again. "Let me get you some water and call the nurse."

After pressing the call button for the nurse, I pour a small cup of water from the rolling table beside the bed. Adding a straw, I bring it to his lips and tell him to take small sips.

"What can I get—" Vincent, one of the night shift nurses who tends to Fletcher, walks in the room. "Oh, Mr. Lockwood. You're awake." A bright smile highlights Vincent's face as he steps closer to the bed. He checks Fletcher's vitals on the monitor and notes them in his chart. "I'll page Dr. Kensington. Take it easy until she arrives. Not too much water, might make you nauseous." Vincent steps toward the door but pauses at the threshold. "Glad to have you back, Mr. Lockwood." His eyes meet mine for a blink. "We've all missed you."

Once alone, I bring my attention back to Fletcher. He

finishes the water and I set the cup on the table. Without hurry, I trace the line of his jaw with delicate fingers. Revel in the labored sound of his breath as I skim the wiry strands of his beard. Close my eyes and sigh as the monitor beeps faster, more erratic with his heartbeat.

The smallest gestures have always meant the most. Material possessions have their place in the world, but I much prefer what money can't buy. A lover's caress — irreplaceable. Their unique heartbeat — a song only you know. The invisible bond that ties you together and refuses to let go.

Fletcher has stamped his imprint on my soul. Not that he needed to, the mark had been there all along. Waiting in the recesses for his arrival — or maybe his return. They say soul mates live countless lives. Each life different from the previous and a lesson until your souls are ready to meet again.

If almost losing Fletcher was a test for my soul, I need to talk with whoever is in charge. Because that better not happen again. Ever.

"I've missed you. So much." I open my eyes and land on his, the sparkle slowly returning to his forest green irises.

Slowly, he lifts a hand and cups my cheek. "Missed you too." A small smile tugs at the corners of his lips. "I met someone while I was asleep." I jerk back an inch to see him better. "Real nice guy. I'll tell you all about it soon."

Before I probe him with questions, Dr. Kensington

walks in and steals the spotlight. She goes through a mental checklist, asks about his pain levels and does tests for mobility, sensation, and mental clarity. When she mentions the treatment plan, I forget everything else and zero in on Fletcher's future care. If all continues to improve, the doctor will let Fletcher leave in two days. On Christmas Eve.

All I want for Christmas is to be home, with Fletcher's arms around me and to never let go. That gift would outshine any material possession under a tree.

THIRTY FIVE

Fletcher

HELPLESS. That's what overwhelms me more than anything as I sit up from the hospital bed and tug on a shirt and jacket. My muscles burn as I move my limbs. The throb in my skull a bit duller today, but present. My inability to do regular, day-to-day activities is frustrating. But I shove all of it aside and focus on the positive.

You're lucky to be alive. Count each and every one of those stars.

I chuckle at Madeline as she shimmies a sock up my leg without the cast, then finagles the shoe on.

"Are you making fun of me?" She stands tall and props her hands on her hips. *Damn, she is adorable.* "Because I happen to be your nurse too."

Widening my legs, I reach for her waist and drag her

closer. I lift a brow, lean forward, and whisper in her ear. "Does the job come with a cute nurses' outfit?"

She pulls back and slaps my chest. "Fletcher," she says with a giggle then tilts her head. "Only if you're good."

Well, hello nurse.

Unfortunately, my devious thoughts get disrupted when Madeline's parents enter the room.

From what Madeline said, her parents and mine have been in and out of this hospital room every day for nearly three weeks. They offered several times to watch over me so she could go home, take a break, eat or walk the halls. But she refused to leave my side or the room. She used the bathroom with the door open, dry washed her hair, had family bring her the occasional change of clothes and check on the house.

If our roles were reversed, I would have done the same without a doubt.

Madeline wheels me out of the room and down the corridor toward the elevator. With each step and roll forward, the weight of what brought us here lightens. The fact that we almost lost each other, and far too soon, has eaten away at me since I woke. But with each breath I take, with each beat of my heart, I vow to not let what *could have been* ruin what actually is.

We survived a horrendous accident. One that had the potential to be fatal. I like to believe fate intervened. After all Madeline suffered, fate stepped up and said *not again.* Which is when Chris appeared. I will be interested to see Madeline's reaction when I tell her about meeting him.

Everyone at the nurses' station waves as we pass. Cheers, well wishes and goodbyes given with bright smiles and palms over the heart. The elevator doors ding open and it isn't long before we exit the hospital and Jonathan drives us home.

Home.

The packing of my house in Los Angeles got disrupted by the accident. To my surprise, Mom and Jonathan spent the last two days in my house. I told them it wasn't necessary, that I would handle it when I healed but they didn't listen. And next week, boxes of everything I hold dear and the basic necessities of life will be delivered to Madeline's house.

Our house.

Weeks ago, Madeline and I second-guessed if our relationship moved too fast. How many people move in together after only spending such a short amount of time together? Most people in my circle spent years single or casually dating.

"How can you settle with one person when you haven't experienced many?"

For years, the words of a former colleague rang in my head. Words he said after my longest relationship ended. And for a time, I took his words as truth. That I needed to experience all life had to offer. Date and hookup, but never commit. Only problem… it never *felt* right.

Now, I understand why. Because that isn't who I am and I hadn't found Madeline.

Jonathan parks in the driveway and fetches crutches

from the back while Madeline helps me out. Crutches and I will be best pals for the next three to five weeks. Dr. Kensington said it may be the former since I spent the last three weeks in bed.

Madeline rests her palm on my lower back. "Welcome home." The timid, sweet melody of her voice eases the last of the tension in my muscles. The soft smile she bestows upon me kick-starts my heart as I take the first breath of our life together.

Our forever.

"Happy to finally be home." I lean on a crutch, cup her cheek and kiss my woman.

Over. It.

I love my parents. I love my parents. I love my parents.

I chant the mantra for the millionth time this week. Christmas passed with less enthusiasm. Being home was the best gift. My parents, though… they didn't leave. Not even to spend time with Ann, citing their time was better spent here to help out.

Madeline and I didn't need help. With the exception of faint scrapes and bruises, Madeline healed from her injuries. Most of my day was spent snuggling Madeline on the couch, either watching a movie, reading a book or resting. Not a single complaint spilled from either of our mouths.

Happy as I had been having the help, it was time for them to leave. I love my parents, but I now understood the term "helicopter parent" better. And I silently vow, if Madeline and I ever become parents, to never hover so close. It is one thing to be caring and attentive, it is another to be less than five feet away at all times.

Plus, I want Madeline to myself on New Year's Eve.

"We don't mind staying longer," Mom states as she dunks a forkful of waffle into maple syrup. "It's no trouble."

Jonathan peers at me from the corner of his eye, silently chuckles, then sits up straighter. "Fran, we do need to get home. We have a bit to catch up on. Plus" — his eyes dart between me and Madeline— "they'd probably like a little time to themselves." Mom opens her mouth to, no doubt, suggest why they should stay longer and Jonathan holds up a hand. "Fran, they need time to settle. Alone."

Thank you for having my back.

Mom looks between us as we toss on apprehensive smiles. "Oh." She covers her mouth with her hand for a moment. "Oh, I… I… sorry. I wasn't thinking… Didn't mean to…"

Reaching across the table, I lay a hand down, palm up, and wait for Mom to take it. When she does, I give her a gentle squeeze. "You're fine. But it would be nice to get back to normal." I release her hand and sit back. "And we're healed enough to handle things on our own."

Mom sips her coffee. "Jon and I will head home today." She nods in reassurance. "If you need anything before we go, say the word. Grocery run, clean up, anything."

"You got it."

I love my parents more than anything. Love that I have them and they took so much time out of their schedule to help. But now, it is time to see them off. Because tomorrow, I have plans.

THIRTY
SIX

Madeline

Why is Fletcher acting strange?

After buying us groceries yesterday, we shared good-byes with Fletcher's parents. Since they left, Fletcher has been on edge. Is he in pain and keeping it to himself? He hasn't complained once about his injuries since we arrived home. Hope he isn't putting on a brave face.

"Everything okay?"

I hand him a mug of oolong tea and park next to him on the couch with a mug of steamy cocoa. He side-eyes me before his shoulders drop and he delivers my favorite smile.

"Yeah. Just thinking."

"About?" I drag out the second syllable.

He sips the tea then sets the mug on the table. Shifting to face me, he rests a hand on my thigh. "I want to tell you something, but don't want to freak you out."

I hold Fletcher's stare for seconds, maybe minutes, unsure how to respond. The gold flecks in his rich green irises shimmer like the sun filters through the evergreen canopy. Deep affection and thrill and a smidge of trepidation hold my gaze. But he waits for me to respond.

"Okay," I answer quieter than expected.

Fletcher steals my mug and places it on the table. He wraps my hands in his, licks his lips then swallows.

"When I was unconscious or in a coma or whatever, I met someone."

The memory of him saying this when he woke in the hospital floods back in. At the time, I didn't know if he was loopy from the morphine and his mind played tricks on him, so I let it go and didn't think twice. But now that he has brought it back up, color me intrigued. I nod for him to continue.

He takes a deep breath, holds it for the count of three then releases. "I met Chris."

I freeze—not just my body stiffening. I go cold head to toe. A sting hits the back of my eyes a second before Fletcher turns blurry. *I met Chris.* How? Does this mean Fletcher died at some point? Oh, God. *Oh, God.* I slap a hand over my mouth as a sob rips from my chest.

Flashbacks of the accident and Fletcher not responding to my cries punch me in the chest. The smells and flashing lights. The pounding on my chest and faint call of my name. The pain… not just the physical, but also my shattering heart.

I almost lost Fletcher. So close. *Too close.*

In a flash, Fletcher has me in his arms. He drags me into his lap and hugs me close to his chest. I bury my face in the crook of his neck as an endless stream of tears spills down my cheeks. One arm holds me close while the other hand trails up and down my spine.

"Let it all out, Maddie. I got you."

And I do. For long minutes, I ugly cry burrowed in Fletcher's chest. What other way is it possible for Fletcher to have seen Chris if he wasn't on the brink of death? Other than the photographs on the walls, Fletcher has never seen Chris, never met or spoken to him.

When my ducts dry out and the tremors fade away, I lean back and wipe my cheeks and nose on my sleeve. Fletcher keeps me tucked to his chest as he lifts a hand to my cheek and wipes any remaining tears away with his thumb.

"Wh-What did he say?" I stammer.

The corner of his mouth kicks up for a beat. "To get back to *our girl.*"

I close my eyes as my heart triples in size. *Such a Chris thing to say.* My eyes fly open. "Were you…" Thinking the word is bad enough, but the notion of speaking it aloud sends bile up my throat. "Were you dead?"

Unsure of *when* Fletcher met Chris, it is quite possible Fletcher died at some point. That we both did after the accident. The memory of blunt force to my chest before I opened my eyes to the EMT has me believing they performed CPR. I had been in such a fog. All I remember after was screaming for Fletcher. Now, though, I recall the EMT saying Fletcher had been resuscitated. So, yeah, at some point, for who knows how long, Fletcher had no pulse.

"When I saw Chris?" I nod in response and he shakes his head. "No. At least that's what Chris said when I asked the same question." Tears pool my eyes again. "He said I was in a coma until I healed enough to wake."

I blot my eyes with the sleeve of my shirt and sniffle. "What else did he say?"

This conversation ranks as the oddest I have ever had. But I want every detail.

Yes, I spoke with Chris often. Saw him around me on a regular basis. Naturally, I had always been aware there was no actual conversation happening. That I used Chris's voice and mixed it with what I *imagined* his response would be. And when I saw him, he always looked the same. Same clothes, same hairstyle, same memory. A happy memory of our last vacation. His skin golden from the sun and a bright smile on his face.

That said, I need to know how Chris interacted with Fletcher. How he looked and what they spoke about.

"It wasn't an in-depth conversation. No guy talk." He chuckles. "More along the lines of him saying you needed me and that I had to wake up. He coached me, I guess."

I wipe my cheeks and laugh. "God, that sounds like Chris. Always helping other people before himself."

Fletcher takes my hand and looks me square in the eye. "We didn't talk much, but there was this… aura about him. He was such a good man, Maddie. And he loved you fiercely. I felt it." *Good grief, if the tears would just stop, that'd be great.* "But I'd like to add…"

His pause shoots adrenaline in my bloodstream. You can't just say something like that and let it dangle in the wind. "What?"

Fletcher tucks loose strands behind my ear. "He may have loved you fiercely, but it's vastly different than how I love you."

My brows pinch tight. "How so?"

"We didn't say much, but it was like osmosis or something. I just *knew* things. You met Chris through Katie." I gasp, knowing I have never mentioned this to Fletcher. "After the third date, Chris asked you to be his girlfriend." *Oh my…* "On your six-month dating anniversary, he knew he loved you."

I may keel over any minute. Hearing this from Fletcher's lips, it's too much.

"Not to sound like I'm trying to show him up. I never could." He pauses and I nod. "Madeline, I loved you before we met. Weird, I know, but it's true. The moment I saw you… God, it was like coming home after being lost my entire life. Like my soul found its missing half, only we didn't quite know how to piece ourselves together yet."

"Fletcher…" I say, breathy.

He frames my face and kisses me with a new level of tenderness. "Maddie…" Since waking up in the hospital, I love the ease at which Fletcher calls me Maddie. "I plan to be here until our skin wrinkles and we die happy and old —very old—at the same time."

"I like the sound of that." My heart inflates with immeasurable love. "What if we weren't completely alone?"

Confusion mars Fletcher's brow. "Not sure I follow."

Since Fletcher came back in my life this summer, so much clicked into place. At first, I felt guilty for having a connection with Fletcher that superseded what Chris and I shared. The more time I spent with Fletcher, though, the more my guilt waned. Without effort, I got swept up in him, in us. And many things fell to the wayside.

Like my quarterly doctor's appointment. The one I go to like clockwork for my shot. *The shot.*

"When we were admitted to the hospital, they ran routine bloodwork before administering pain medication. Standard procedure for women of childbearing age." Fletcher's eyes widen and he stills beneath me. *Please let this be good news.* "And it turns out, I'm pregnant."

His wide eyes glisten and, before I register the change in his expression, Fletcher smashes me to his chest. A second later, he softens the embrace.

"Shit. Sorry. I shouldn't have hugged you that hard. Shit."

I laugh at his minor panic attack. Bringing a hand to

his cheek, I lean in and kiss him until his body wilts and arms band around my waist.

"It's okay. Although, the doctor did say I need to take it easy. Pregnancy in your late thirties can be risky. Plus the accident."

"The sooner this cast comes off, the better. Then I'll be the one doing everything."

"I'm not made of glass, Fletcher. It's okay if I do everyday things."

Fletcher rests his hand over my abdomen, rubs small circles and follows the motion with wonder-filled eyes. "Hey, lil' bean." My vision instantly blurs and emotion clogs my throat. "Daddy here. We haven't met yet, but as soon as I know your birthday, I'm counting down the days until we do." My heart hammers against my ribcage. "Make sure you stay safe inside Mommy. We need her." Be still, my heart. "One more thing. Mommy needs to say yes."

Huh?

Fletcher leaves his hand on my belly but meets my confused gaze. "I planned to do this on New Year's at midnight. Corny, but I don't care." Fletcher digs into his sweatpants pocket, pulls out a tight fist then pauses between us. "Madeline, I love you."

"I love you, too."

"Weeks ago, I planned this moment. Had it all worked out. Nice dinner, special dessert, a song I wrote only for you." *Is he...* I slap a hand over my mouth and stop breathing. "Maddie, please breathe." His eyes drop to my belly. "For the baby." *Oh shit.* He chuckles, then continues. "But circumstances change. We can still have a nice dinner and dessert. And I plan to serenade the hell out of you and lil' bean." *Cue ovary explosion.* "But I'd love to do so as your husband."

"Oh my god." *Oh. My. God.*

"Madeline, will you and lil' bean marry me?"

THIRTY SEVEN

Fletcher

"Do you want to know the gender?"

Madeline peers up at me from the exam table, cheeks aglow and eyes glistening with adoration. *Never more stunning.* Before the appointment, we went back and forth over whether or not we should learn the sex of the baby. With the high-risk pregnancy, we worried knowing the sex might devastate us, should something happen.

Then we took a different tactic.

What if learning the sex, what if giving she or he their name, was our way of telling the universe this baby would bear full term? That our lil' bean would arrive safe and sound and loved more than ever.

"Please," Madeline answers, our eyes locked.

The ultrasound technician moves the wand over

Madeline's belly then stops. "There." She points to the screen and we both shift to see what she points out. When she presses a button, the image freezes. I have no clue what I am seeing, but I refuse to look away. "Congratulations, Mom and Dad. It's a boy."

A boy! We have a son.

The technician prints out the image twice, cleans Madeline's belly, then excuses herself a moment. I help Madeline clean the remaining goo off her belly and sit her up.

"Is it okay if I still call him lil' bean a while longer?"

Madeline smiles up at me and steals my breath. "I love that you call him lil' bean. So, yes." She rubs her hand over her belly. "That okay with you, lil' bean?"

Damn, I love this woman. More and more with each passing day.

I offer her my hand and help her off the table. We sit and wait for the doctor to return and go over the pregnancy plan and precautions we need to follow. We leave the office with loads of information and beaming smiles.

Happy as I am, the day will be a thousand times better in mere hours.

"Thanks for making it on such short notice," I say to Mom and Jonathan.

"What's this all about?" Mom looks between us with deep worry lines marring her forehead.

Not a day has gone by in the last three weeks that Mom hasn't called or sent a text message. I suppose your child having a near-death experience puts you more on edge. Ages you decades in a matter of minutes.

Come late summer, Madeline and I will learn the emotional spectrum of parenthood. Pure jubilation as his little fingers clutch my pinky. Amazement as I take in his features, seeing pieces of myself and Madeline reflected in his face and smile and eyes. Delight as we witness him grow and learn, laugh and love. Trepidation as he endures his first fever or skins his knee playing in the yard or falls from a tree.

The natural impulse to protect Madeline shot through the roof when the word *pregnant* entered our lives. It isn't solely the accident that has me in full-on defense mode. After all Madeline has undergone, her strength and perseverance stand stronger than ever. I admire her resilience, her need to stand tall. Now, though, she isn't alone. With me in her life, she never will be again. And she doesn't need to push herself. Doesn't have to bear the weight of everything on her own. And definitely doesn't need to stress our lil' bean.

"We wanted everyone here since the holidays were a bust."

Earlier this week, we called our families and asked

them to join us for a get-together. Neither of us gave specifics. We kept the details vague. Christmas 2.0 was a good excuse, so we ran with it.

Madeline and I share a brief smirk as we guide my parents, stepsister and Madeline's best friend, Nadia, to the living room. In the corner, a small artificial tree laden with silver balls and twinkling white lights brightens the room. Five small wrapped boxes sit under the tree—one for each set of parents, one for Phillip and Sylvia, one for Ann, and the last for Nadia. Faint classical music plays in the background. Savory herbs, roasted vegetables, and cinnamon apples waft throughout the house.

Hellos, hugs, and easy smiles are exchanged as if our families have known each other for generations. As we take our seats, I scan the room and absorb the affection we all share. Honor how easily our two worlds came together. Chatter, laughter, and love float through the air with ease.

Beside me, Madeline's knee bounces as we prepare to share our news. I rest a hand on her thigh, draw circles with my thumb over her exposed skin, and kiss her temple. A muted sigh leaves her lips as she melts into my embrace.

"Thank you," she whispers.

"Always. Ready for this?" Our eyes lock—her unwavering love stares back—and she nods. "Can I have everyone's attention?"

Conversations taper off and all eyes swing my direction. For the first time in years, stage fright engulfs every one of my muscles and nerve endings. Seven sets of eyes zero in on the slight pinch of my brows, the bead of sweat on my temple, the nervous twitch of my lips, and hard swallow of my throat.

"What's wrong?" Jonathan pipes up.

I cut to him and subtly shake my head. "No." Madeline takes my hand and a wave of relief wipes my anxiety away. I clear my throat. "Nothing. Nothing is wrong. We have news."

Both of our moms scoot to the edge of their seats in unison. Jonathan leans forward and clasps his hands while Robert takes Jeannie's hand. Phillip, Sylvia, and Ann freeze and give their undivided attention. Nadia focuses her gaze on Madeline, trying to read the situation. Madeline gives me a gentle squeeze and I take a deep breath.

I twist to hold Madeline's warm gaze and feel grounded on the spot. *I love you,* I mouth and she mirrors the sentiment. Resting a hand on her lower abdomen, I face our family. "We're pregnant." I don't breathe during the silence that follows.

Why is no one speaking?

Mom shoots up from her seat, eyes on me and Madeline, expression unreadable. In one, two, three steps, she stops within inches and squats. Her eyes dart from me to Madeline and back again. The way she regards us… I have never seen her like this. Speechless and somber.

Then, without hurry, one corner of her mouth curves

up. The other corner soon follows and I release my held breath. *Thank God.*

She extends her hand, but stops inches from Madeline's belly. "May I?" Madeline nods. I remove my hand and Mom replaces it. "Hi, little one. I'm your Grandma Frances."

Madeline's eyes glaze over as she peeks up and meets my eyes before scanning the room. One by one, our family greets the future generation and extends us congratulations. When the excitement tapers off, we relocate to the dining room and enjoy an early dinner.

After dinner ends, Madeline and her mother bring dessert to the table while I bring the gifts from the tree. I set each in front of their respective owner. Once everyone has cobbler and ice cream, the gifts get unwrapped. Jonathan picks up the box for him and Mom, shaking it then handing it over. Mom peels back the paper, pops off the lid and removes a slip of paper.

"What's this?" She flips the small note in her hand then holds it up. "It says 'our.'"

I hold up a hand. "It'll make sense in a moment."

Counterclockwise around the table, the gift boxes get opened. With each unwrapped box, a new slip of paper is revealed and another pair of confused eyes stare at us. Ann, the last to open, peels back the paper as the doorbell rings.

"Excuse me?" I rise from the table, kiss Madeline's crown and go to answer the door.

As I open the door to welcome our final guest of the

evening, Ann shrieks in the dining room. "Fletcher! Are you serious?"

Approaching the table, I chuckle. "Everyone, this is Yvonne." Going around the table, I introduce our family. "If you'll all humor me." I look to Madeline as she rises from her chair and hooks her arm in my elbow. "I need you to read your papers in order. Frances, Sylvia, Mom, Ann, then Nadia."

Everyone except Ann, who hasn't read her paper aloud, narrows their eyes. "This is the strangest Christmas ever," Mom mutters.

Madeline laughs as she removes her oversized cardigan—the vest blanketed the majority of her dress while the sleeves masked her hands all evening. As each note is read, Madeline's blush, knee-length dress and sparkling engagement ring come into view.

"Welcome."

"To."

"Our."

Ann shakes her head on a laugh. "Wedding."

"Ceremony." Nadia's eyes fill with love as they regard Madeline. "So happy for you," she whispers.

"Thank you," Madeline tells her.

Wood grates tile as chairs stagger backward. Our parents crowd around, a blend of confusion and happiness etched in the lines of their faces. Madeline meets her mother's gaze, tears in both their eyes, then embraces her daughter.

"So happy you found love again, sweetheart. I love you."

"Thank you, Mom. Love you, too."

And at seven twenty-one in the evening, on the twenty-second of January, in front of the people we love most, Madeline and I vowed to love one another for eternity.

THREE YEARS LATER

EPILOGUE

Madeline

"Higher, Daddy. Higher."

Hysterical giggles ripple the air from the wooden swing set to the back porch. A smile splits our son's face in half. His little hands fist the vinyl-covered chains connected to the toddler seat. His little legs kick with glee.

"Is this higher?" Fletcher asks as he gives another push.

"Higher, higher."

Fletcher puts a smidge more gusto into the next push. Squeals of delight ring out and wrap around my heart. I love all his little noises—pouts and grumbles included.

"He's beautiful, Maddie." Chris's soft timbre reverberates in my ear. A voice I hear less and less as time passes.

As time goes by and life progresses, a greater level of

peace fills my heart. Losing Chris will always be a part of me. To think otherwise would be to ignore all the pieces of my life that led me to where I am now. To Fletcher, our son, and the life and love we share.

I smile. "He's perfect."

Fletcher gives the swing another push then tosses a smile my way. Heat splashes my cheeks that has nothing to do with the summer sun on my skin. I sip my water, set the glass down, and lick my lips. I never expected father-hood to make Fletcher more attractive, but nothing has made my mouth water more.

"Are my guys ready for lunch?" I holler from my seat.

"Lunch, lunch, lunch." I laugh at his little chants.

Fletcher slows the swing, unbuckles the belt and sets TJ on the ground. His little legs sprint across the lawn to the porch.

"Topher James, no running in the house," I call out as he passes.

The closer it came to Topher's birth, the more Fletcher and I pondered over a long list of names. I'd kept track of all the names we thought of in the notepad on my phone. Out of the blue, a week before Topher was born, Fletcher said something I will never forget.

"Would you be uncomfortable if we named the baby Christopher?"

The question shocked me more than anything. Although I loved the idea and that Fletcher wanted to pay tribute to Chris—we wouldn't be where we are now without either of our pasts—I didn't want our son to ask why he shared my first husband's name when he was old enough to understand.

So, we settled on a shorter version. Topher. For us, it pays homage to Chris. For our son, he has a name all his own.

Fletcher steps onto the porch and helps me up from the chair. "How're you feeling, Mommy?"

As we walk inside, I spot TJ pulling out his chair at the table. Fletcher steps over, plucks him from the ground and secures him in the toddler seat before scooting him in. I fetch the premade plate of cubed fruit and cooked vegetables and his water cup. With food to occupy him, Fletcher and I make our lunch.

"Good. A little tired."

"Maybe after lunch, we should have a nap, too."

I lean into Fletcher's side. "Sounds like heaven."

We join TJ at the table, eat lunch, then put him down for his midday nap. Fletcher grabs the baby monitor and we wander to our room. The second my body hits the sheets, my muscles sigh in relief. Fletcher lays down behind me, his front to my back, and wraps an arm around my belly.

"How's our little gymnast?" Fletcher rubs my expansive belly as he presses a kiss to my shoulder.

"Tumbling up a storm today."

"Get some sleep." The circuit his hand makes over my very pregnant belly soothes me and our daughter. "I'll tend to TJ when he wakes."

I startle awake. The urge to pee overrides every other

bodily function. Fletcher is no longer behind me in the bed. The soft sounds of a nature documentary echo through the walls. Scooting to the edge of the bed, I sit up then hobble to the bathroom with as much speed as my legs can muster.

After I do my business, I rise from the seat and clutch my belly as pain rips through my midsection. "Argh," I yell and grip the vanity like a vise. "Fletcher!"

The bedroom door stopper smacks the baseboard as Fletcher runs into the room. "Maddie! Where are—" He rounds the corner and stops dead in his tracks. "Is it time?"

Another contraction has me bent at the waist. "It… maybe… yeah, I think it's time." I fist the counter and my shirt suddenly feels way too tight.

"Alright. It's time." Fletcher takes my hand and guides me to the bed. "Sit here a second while I get TJ's shoes on."

Fletcher darts from the room and I hear him talking to TJ. A minute later, he has our little man on his back as he reenters the room. Fletcher helps me up from the bed and we make our way to the garage; our hospital bag already in the car.

The drive to the hospital is a blur of pain, Fletcher on the phone with my parents, and TJ asking how long it will be until he meets his baby sister. I do my best to answer TJ and not freak him out as each contraction has me on the cusp of curse words.

My parents make it to the hospital before us and take

TJ. Since we preregistered a week ago, we take the elevator to the labor and delivery floor. The moment we step out of the elevator, nurses are at our side and I get wheeled into a room.

Everything happens in a flash. As I disrobe to put on the hospital gown, warm, sticky liquid pools around my feet and fire spreads through my abdomen and pelvis. Fletcher and a nurse help me onto the hospital bed. The urge to push amplifies as another contraction takes over.

"I need to push," I bite out.

The doctor strolls into the room with a bright smile on her face. "Mrs. and Mr. Lockwood, I hear your little gymnast is ready to meet you." She sits on the stool at the foot of the bed and lifts the gown. "It's time."

More than an hour of the most intense labor passes before I hear the sweetest sound. Cries rip through the air seconds before our little girl is laid on my chest. The second we are skin to skin, she quiets.

I hug her close, swipe the tip of my finger over her brow, and peer up at Fletcher. "Hey there, sweet girl. I'm your mommy."

Fletcher bends closer. "And I'm your daddy. We're so happy to meet you, Stella Mae. Mommy and I love you."

I turn my head to face Fletcher. "Look what we did." A bright smile lights up his face and kicks my pulse up a notch. "Thank you."

"You just experienced hours of pain, gave birth to our daughter and you're thanking me?"

I nod subtly. "Without you, I wouldn't have TJ or

Stella. I wouldn't know love like this." I take his hand. "Thank you for giving me such a wonderful life. For loving me."

Fletcher kisses my forehead, then lays his cheek on mine. We peer down at our daughter in awe. "Our love has no bounds, Maddie." He inches back, tips my chin up and holds my gaze. "Our love is transcendental."

And then Fletcher kisses me as if nothing and no one else exists.

Not ready to say goodbye to Fletcher and Madeline? Download their bonus story on my website:

www.persephoneautumn.com/bonus-content

THANK YOU

Thank you so much for reading **Transcendental**. If you would take a moment to leave a review on the retailer site where you made your purchase, Goodreads and/or BookBub, it would mean the world to me.

Reviews help other readers find and enjoy the book as well.

Much love,
Persephone

MORE BY PERSEPHONE AUTUMN

<u>The Click Duet</u>

High school sweethearts torn apart. When fate gives them a second chance, one doesn't trust they won't be hurt again. Through the Lens (Click Duet #1) and Time Exposure (Click Duet #2) is an angsty, second chance, friends to lovers romance with all the feels.

<u>The Inked Duet</u>

A man with a broken heart and a woman scared to put herself out there. Love is never easy. Sometimes love rips you apart. Fine Line (Inked Duet #1) and Love Buzz (Inked Duet #2) is a second chance at love, single parent romance with a pinch of angst and dash of suspense.

<u>The Artist Duet</u>

A tortured hero with the biggest heart and a charismatic heroine with the patience of a saint. Previous heartache has him fighting his desire to be more than friends with her. But she is everywhere, and he can't help but give in. The Artist Duet is an angsty, friends to lovers slow burn.

<u>Depths Awakened</u>

A small town romance which captivates you from the start. Two broken souls have sworn off love. Vowed to never lose anyone else. But their undeniable attraction brings them together and refuses to let go.

Every Thought Taken

As young children, an unshakable friendship brought them together. As teens, they discovered an undeniable love. Then life pulled them in different directions—into darkness and light—and slowly ripped them apart. Years later, he returns home in the hopes of a second chance with his first love and to conquer the demons of his past.

Distorted Devotion

Swept off her feet by love, life takes a dark, unexpected turn. Now the love of her life may be the cause of her death. Check out this gripping, romantic suspense.

Undying Devotion

A long-term couple with a secret life. Their friends envy the bond they share, but remain oblivious to their lifestyle and how deep the bond lies. A turn of events has her wanting to spill every secret.

Beloved Devotion

She asks the love of her life to marry her. When her girlfriend hesitates, then says yes, she is determined to learn why. As the pieces start to fall in place, she discovers she doesn't know her fiancée at all.

TRANSCENDENTAL PLAYLIST

Here are some of the songs from the *Transcendental* playlist. You can listen to the entire playlist on Spotify!

This Year's Love | Jasmine Thompson
Immortal Lover | Andrew Bayer, Alison May
In My Last Life | Andrew Bayer, Alison May
Your Eyes | Andrew Bayer, Alison May
exile | Taylor Swift, Bon Iver
my tears ricochet | Taylor Swift
invisible string | Taylor Swift
Love Like This (Acoustic) | Kodaline
Carry You | Novo Amor

CONNECT WITH PERSEPHONE

Connect with Persephone
www.persephoneautumn.com

Subscribe to Persephone's Newsletter
www.persephoneautumn.com/newsletter

Join Persephone's Reader Group
Persephone's Playground

Follow Persephone Online

instagram.com/persephoneautumn
facebook.com/persephoneautumnwrites
tiktok.com/@persephoneautumn
goodreads.com/persephoneautumn
bookbub.com/authors/persephone-autumn
amazon.com/author/persephoneautumn
pinterest.com/persephoneautumn

ACKNOWLEDGMENTS

All the hugs to my family! For continually believing in me. For cheering me on. For telling me how proud you are of all the things I have accomplished in my author journey. Thank you! I am forever grateful. And I love you!

To my rockstar editing team—Ellie and Rosa. Thank you for correcting lie, lay, and its variations in my manuscript that were not used correctly. Thank you for polishing up my books and making them better. And thank you for all your insight and love!

To Kat, queen of all things amazing! You always make the outside of my books pretty. Thank you for listening to my craziness and weird ideas then turning them into something readers will love. Can't wait to squeeze you again!

To my author friend... Thank you for every ounce of support. Whether it's just to chat or to guide me in a better direction. I appreciate having each of you in my circle.

To every person reading one or all of my books... THANK YOU! Being an author is equal parts amazing and chaotic. Every time you choose to read my books, my heart melts a little more. I appreciate each and every one of you.

ABOUT THE AUTHOR

USA Today Bestselling Author Persephone Autumn lives in Florida with her wife, crazy dog, and two lover-boy cats. A proud mom with a cuckoo grandpup. An ethnic food enthusiast who has fun discovering ways to veganize her favorite non-vegan foods. If given the opportunity, she would intentionally get lost in nature.

For years, Persephone did some form of writing; mostly journaling or poetry. After pairing her poetry with images and posting them online, she began the journey of writing her first novel.

She mainly writes romance, but on occasion dips her toes in other works. Look for her poetry publications and a psychological horror under P. Autumn.